PIERRE'S STORY

Sequel to "I Was, I Am, I Will Be"

By John Coventry and Trish Faber

There is a very thin line between the truth and fiction, some of the events are true, and others have been added as fictional events. This is a work of fiction. In order to maintain their anonymity, in some instances the names of individuals and places may have changed, as well as certain events, and some identifying characteristics and details such as physical properties, occupations and places of residence. The authors have tried to recreate events, locales and conversations from researched documents and people's memories of them.

CHAPTER ONE

The crisp morning air from a late August cold snap, rustled the thin satin curtains, just enough for a glint of sun to poke through and illuminate the beauty of her glistening skin. Soft and tanned, it stretched perfectly over her toned frame, and smelt like the lavender which grew wildly in the surrounding French countryside. Sensing the slight breeze against her bare shoulder, Michelle snuggled even closer into the nape of my neck, her long dark hair tickling my chin, her warm breath teasing my senses.

"I love you John Coventry. I will love you forever."

I enveloped her words with my lips as she slithered her frame on top of mine, our bodies meshed together in an absence of time and space. Her beating heart pulsed against my chest, igniting my blood in a firestorm, as it raced to my own heart, forging our love and making us one. At that moment, nothing else mattered. I was exactly where I was supposed to be, where I needed to be, where I wanted to be.

Sitting on the nightstand, and cast in the shadow of the rising sun was a single bearded iris drooped lifelessly over the side of a tall glass vase, its brilliant royal blue petals distressed and aching for a drink. A small crack originating from a chip in the rim of the vase threatened to snake its way to the base, thwarted only by a thick layer of dust and grime. The room was past its prime. Flakes of paint hung perilously from the yellowing walls and the old, hand fashioned doorframes were wrought with chinks and chips, holding memories of all those who had stumbled through on their way to somewhere else.

I had no idea how long Michelle had lived at the farmhouse or if she even considered it her permanent address. I had my doubts. Besides some clothes shoved in a few of the drawers, and a scattering of toiletries perched on the chest, there were no discernable signs of any sort of permanence. No pictures or memorabilia, not even a postcard from a long-lost cousin wishing her Merry Christmas. It was as if she only existed in the here and now, which although unnerving, was fine by me, because in the now, she was in my arms and kissing my lips. She was a ghost, moving through life with no footprints, except the ones she left on my heart.

"How about we just stay right here," I said stroking the side of her soft cheek with the backs of my fingers. "Who would miss us?"

Michelle laughed then bolted upright, shattering the tender moment. "Was that a car door?"

"I didn't hear a thing," I answered.

She jumped from the bed and ran to the window, throwing back the curtain, exposing her nakedness to the world below. "He's back!"

"Who's back?"

"No time to talk! Have you seen my shirt?" She scrambled about the room, searching for the clothes we tore off last night.

"Who's back Michelle?" I said throwing my legs off the side of the bed.

"No, no John, you stay here. It's just business." She put her hand to her mouth, blew me a kiss, and darted out the bedroom door, her feet pounding down the old wooden stairs.

I never knew what to expect from Michelle. One minute she would be in my arms, the next she'd be off, caught up in her cause. I never understood her reasoning, and she could never convince me that her politics were just. Her dedication was frightening; obsessive to the point where I knew I mattered, but was definitely not her first priority. The pain of that realization stung deep, like an open wound never quite able to heal. Our lives could be so much more, if only she'd open her eyes and see the possibilities. I wanted more, she wanted what we had, and there was no compromise, no moving forward. As much as I hated the situation, I would make the sacrifice. Snippets of time with Michelle were my salvation, and in the craziness of my world, I needed all the salvation I could find.

The animated voices resonating through the rafters piqued my curiosity about the farmhouse visitor. Tossing on my jeans and blue button down shirt, I carefully creaked open the bedroom door for a listen. Michelle and her 'business friends' were guarded in their conversation when I was around, so I figured a little prudent eavesdropping wouldn't hurt. I didn't recognize the new man's voice but that didn't really mean much. He could have been one of the machine gun-toting thugs that hung around the farmhouse. They seemed to come and go in shifts, arriving early in the mornings before dawn, staying for a few days, and then leaving again at night, presumably under the cover of darkness. Michelle had no idea I knew about the storage shed discreetly tucked amongst the green and red bushes, or how I'd witnessed the men loading and unloading crates of weapons and explosives. How she could be a part of the extremist violence the terrorists perpetrated was beyond me.

From what I could gather, the man was relaying information about a bombing that was going to occur. Or had it already occurred? Large casualties? Damn it! Why hadn't I paid more attention to my French lessons back in school?

Guns…street…government? An attack with guns on the street against the government? Explosion…bodies? Their voices were racing as fast as my heart.

"Yes! Yes! Jean-Luc! Finally! They will take notice of us now!"

The smug tone of Michelle's voice made my insides turn and want to scatter. I desperately needed some air. The minute my foot touched the top stair, the room below went silent.

"John? Are you all right?" said Michelle.

"I'm fine."

"John?"

"Just let me be Michelle."

Normally, the sight of seven stern men, much larger and weightier than me, with loaded machine guns strung over their shoulders, and pistols tucked into the waist of their pants was unnerving, but today I didn't care. The sooner I got out of that small, stuffy farmhouse and into the fresh countryside air, the better. The room reeked of stale blood and indifference - a sickening combination.

"John! Wait! What's wrong?"

"Nothing Michelle, nothing. I'm going for a walk while you finish up your very important business conversation."

The morning dew still lingered on the tallish grass, flicking drops of moisture over my sandals and onto my bare toes with every step. I didn't know if Michelle would follow me, and now that I was away from the farmhouse, I wondered if running out of there was the right thing to do. What if Michelle's friends saw me as a liability? The bullets in their steel guns couldn't discern my heart from the next, just as the steely ice in their souls couldn't discern right from wrong. I trudged along the well-worn path that veered off from the farmhouse, through a field of beautiful and bright wildflowers, to the edge of the forest. The tall trees formed a perfect canopy of branch-laden shadows skirting across the damp, mossy forest floor, intertwining through the vines and short brush. Walking in the woodlands gave me an instant sense of peace and reminded me of walking through the luscious gardens back home at 'Townfield', the family estate in England. Simpler times seemed so long ago.

"John."

My heart jumped. "Michelle, I'm sorry…I didn't even hear you behind me."

"I can be like the shadows when I want to," she smiled, teasing me with her sea-green eyes, knowing I didn't have the capacity to resist. "Why did you leave so quickly before?"

"You don't know?" I said. I walked a little further down the path, perhaps looking for a fight.

"Of course I don't know! Why are you acting this way?"

"What way Michelle?" I turned and confronted her confused face. "Do you think I'm that naïve? That I don't know what you and your business friends were talking about?"

A soft smile broke from the corner of her lips. "John you know that has nothing to do with you and me. Why do you let it bother you so much?"

The tightness of her jeans revealed every inch of her swaying hips as she glided towards me, her movements smooth and sultry. I was frozen, my mind pleading for me to keep walking, my heart enthralled by her magnetism.

"My dear virgin boy. Perhaps you are not so virgin anymore non?" I hated when she used that irritating nickname for me. She thought I was so naïve about her terrorist world. She was wrong. She placed her hands gently against my chest, and I could feel her energy radiate throughout my body, healing my anger, and softening my stance.

"This is what I wanted to protect you from John."

"From your life? You're trying to protect me from your life? Because this is who you are…the guns, the explosions…the killing. This is you. And there's nothing I can do to change that…and as much as I want to walk away and as much as my brain is telling me to walk away, I can't…because I love you. So now I'm stuck. Worrying about you when we're not together, worrying about you when we are together. Trying to comprehend what you and the Action Directe are doing…I don't understand it. Bombing and killing? For what? These are innocent people Michelle?"

"No one is innocent John. We do what we do because we have to."

"It's terrorism Michelle!"

She gripped her hands into my shirt and pulled me close, her breath hot on my neck. "Is it terrorism when I do this?" Her tongue licked the corner of my ear as her lips found a home beneath my hairline.

"That's not fair," I groaned. "You know what I mean."

She ignored me and continued her conquest of my neck, deftly opening the buttons on my shirt and sliding her hand underneath to caress the hotness of my skin. I couldn't hold out much longer. As much as this woman maddened me with her politics and beliefs, I loved her, and wanted to spend the rest of my life with her.

"Let's just leave all this Michelle, and go away. Somewhere where no one will find us and bother us. Let the Action Directe fight the cause without you! Please Michelle!"

"You know I cannot do that John. My heart cannot leave the Action Directe as much as my heart cannot leave you!" I wanted to ask her to choose but I feared I already knew the answer - the cause would always be more important. "Let's just enjoy the time we have together John. Who knows where life will take us? Maybe it will all work out and maybe we will grow old together…I don't have all the answers…I just know that I love you, more than I have ever loved any man."

I didn't doubt her love but she was lying about the happily ever after. I just didn't see it, and I know she didn't believe it.

"I love you too Michelle, and no matter what happens or where life leads, I will always love you. Remember that."

"We will always have each other John. I will always be right here." She opened my shirt wide and lightly placed her lips on my heart. "Wherever, whenever…I will be right here."

"Oww!" I laughed as she pinched my nipple in her teeth.

Her eyes danced with mischief. "You didn't think I was going to stay all sappy on you did you?"

"Of course not!" I pulled her close and found her lips eagerly awaiting mine. "You drive me crazy woman."

"I'd rather I drove you mad!"

We kissed wildly, like two teenagers exploring their love for the first time, hands grasping, reaching, wanting to feel as much of each other as possible; laughing hysterically as we tripped over a knotted vine and fell backward into a pile of brush. In that moment, life was perfect. A crackle of gunfire broke the peacefulness.

"God damn them for target shooting at the birds again!" said Michelle easing away from our embrace and turning up the path. "They can be so stupid!" A wicked explosion of glass resonated over the treetops, followed by shouts and the peppering of machine gun fire. "That's not target practice!"

She was gone through the woods before I even had a chance to comprehend what was happening.

"Michelle! Michelle! Stop!"

The veins in my neck were poised to pop. She wasn't listening and just kept running - running straight into the fire. I chased after her, throwing off my sandals, the harsh forest floor assaulting the bottoms of my feet. I had to reach her. I had to save her from them. Save her from herself. As I tore into the open field, my heart stopped. Swarms of hooded men with machine guns blazing swooped through the entire area, shooting anything and everything that moved. I couldn't tell if they were police, Special Forces, or some other terrorist faction intent on taking the Action Directe out of commission. Flames leapt from the roof of the farmhouse as the terrorists returned fire from the smoke-filled windows, making one gallant last stand. For a brief second I lost track of her, scanning my eyes through the horror, until I saw her standing in the middle of the path, an automatic pistol booming from her steady right hand.

"Oh my God! Michelle! No!"

I ran as fast as I could, bullets screaming past my ears. I had to reach her. I had to stop her. I saw him coming. A big brute of a man, flashing a menacing smile, like this was all just a game; his heavy black boots ripping the lush grass as he clunked towards her. She didn't see him. Why couldn't she see him? He cocked the pistol, a semi-automatic Desert Eagle. I reached out to grab her. She took a step forward and my hand flailed at the air. The crack of the gun. Once. Twice. Silence. She fell back into my outstretched arms, blood gushing from a gaping hole in her abdomen. I cradled her weakening frame, pressing my body against hers, sending every ounce of my strength to rescue her fading pulse.

"Oh Michelle. My God what have they done to you?" Her hair, matted with sweat and blood, stuck to my fingers as I brushed it away from the corner of her mouth.

"Remember me John."

"No Michelle, no…everything is going to be fine."

The colour drained from her beautiful face, her dry lips barely able to form the words. "Keep me with you always."

With exaggerated effort, her bloodied hand reached blindly for my fingers, clutching them tightly, holding on for life and for love. My mind raced through all the moments I'd held her in my arms before, so full of vigor, so full of passion.

"Please don't leave me Michelle! Please hold on! I can't live without you! My God! My God! My God! No!"

"I love you John." The words were painful to hear, her voice just a shadow, her soul seconds away from its final journey.

"I love you too babe. Always. Always you will be in my heart."

Her grip on my hand slowly loosened, one agonizing finger at a time, plummeting my heart to the pit of my stomach. With a final heave of her chest and a slow ooze of blood from the side of her mouth, she was gone. The woman I loved, the woman I adored, the woman I planned my entire life around, lay limp and lifeless in my arms, the pain of her final moments etched forever in her bloodstained tears. My body yearned to scream out in anguish and anger but was paralyzed by the wisp of smoke drifting from the burning iron shaft pointed straight at my head.

"So good to see you again laddie!" said the monstrous man pulling back his balaclava. "I know you've missed me!"

My chest exploded with terror, pounding, pounding, pounding. How did he find me? That voice. That fucking Irish brogue. Pounding, pounding, pounding. I couldn't think. I couldn't breathe. Pounding, pounding, pounding.

"Say yer prayers laddie. Yer going to need them in hell!"

"No Brian! No!"

I awoke with a start, jumping from the bed, clutching my chest, my clothes dripping with sweat. Pain ripped through my temples like an out of control freight train; the empty bottle of Whisky tipped sideways on the night table, no longer my

friend. I needed a fucking cigarette. Fumbling for my
Dunhill's, I managed to shove one in my mouth before
dumping the pack on the floor, my hands trembling and
unsure. The only cure for my shakes was more liquor. I called
down to the bar and ordered up another bottle of whiskey.
With much difficulty, the flame from the lighter found the end
of my cigarette, my deep inhale igniting the tip into orange
embers. Inhale, exhale, breathe. Two cigarettes later, a knock
on the door jarred my rhythmic trance.

I opened the door and the waiter entered, wheeling my
much-needed bottle of whiskey and a tub of ice in on a trolley.

"Let me pour you a glass Mr. Coventry."

"That would be great, thank you," I said running my fingers
through my sweaty hair. He took a fresh glass, popped in some
ice cubes, and poured a few ounces.

"Will that be all sir?"

"Yes, thank you." I signed the bill and handed the young
lad a twenty-dollar tip.

"Thank you! You have a nice evening Mr. Coventry! And
welcome to Los Angeles! The Beverly Hills Hotel is happy to
have you!" Without counting, he tucked the money inside his
tailored uniform coat and strutted down the hall.

I closed the door behind him and collapsed onto the bed.
My senses were spinning from the alcohol, from the
nightmare, from everything. I tossed back the drink and
poured another. The image of Michelle dying in my arms was
as vivid as my own scraggly face in the hotel mirror. The sound
of the shots, the blood, her words, they all echoed in the
hollowness of my heart. But Michelle had been dead for years,
killed in France, while I was at home in England. At least that's
what Rondell had told me, and really, I had no reason to think
she would lie. Sure, she was a terrorist like Michelle, but she
was also her best friend, and I know she loved her immensely.

I had tried to put the whole thing behind me and move forward. Coming to Los Angeles was going to be the next step in my recovery. Then just before I left, the nightmares began. At first, they were subtle. I would see Michelle walking beside me, smiling and laughing, but there would be no sound, just an image, an image of us together, happy, the way we used to be. When I reached out to touch her, she would disappear, and I would wake up, tears streaming down my face.

Sometimes, I would see the face of a child, his dark curly hair, and brown eyes staring back at me in the shadows of the night. When I reached out to touch him, he would run away, looking back with a cheeky grin, almost taunting me with his presence. Other times, I would see him sitting alone in a room crying, clutching a small brown bear close to his chest. My arms kept reaching out to hold him, and to comfort him, but I couldn't break through the invisible barrier that kept us apart. I knew I was envisioning Pierre, my son with Michelle, the son I never knew, and I thought I'd reconciled the idea of him living with Rondell in Germany, but I couldn't shake the constant thoughts of loss.

I don't blame Rondell for taking him; after all, his mother had been killed by God knows who, and she had to get the hell out of there for somewhere safe. Still, I struggled with the knowledge that I had a son out there, and he probably had no idea who I was or why I wasn't with him. I can't say for sure how I felt about him, since I didn't know him from any other child on the street, but there certainly were times I felt a true emptiness in my heart. Maybe it was the longing for what could have been - with him, with Michelle, having a family of my own. The child that appeared in my dreams only made me miss them even more. Someday I would make amends. I didn't know how, and I didn't know when, but someday I would make things right with my son.

Tonight's dream scared the shit out of me. Holding Michelle in my arms never felt so real, and she never seemed more alive. And then she was gone. I heard the shots. I felt her pain. I still feel her loss. And Brian? What the hell was he doing there? Laughing and taunting me with his sinister smile. Fucking IRA terrorist. What on earth was my subconscious trying to tell me? I already felt uncomfortable when someone gave me more than a passing glance, and the slightest trace of an Irish accent sent shivers racing through my spine. Unless something had happened to sour their partnership, I was quite sure Brian had nothing to do with Michelle's murder. My own fear and anxiety placed him in my nightmare. The threats, the beatings, the promises of death, all tend to make a person a little skeptical and on edge. I didn't want to feel that way, I wanted to be strong and resilient, but scars only ever fade, they never go away.

Los Angeles was going to be the start of something new, something better. Just yesterday, I was in England, living a life stilted and weighed down by past transgressions. The "involuntary" relationship with British Intelligence left me battered, bruised, and constantly looking over my shoulder. I was only supposed to help them find out about the drugs, they never mentioned anything about getting involved with members of the terrorist IRA, Baader Meinhoff Gang, and the Action Directe. That was all a huge and not so welcome surprise. Fucking bastards. I almost had as much hate for them as I did for the terrorists. But I'd made a vow on the plane that things were going to change. The days of shifting blame and depending on others for my own well-being were over. Never again would I allow someone else to control my life. In America, my name meant nothing – and that's just the way I wanted it. Anonymity would be a breath of fresh air.

CHAPTER TWO

I folded up the thick worn newspaper and set it on the tempered glass table in front of me, my brain too scrambled to read. The sun pounded on the back of my head, intensifying my already staggering headache. But it was a glorious morning in California, and I was relishing sipping my morning coffee on the outdoor patio of the world-famous Polo Lounge Restaurant in Beverly Hills. It was definitely a change from the drab and dreary rain of England. Taking another sip of coffee, I let my eyes wander.

With its peachy pink colours, The Polo Lounge had a magnificent 'Old Hollywood' type of feeling. Movie stars since the beginning of movies, have graced its tables, drank at its bar, swam in its pool, and made deals that turned bit actors into superstars. Hollywood history hung in the air like a thick, mysterious mist, encompassing visitors with its grandeur and elegance.

I tilted the china mug and let the last few drops of coffee find their way down my whiskey burnt throat. Trying to rid my body from the shakes, I thought maybe the coffee would somehow help. It didn't; nor did the buttery French croissant, its richness clashing with the wild spirits churning in my gut. My body craved something a little stronger than cocoa beans. I motioned for the waiter hovering in the background.

"Excuse me. Bloody Mary, heavy on the vodka?"

"Right away sir." I eased back into the chair, my body stiff and sore from the long flight the day before. The green and white cushions fit perfectly into the nooks and crannies of my back. The young, slim man wearing a Beverly Hills Hotel badge set the drink on the table beside the chair, then discreetly disappeared. I took a large gulp of the Bloody Mary, the vodka kicking the back of my throat, overpowering the lingering flavour of java.

With a second gulp, my eyes caught a glimpse of a stunningly beautiful woman inside the indoor Lounge area. Her Mediterranean cheekbones and long flowing, silky brown hair only complimented the smooth and luscious olive skin that shone as if the Gods blessed her. I marvelled at the length of her legs and the curve of her hips as she leaned over the bar to talk to the blond haired man serving up the drinks. The bartender lifted his muscular arm, pointing to a table across the room. As she turned, she noticed me watching her, and flashed a little smile, showing just a glimpse of her brilliant white teeth, her eyes twinkling against the lights of the chandeliers. Before I had the chance to smile back, the woman was gone.

Snickering, I picked up the newspaper, found a lounge chair by the pool, and stripped off my shirt, tossing it on the side table. The warm California sun felt good on my bare English skin. Digging the pack of Dunhill's from my back pocket, I lit up a cigarette, inhaling slowly and deliberately. It was turning out to be a perfect morning and the poolside views were incredible, from the pink arches and white awnings of the hotel building, to the flawlessly placed palm trees standing guard. The shimmering aqua blue waters of the over-sized pool proved to be perfect fodder for a man desperately needing to move forward with his life.

Stamping out my second cigarette, I removed my dark tinted, metal framed glasses and set them on the table beside my empty drink. A few steps landed me at the pool's edge, and with a quick retightening of my hunter green swimming trunks, I was in the pool, my arching dive rippling the tranquility of the still water. Years of family vacations in the south of France and other seaside resorts honed my powerful swimming stroke. Swimming had always been a release for me, a place where I could challenge my strength against the current, and push my body to the brink of physical exhaustion. While the climate-controlled water of this pool certainly didn't mimic the feisty ocean, it gave me a chance to concentrate solely on my breathing, pacifying my demons - at least for the time being.

"Need one of these?" It was the pretty woman with the high-cheek bones. She held out a towel.

"Why yes…thank-you," I said hoisting myself onto the edge of the pool. I rubbed the towel through my dark hair, then let it drape around my toned shoulders. I couldn't help but notice her eyes roaming up and down my water kissed body. "Just had to cool off in the pool there. I'm not used to it being so hot!"

The woman laughed and held out her hand. "I'm Cassandra."

"John…John Coventry," I answered taking her hand in mine. "Can I buy you a drink?"

"I'd like that."

I grabbed a neighbouring lounge chair and cozied it up beside mine. "Please, have a seat. What can I get you to drink? I'm having a Bloody Mary."

"A lime margarita would be great. Thank you."

"It's my pleasure."

"So where are you from? Your accent sounds British but I just can't figure out where in Britain. London? Cambridge perhaps? You definitely have the look of an English gentleman."

"I'm from the Liverpool area.

"Really? You sound so much more refined than others I've met from Liverpool."

The stereotypical comment made me smile, not everyone in Liverpool worked on the docks. The only thing Liverpool was famous for was the docks and the Beatles, and they left the city as fast as they could for the wealth of London and the south.

"In any case," she continued. "I find your accent so intriguing. Trust me, American women love a man with an accent!"

"I've heard they love a man with money!"

Cassandra smirked. "We love both. I'm just giving you fair warning. Once Beverly Hills hears there's a new Englishman in town, you're going to be swamped with offers - dates, parties, and probably even a few marriage proposals! I'm just glad I got to you first!"

She tossed her long hair forward as she placed her hand on my knee and laughed. I wasn't uncomfortable with the touch, just a little unnerved by the tingling sensation drifting up my thigh.

"So tell me about this place," I said changing the subject. "The world famous Polo Lounge."

"Ah…the Polo Lounge," said Cassandra. "I love coming here… There always seems to be someone you know and at least five people you're dying to meet. Are you a big movie fan John?"

"I can't say that I am, no. Not that I dislike them, it's just not something I was ever that interested in."

"That's a shame. The Polo Lounge is such a great place to come and people watch, especially in the old days. All the big Hollywood heavyweights hung out here…from Charlie Chaplin to Clark Gable to Marlene Dietrich to Bogart and Katharine Hepburn. You name it…they've probably swam in that pool, had drinks at the bar and slept in the hotel." She paused and took a sip of her drink. "In this town, it's all about who you know, and how much money you flaunt around."

"I suppose I'm shit out of luck then aren't I?"

"Why's that?"

"Well I only arrived yesterday, and besides the manager and a few other staff here, I haven't met a soul!"

"You've met me haven't you?"

"Yes I guess have," I laughed.

"I know lots of people John…people that would just love to meet you, and your wonderful British accent. Let me show you the sites and introduce you to a few friends."

"That sounds like fun."

"You're a fun guy to be around. In fact, I'm going out to a party tomorrow night in the Pacific Palisades. Would you like to come?" She grinned, "Unless of course you're not up for a party?"

"I'd love to," I said grinning back. "I'm always up for a party."

"Well I promise you won't be disappointed," she said flipping back a piece of hair that had fallen across her face. Her hazel eyes glanced down at the gold studded watch dangling on the end of her wrist. "Shit! I've got to get going. I'm supposed to meet a girlfriend down on Rodeo Drive for a manicure. Meet me in front of the hotel around seven pm."

"I'll be waiting." I stood politely as Cassandra rose from her chair.

She noticed the gesture and a sassy grin appeared from the corner of her mouth. "I'm so glad I met you today John. I think we're going to be fast friends." She bent in and placed a slight kiss on my cheek, her lips moving close to my ear. "Just remember, I saw you first!" She kissed me again, then sashayed across the pool deck and into the main building.

I let my brown eyes trail her shapely behind as she walked away. I really couldn't believe my luck. I hadn't been stateside for more than a day and already I'd met a beautiful woman, and tomorrow was off to a party in the exclusive Pacific Palisades. Definitely a far cry from the life I was living back in Britain. I had come to America for a new start – to put the events of the past where they belonged – in the past. For the first time in a long time, I felt comfortable. I could be myself and go about my business without fear of judgment or ridicule. I had no expectations of a relationship with Cassandra, or even sex for that matter, I was just glad I'd met someone who saw me as me, and not someone with a shamed existence. Changing the past wasn't an option, but I also didn't have to let it control my future. Things would be fine, if only I could stop the nightmares from appearing every time I closed my eyes.

"So who exactly is throwing this party?" I said pushing back my wind swept hair as the sleek white convertible flew down Sunset Boulevard heading toward the coast. Cassandra had picked me up exactly as promised, at seven pm in front of the Beverly Hills Hotel, looking more beautiful than the day before, her flowered mini-sundress barely covering the upper portion of her thigh.

"Barbara Saberton. I've known her for years," she answered. "She's a big Hollywood socialite who always throws the best and most distinguished parties. Tonight you'll meet your fair share of movie stars as well as some major movers and shakers. Be on your toes John. In this town, opportunity exists with every glass of champagne."

"And which category do you fall into Cassandra? Movie star or mover and shaker?"

A devious smile arose from her lips. "Well by trade I'm an actress, some television and a few feature films, but I've also been known to do a little moving and shaking."

I liked this woman. She seemed flirty, fun, and not at all pretentious; a breath of fresh air. Just before Sunset Boulevard meets the Pacific Ocean, she turned up a steep road that led into the hills. House after house sprawled across the different painted lush green lawns, monuments to money and fame. Growing up in England, I was used to seeing the wealth and opulence of old country estates and historical Royal residences, but I had to admit, I was impressed at this American scene, even though it appeared so over the top. Unlike England, this was a different sort of wealth, more of a flashy wealth, where it seemed every house tried to outdo its neighbour in size and grandeur. Subtlety was not on display. The smell of new money was as thick as an early morning occan fog. Most people here were not born into wealth and power; they created it, and with that creation came an egotistical sense of entitlement.

Cassandra pulled the convertible through an open set of huge cast iron gates that stretched half way up to the sky, stopping behind a long white stretch limousine. Like magic, a young clean-cut man in a burgundy buttoned-up waistcoat appeared at the side of car.

"Mrs. Saberton is pleased to have your presence at her gathering tonight. May I park your car?"

We stepped out of the car and Cassandra handed the man her keys. "Take care of my baby."

Beautiful and elegant tiny white lights guided us through the grounds of the Saberton mansion. The laughter and din of partygoers wafted through the air, inviting the new arrivals to come join the festivities. It was a gorgeous, warm evening, and the sky dazzled with the brilliance of twinkling stars and the reflection of the huge flaming torches lighting up the garden area. Waiters in smart red jackets were serving wine and canapés, while dozens of croaking frogs sang their approval from the nearby pond.

"Would you look at that," I said admiring the ocean view from the garden. "It's fantastic…I think I could be quite happy in a place like this!"

"It's something isn't it?" said Cassandra taking my hand and skilfully manoeuvring her way through the guests. "C'mon…I want to introduce you to Barbara."

Barbara Saberton was an elegant looking woman of about sixty years of age, with blond hair, a pale complexion and a self-assured smile. Her perfect make-up highlighted the expensive skill of a plastic surgeon's delicate knife. Dressed in a posh long blue gown with embroidered gold embellishments, and diamond studded gold shoes, Saberton was the epitome of Beverly Hills beauty. A sleek black Doberman darted around her feet.

"Down Max," commanded Barbara in a strong accent. I wasn't quite able to distinguish whether the accent was Swedish or German. The dog snarled and sat back down, never taking his sinister eyes off mine.

"Cassandra, how lovely to see you," said Barbara leaning forward to embrace her.

"Lovely to see you as well Barbara. You're looking ravishing as always tonight." Cassandra turned toward me. "This is John Coventry, my new friend from England. He just arrived in the States a few days ago. I hope you don't mind I brought him along."

"My God of course not," said Barbara holding out a hand weighted down by several huge diamond rings. "You can bring whomever you like to my parties, especially when they're as cute as him. I love an accent!"

Blushing, I gently took her hand in mine. "Thank you Mrs. Saberton. It's a pleasure to meet you. I must say you have quite a lovely garden…and the view is incredible."

"Thank you dear. Please make yourself comfortable and have a wonderful time." She cordially let her hand slip away and turned to Cassandra. "This one is a keeper dear! But we'll talk about it later. I hear someone calling my name. That Jacobs fellow has probably found his way into the pool again…fully clothed. I'm not sure why he's still on my guest list," she laughed.

"Because he's fabulously rich?" answered Cassandra.

"You know me too well young lady." She laughed, then floated regally across the floor, offering her hand and a few cheek kisses to the passerby's as she melted into the crowd of diamonds, designer dresses and Armani suits.

"She's something else isn't she?" said Cassandra handing me a glass of champagne.

"Yes she is," I said taking a sip. "She certainly seems comfortable in her role as hostess."

"It's pretty much just another day at the office for her. I think she lives for her parties as much as we do!"

Judging by the light-hearted ambiance of the room, I tended to agree. Then again, this was California, where a laid-back, carefree sort of attitude was a religion.

"Oh my God," I said gently grabbing Cassandra's sleek arm. "That man over there is the spitting image of that fellow from Star Trek…Patrick Stewart."

"Really? You think he looks like Patrick Stewart."

"Oh yes! The man looks just like him!"

"Well it looks like him because it is him," Cassandra laughed. "Would you like to meet him?"

"Of course! Are you kidding me? I don't know many movie stars but I do know him!"

Cassandra linked her arm in mine, guiding us through the maze of guests, stopping every few people to say a word of hello or give an introduction.

"I'm not sure I'm going to remember all these different names."

"You were forewarned!" she laughed. "I told you yesterday I was going to parade you around, and I'm not one to go back on my word." She gently touched the man's arm. "Sorry to interrupt Patrick, but there's someone here I'd like you to meet."

I had long been an admirer of Patrick Stewart and his work, seeing a few of his performances in the Royal Shakespeare Company out of London. The thought of meeting him in person set off a few butterflies in my stomach.

"Patrick, this is John Coventry. A fellow countryman I believe."

"Really?" said Patrick holding out his hand for a shake. "Where abouts in England are you from?" His wide grin instantly put me at ease.

"The Liverpool area," I replied returning the friendly gesture.

"Brilliant. I'm from Mirfield, West Yorkshire. Ever heard of it."

"I certainly have. I used to travel to Middlesbrough quite a bit for business and passed very close to your little hamlet."

"Middlesbrough? What on earth kind of business did you have up there?"

I had to think quickly. I couldn't exactly tell Patrick Stewart I'd travelled to Middlesbrough several times to drop off some crates full of drugs, guns, and God knows what else.

"Finance," I stumbled. "Dealing with foreign currencies and such. I had a few clients up that way."

"Oh I see…sounds quite interesting."

"Yes quite," I answered. I hated having to lie, but in this case, I had no choice. The less people knew about my past, the better.

"Well I'm very pleased to meet you John. Hold on a second, there's someone I want to introduce you to."

Patrick turned to his right and caught the attention of an older gentleman, a little taller than myself with broad heavy set shoulders. His whitish hair was combed back, revealing a distinguished forehead and bright sparkling eyes.

"John, this here is my friend Buzz Aldrin and his beautiful wife Lois."

"I remember watching you walk on the moon when I was a youngster!" I said reaching for his outstretched hand. "This is quite an honour Mr. Aldrin, and such a pleasure to meet you Mrs. Aldrin."

"Please call me Buzz and my wife Lois. Lois always says Mrs. Aldrin was my mother, isn't that right honey?"

Lois smirked and affectionately took my hand in hers. "Don't listen to him! It's so nice to meet you John."

Wearing a full-length red-velvety evening dress, with diamond drop earrings, Lois Aldrin was the perfection of charm, and I spent better part of an hour chatting away to the "moon-man" and his wife. I was glad Cassandra invited me to the party. Already I'd met some great people, exchanged a few phone numbers and had many promises of future engagements, including a dinner engagement with the Aldrin's next week. It was a good way to start my new life. But as much as I wanted to be open and honest with everyone, I was always on guard, never wanting to say too much or give any indication that I had anything to hide. We all have secrets in our lives, some more explosive than others, and there was no way in hell I was going to jeopardize anything with a flippant slip of the tongue.

Guests filtered into the dining area, a large stately room daintily covered with small floral patterned wallpaper. The creamy shade perfectly accented the rich cherry side serving tables and floor to ceiling buffet. No expense spared, the three-rung crystal chandelier glistened like a full moon, spraying the ceiling with starlit twinkles, and spotlighting the enormous spread of succulent seafood laid out on the pristine white table cloth below. Piles of oysters, shrimp, crab, and muscles were all colourfully nestled on a bed of crushed ice, surrounding the most exquisitely detailed ice sculpture of a fish, complete with water spouting from its partly opened mouth. The scene was a pure Picasso to my taste buds. Taking a cue from the other patrons, I stacked my plate high with goodies, and then joined Cassandra at a table on the terrace.

"This is one of the most incredible displays of seafood I've ever seen," I said sucking back an oyster. "Honestly, I don't think I'm going to be able to stop myself."

"I know what you mean," said a man sliding his rump into a chair across the table. "Name is Robert King."

"John Coventry."

"Ah…a Brit I see!" The man took a deep puff from his cigar. "I've always liked the British. I suppose I should call you Lord Coventry then."

A smallish sort of plump man, with balding hair, Robert King looked to be around fifty years old. He puffed constantly on a cigar and the smoke circled about his head like a halo.

"I can assure you that I am definitely not a British Lord," I laughed. "Just a regular citizen."

"Are you sure about that? No hidden secrets?" said King said with a grin. "Normal citizens from foreign countries usually don't find themselves seated at a table at one of Barbara Saberton's parties. There's something more to you sir, and I think I'll call you Lord anyways. I like the sound of it."

I didn't quite know how to respond. I didn't want Robert King to assume I was anything more than I really was, but then again, this was Los Angeles, and everybody was an actor, always playing a part, whether the camera was rolling or not.

"I don't suppose I can stop you, but I'd much prefer you called me John."

"Sure thing Lord Coventry," he answered arrogantly. "I'm the guy you want to know, if you ever want to get anything done in this town!" A quick foray into his suit jacket produced a business card. "Give me a call sometime if you ever need anything…like I said, I know everyone who's anything, and trust me, they'd all love to meet a Lord like you!"

Ignoring the ridiculous Lord reference, I shoved my fork into my mouth. "Will do Robert." I didn't want to cut him off or be rude, but I was starving and he was interrupting my much-anticipated date with a second and third oyster, not to mention a few mussels and scallops. King chatted on throughout the entire dinner, and while I was pleased I'd met a seemingly important person, I wasn't sad when he finally finished his plate and moved on, taking his cloud of cigar smoke with him.

"He's quite a character," said Cassandra. "Smokes too many cigars. The smell is what gets me after a while."

"He does seem to enjoy them doesn't he?"

"I'm not sure I've ever seen him without one."

"Speaking of smoke, I think I might step back out into the garden for a cigarette," I laughed. "Care to join me?"

"I'll be out in a second," she said rising from the table. "I just spotted an old friend I haven't seen in a while."

"Take your time," I answered. "I'm quite fine milling about on my own."

"You are a sweetie," she said putting her impeccably manicured fingers on my shoulder. I'll come and find you in a bit."

I gazed as she sauntered into the adjacent room, then made my way outside to the garden, plopping into a chair to watch the ocean wrestle with the night breeze. Taking a drag of my cigarette, I closed my eyes. It'd been an amazing night so far, and I'd met so many different people and faces, that I was having trouble keeping it all straight. The copious amounts of wine didn't help.

The cool ocean mist felt good on the hotness of my face, burnt from two consecutive days spent poolside in the Polo Lounge. I was happy, happier than I'd been in a long time. I loved England but the mundane routine and the loss of never seeing our son had been dragging me down. Most of my old friends found ways to forget they'd ever met my acquaintance. Not feeling sorry for myself, I was just recounting the facts. With a bit of a nest egg and an empathetic push courtesy of my mother, I was eager to make a new life, build a new future, and perhaps my own fortune. How I intended to make that happen was still in the planning stages.

Restless and tired of waiting for Cassandra, I doused my fourth cigarette on the grass and ventured out into the beautiful torch lit garden paths. I took the long way back to the house, enjoying the palm trees and the nocturnal serenade from the frog chorus. A tug at my tie and a flick of a few buttons on my shirt allowed the still warm night air to dry up the beads of perspiration forming at the base of my neck. I strolled around the side of the pool, its backlit waters offering a sparkling invitation, and entered the house through the side patio door. Seeing Cassandra deep in conversation with Barbara, and not wanting to disturb them, I continued my explorations. The stainless steel kitchen bustled with the catering and the wait staff, as I pardoned my way through, fending off impolite scowls with my English charm. Making my way towards the main reception area, I noticed a narrow flight of stairs leading down. Memories of sneaking through the secret passageways and forbidden rooms in my childhood home in England made me snicker as the curious eight-year-old boy with the insatiable imagination resurfaced.

Wary of getting caught, I took a quick peek over my shoulder then descended the stairs, carefully bending my five foot nine inch frame forward as the ceiling crept closer to the ground. I craned my neck up the stairs to check on the whereabouts of the Satan dog Max, then clasped the door handle in my sweaty palm and turned. I felt my adrenaline serge. The old metal hinges creaked like they were thirsty for some oil, causing me to pause and listen. Hearing only my pounding heart, I opened the door, stepped into the blackened space, and closed the door behind me. Fumbling for the light switch, I hit the jackpot, and the room exploded into a glowing shade of red.

"Well, well, well, what do we have here," I said laughing. "I see you have a few secrets of your own Mrs. Saberton. Hollywood socialite by day and fetish dungeon master by night!"

I wasn't prudish by any means but I'd also never seen anything quite like it. In the middle of the room stood a rack with two sets of leather straps tightly fastened to each end, and dangling from the spackled walls was a wide variety of sadistic implements of torture – whips, canes, chains. I had no idea what some of the 'pleasurable equipment' did and really had no desire to find out. As my eyes grew accustomed to the reddish glow, I noticed several framed, erotic-themed photographs gracing the blood toned walls, faces and bodies clad in leather masks and outfits, seductively posing for the camera.

"Holy shit…There's even a picture of the damn dog Max wearing a leather mask."

I took one more glance around the room, turned off the light, then silently crept back up the stairs in need of a very stiff drink. I wanted to find Cassandra and get the hell out of there before Barbara suggested the party move on to the basement.

"Did you have fun?" said Cassandra placing her hand on my thigh as we drove down the highway.

"I had a splendid time. Thanks for inviting me."

"So did I," she answered. "Although we didn't get much of chance to talk. I want to know all there is to know about you Lord Coventry!" Her silky hair brushed the side of her face as she laughed.

"Not you too!" I laughed.

"I'm just shitting with you…although the prospect of dating a Lord really does sound appealing!" Her raised eyebrow mirrored the definition of her cheekbone.

I didn't know if she was serious or kidding. The wound from my last love still tore at my heart, and I wasn't in the mood to be played for a fool.

CHAPTER THREE

Rondell leaned back in the soft pillows of the old tattered couch, her strong stout fingers cupped around the chipped white coffee mug. The brilliant morning sunshine had cut her slumber decidedly short and she was feeling cranky and a little on edge. She heard Pierre stirring in his crib upstairs, probably playing with the tiny stuffed tiger Michelle had picked up during her last venture into Paris. Where was she anyways? It wasn't like her to leave him playing alone for so long, especially first thing in the morning. Usually by now she'd have him on her big bed, snuggling, laughing and telling stories. Michelle loved the way his brown eyes sparkled with anticipation, his little body so full of life and energy, ready to start the day.

Rondell wondered if she'd ever have the chance to be a mother like Michelle. Before Pierre was born, neither one of them had thought too much about having children, never seemed to be the right time, never seemed to have the right partner. Even after Michelle met and fell in love with John, she still wasn't ready to settle down. Starting a family was the last thing on her mind. That all changed when she cradled her newborn son in her arms, kissing his tiny nose and gently caressing the wrinkly skin on his forehead. It was pure bliss.

Letting out an extended yawn, Rondell eased off the couch, setting her half-empty mug on the small side table. A booming blast shook the old farmhouse sending shards of glass catapulting through the air like knives. Rondell dove to the floor, her foot jarring the end of the table, sending the coffee mug and its contents splattering to the floor. Gunfire pounded through the smoke billowing from the upstairs windows. Rondell reached for her gun and snaked across the wooden floor to the window.

"God damit! Police!" They were everywhere, riot gear on and maneuvering in skilled teams through the paths surrounding the farmhouse. "Jesus Christ!"

She ducked her head and took a deep breath before she ventured another look. Thomas, Jacques, and Simon all lay dead or dying in the front yard, defeated in the kill or be killed battle, their blood staining the innocence of the green grass. Just as she was going to charge through the front door, Rondell saw Michelle running towards the farmhouse; her long dark hair raging against the wind, her face distorted with fury, her trigger finger exploding bullets from her gun. She had no fear as the return fire ripped her abdomen open, spilling a once vibrant life onto the dewy ground below. Rondell screamed in horror, her hands shaking, her body convulsing against the bloody scene. She couldn't move. She couldn't think.

The black smoke from the burning roof pushed its way down the stairs, choking out the oxygen in Rondell's lungs. Police bullets rang off the farmhouse walls like a pinball game. She had to make a decision. Join the fight or get the hell out of there. A bone-chilling scream cut through firestorm.

"Oh my God Pierre!"

She dropped her gun, pulled the neck of her shirt over her nose and mouth and stumbled towards the stairs, bloodying her knees against the tough grain of the old wooden floor. The child's cries intensified, sending a shock of panic through her trembling body. The flames were already peeking into the stairwell, licking the banister, like they were laughing and toying with her, as she peered up. With a deep inhale, she held her breath and bounded up the stairs, unable to see and not knowing what to expect.

Pierre's room was ablaze, the flames tearing through the ancient dry roof like it was paper. Crawling on all fours she ripped the outer blanket from Michelle's bed, grabbed the knapsack from the chair, then turned towards the crib at the far end of the room. Wiping her eyes with the blanket, she crouched low, hooking the knapsack over her shoulder. Fear gripped her heart as a huge burning beam crashed against the bed, half crushing it to the ground and igniting the mattress. Pierre's excruciating cries had grown quiet. She had to hurry. Digging deep into her cache of courage, Rondell crawled across the floor, the wood hot and smoking with every inch.

Reaching the crib, she snatched up the child, his limp body sagging in her arms. She wrapped him in the blanket and pulled him tightly to her chest. Staying as low to ground as she could, Rondell found the doorframe purely by touch, the room a black hole of smoke. Swishing her hand across the floor in front of her, she found the top step. A few quick maneuvers and she was descending the stairs on her bottom, like a child first learning to walk. With the smoke not quite as thick as upstairs, Rondell could see a tactical squad of policemen ready to pound through the front door. Making her way past the kitchen, she threw open the basement door, and descended into darkness, almost tripping over the last step and falling in a heap on the cold damp floor.

Scrambling in the dark, she unwrapped Pierre from the blanket and held his face close to her ear, listening for the mere whisper of a breath. Hearing nothing, and not knowing exactly what to do for some inhalation, she plugged his nose, and began breathing into his open mouth, praying that the influx of oxygen would clear his poor little lungs. The seconds seemed like hours. Rondell knew it wouldn't take the police long to find the cellar door. She had to get out of there.

"Breathe child breathe!" she whispered. "C'mon Pierre. You can do it." She placed her lips on his and gently pressed her palm against his chest, counting the beats in her head. With a great gasp for air, Pierre coughed. "That's it! Good for you!"

She wrapped him back in the blanket, soothing him with a soft, loving voice. Taking a lighter from her back pocket, she hammered on the pusher until a small flame flickered illuminating the small dirt-walled room. Working quickly, she grabbed one of the cloth sacks from an old wooden shelving unit and slung it over her other shoulder. With the constant threat of a police raid, the farmhouse basement was well stocked with supplies needed for a quick getaway. Throwing the lighter back in her pocket, she switched on a small but bright flashlight she'd retrieved from a wicker bin on the bottom shelf. Pierre began to whimper.

"I know you're scared," she said softly as she flipped a concealed switch on the side of the shelving unit. "I'm scared too. But we're going to be fine. Just hold on tight okay?"

With a slight push, the unit slid to the left, revealing a tunnel about four feet high and three feet wide. Hunched over and weighed down by her load, she ducked into the passageway, locking the shelving unit back in place from the other side. Safe for the moment, she placed a crying Pierre on the damp ground as she readjusted her backpack, hooking the cloth bag through one of the loops. Hearing the basement door open, she gathered her precious cargo against her chest, pointed the flashlight forward and took off walking as fast as she could.

The tunnel was damp and dirty but at least the air was void of smoke. Rondell could already feel her lungs clearing a little but she was worried about the damage done to Pierre. She wanted to stop and comfort him but she knew the police would search the basement for escape routes. Every hideout they'd had over the years contained a few tunnels or hidden exits for occasions just like this. The police always found them. The key was to be out of the tunnel before they came looking.

Quickening her pace, she dodged the roots, almost knocking her head on a partially exposed rock in the ceiling. Her skin glistened with sweat and her throat was coarse and dry. Still dazed, Pierre whimpered against her chest, his tears streaking his soot covered face.

"Almost there little guy," said Rondell slowing down. She panned the flashlight and quivered as a small snake dove back into a hole near the ceiling of the tunnel. Abruptly, the tunnel stopped. "There it is." Angled up against the side of the tunnel was a sturdy wooden ladder. "We'll be out of the darkness in a second honey. Hold on but I need you to be real quiet okay?" She smoothed back Pierre's dark hair and kissed the top of his head. Her arms were tired from carrying the boy and she wished she'd had the time and the presence of mind to grab his sling. She'd just have to make do.

She desperately wanted a drink of water and judging by the violent hacking coming out of Pierre, he could use one too. Holding the flashlight in her mouth, and Pierre on her hip, she flung the knapsack to the ground and reached inside the cloth bag for a bottle of water. The water felt good on her raw throat, easing the burning sensation. She steadied Pierre's neck and put the bottle to his lips. Almost nine months old now and used to drinking from a cup, he instinctively began to suck as she tilted the bottle ever so slightly.

"That's a good boy! Take a nice long drink. Does that feel better?" Pierre lapped at the liquid like a puppy, droplets dribbling down his chin. "Okay that's enough for now," she said screwing the cap back on. "We've got to keep moving. It isn't safe here."

Rondell knew Pierre couldn't understand her words but she felt better talking out loud; it didn't make her feel so scared and alone. Sitting the child down on the dirt floor, she ventured up the ladder, using all her strength to push open the trap door. Streams of light and fresh air poured into the tunnel, and just for a second, Rondell allowed herself to smile. Taking a quick peek over the top, she tossed the bags, and then went back down the ladder for Pierre. Smeared in black soot and dirt, his clothes torn, the child looked straight out of a Charles Dickens novel, yet somehow his sparkling eyes gave Rondell a sense of hope, that somehow they would make it out of this mess alive. How would she ever tell him his mother was dead?

She scooped the child up in her arms and made her way up the ladder, careful to keep her body as low to the ground as possible as she emerged. She had no idea if the police were combing this far out into the woods yet and wasn't going to take any chances. Setting Pierre off to the side, Rondell closed the trap door, concealing it with leaves, brush, and a few fallen branches. A resounding boom shook the anxious birds from the trees and sent her sprawling to the ground, her body instinctively shielding the terrified boy. She wanted to scream. Everything was happening so fast. She could still hear the cries of her comrades as the police bullets found their mark. Flames leaped from the farmhouse, dancing furiously against the pristine blue sky. Frozen in fear, Rondell laid on the forest floor sobbing, her arms and legs dripping with blood from the patchwork of tree branch and thicket scratches.

"So much death. So many friends. And Michelle. My god Michelle."

She couldn't grieve. Not yet. She had to focus. She had to get the hell out of there, although she had no idea where she was going to go. Tucking the blanket in around Pierre's legs, and adjusting the shoulder straps on her knapsack one more time, she turned towards the unbeaten path, facing an uncertain future, able to only exist in the moment. She walked quickly but cautiously, climbing over the fallen branches and dense underbrush of the thick Normandy forest. Every squawk of a bird or shuffle of the leaves sent her diving for cover, her nerves rattled and her stamina wearing thin. Pierre was restless and getting cranky, wanting out of her arms to explore the terrain on his own.

As much as she wanted to continue, she had to think about the child. Taking a quick peek at her watch, she judged they'd been walking for over an hour. The sting in her back and shoulders suggested much longer. Finding a small open space under a canopy of trees, Rondell laid out the blanket and set Pierre down for a rest, her arms welcoming the respite. Digging into her pocket she found a tissue and attempted to clean up the boy's face with a bit of the water from the bottle. Rondell was glad to see some of his energy returning. His lethargy before had scared the shit out of her. She found a small stick for him to play with, then dumped the contents of the army green knapsack and the brown thick cotton bag on the far edge of the blanket.

Michelle always kept the green knapsack stocked with diapers, a few changes of clothes, and some food. Pierre would be okay for at least a few days. The cloth bag contained a small pistol and ammunition, extra flashlight batteries, some matches and a candle, some rope, three packages of dehydrated army type food, three bottles of water and a wallet flap of money. Rondell counted the bills; it wasn't much but it was better than nothing. She opened a jar of peaches and fed Pierre. He was being such a good little boy, cooing and blabbering as she spooned the pureed food into his mouth. She had to give Michelle credit. It was her idea to build the tunnel, and her idea to put supplies in the cloth bags. Thank god Pierre's knapsack was sitting on the chair by the door. She was always one step ahead, like she knew disaster could strike at any moment.

As Pierre played and stretched on the blanket, Rondell repacked all the items into the knapsack, except for the rope and the pistol; she tucked that into the back of her waistband. She took out her pocket knife and went to work on the cloth bag, cutting off both bottom corners, and making a "v" shaped slit in the top of one side. Using the rope, she fashioned a makeshift harness around the bag, which she then attached to the shoulder straps on the knapsack.

"Sorry Pierre," she said picking up the child and giving him a quick snuggle. "We've got to keep moving."

She placed him in the cloth bag, pulling a leg through each of the bottom holes and tucking the bag under his two arms. Placing the knapsack over her head, she settled Pierre into the harness, his back against her chest, securing the cloth bag with the extra rope. Rondell smiled as he kicked his legs and giggled, happy for some freedom. With her arms free and the weight equally balanced on her front and back, she moved through the forest with greater agility, forging her own road, trying to put as much distance between them and the farmhouse.

Stopping every few hours for water and to give Pierre a break from the harness, Rondell made good time. With the sun easing down into the horizon, she stumbled across a sheltered space between two fallen trees on the edge of a small brook.

"Sorry Pierre but this is the best it's going to get tonight."

Setting the increasingly fussy child down on the spread out blanket, she ventured nearby for some leaves and pine needles; anything to make the ground somewhat softer, and the roof a little more concealed. She found a wash cloth in the side of Pierre's knapsack and with care, gave the boy a quick clean up in the cool waters of the stream.   Frightened and uncomfortable, he wailed as she dripped the water over his soot-stained body.

"Shhh, it's okay baby...I know, you've had a rough day...I'm so, so sorry...you're going to feel so much better all cleaned up."

She talked endlessly while she bathed him, her voice soft, smooth, and reassuring, and not at all a reflection of the turmoil she was feeling inside. With Pierre clean, fed, and playing happily in the leaves, Rondell opened a package of "army" food. Her stomach had been in knots all day and although she still didn't feel like eating, she knew she must. How had this all happened? How did the police find the hideout? Were they betrayed? And if so, by whom? What was she going to do? Where was she going to go? Were the police looking for her? Did they ever know she'd escaped? Surely they'd see Pierre's empty crib and wonder...

She so many questions ran rampant in her head, but she desperately needed to sleep, her thoughts incoherent and senseless. Besides being in the forest, she didn't even have a clue where she was or even what direction she was heading. She would sleep for a few hours and then decide. Her mind would be clearer then. It had to be. Snuggling a drowsy Pierre up under the blanket, she waited for night to fall and sleep to come, her hand firmly guarding the loaded pistol. She didn't want to have to use it, but certainly wouldn't hesitate. There was only so much shit she could take in a day.

The darkness descended, shrouding them deep in the shadows of the forest overhang. A single trail of moonlight illuminated the water of the brook as it babbled over the rocks on its continuous journey. Lulled by the melodious chirp of the crickets, Rondell fell into a state of intermediary, not really asleep, not really awake. The minute she heard the rustle of the leaves her senses jumped, the hair on the back of her neck straight as an arrow. Gripping the pistol a little tighter, she raised it from her chest and pointed it in the direction of the noise. The tramping heightened. Rondell silently dug for the flashlight tucked into the side of the knapsack, her hand sweaty and trembling against the rubber on/off switch.

She stretched her ear, straining to hear a voice or any other discerning human characteristic. Nothing. But that didn't mean much. Police units were trained to be silent. Pierre tossed his sleepy body and inadvertently elbowed her hard in the breast, sending a muffled screech from Rondell's throat. Then she saw the flash of light spring against the trees.

"What was that?" said a female voice from across the brook.

"I don't know," answered the male. "I don't see anything. You're not scared now are you?"

"Shine the flashlight over there more."

Rondell quickly tucked herself as deep into the little cove as she could, pulling the brown blanket over their heads. Maybe, just maybe they would blend into the scenery. She could only hold her breath and wait. They didn't sound like police officers; their voices too young and playful. Her body tensed as the light drew closer, edging onto the corner of the blanket. She gently placed her hand over Pierre's mouth – just in case.

"There's nothing over there Suzette but some trees and a big rock."

"Well I could have sworn I heard something!"

The boy laughed. "Probably just a critter walking around…or maybe a snake!"

"A snake? You never told me there were snakes in this forest!" The two voices blended together in laughter as the light disappeared back across the brook.

"So will you kiss me now Suzette?"

"I'm not kissing you anywhere a snake might crawl up my leg!" the girl answered.

"Well what about on the roadway? It's not that far away."

"Oh Adrien! You try so hard!"

The chatty voices dimmed as they faded amongst the swaying trees. Rondell waited until they had completely disappeared before she pulled back the blanket and breathed a sigh of relief. She looked down at the child asleep on her chest, his pudgy little face squished up against her shoulder. So peaceful. So unafraid and unaware of the world around him. Yesterday he was sleeping in a crib; today he's sleeping in the forest. Yesterday his mother was feeding him apricots and singing him his favorite lullaby. Today his mother is dead. And his father? Michelle had sworn that Rondell never tell John that she'd been pregnant or given birth to his son. Rondell was torn.

As far as she knew, John was in England. But how would she get there? And with the child? She didn't have enough money to purchase tickets for both of them and besides, she'd never get through French or English Customs. Trying to stow away on some lorry making the passage through the English Channel would be almost impossible with baby Pierre. But did John even want to see the child? Rondell knew he'd be furious with Michelle for not telling him right away. And now Michelle was dead. She couldn't tell him about her death or Pierre – at least not yet. Going to England and giving the child to his father was out. Too risky. And if the police had found the farmhouse hideout, maybe they'd found the others scattered about France. Going there wouldn't be safe. Rondell was running out of options. She glanced down at Pierre, a small smile etched on his sleeping face. Her heart broke. No. She couldn't subject him to a life on the run. He needed stability. A place where he could run and play, go to school and make friends.

Germany. She would head home to Germany. Her Aunt lived in a small village near Bonn. Rondell knew her Aunt would take them in and protect them from harm's way. Her Uncle, a well decorated soldier, had been narrowly escaped being killed while defending Adolf Hitler's bunker in Berlin as World War II drew to a close. The Aunt was old now but still spry and much respected in her community. Family meant everything to her, and no one would question her niece and 'great-nephew' coming to stay.

Rondell felt somewhat relieved knowing she had plan. But Bonn Germany was a long way from a makeshift canopy somewhere in the forests of Normandy, and she wasn't sure she had the strength or knowhow to pull it off. Yet, feeling the child's heartbeat pound against her own, somehow gave her the courage to push past her fears. She would make a better life for both of them, free from the violence, the terror, and the awful memories. The road ahead would be long and hard, full of the unknown and wrought with uncertainties, but at least it was a road that they were still alive to travel.

CHAPTER FOUR

I tossed my head back, opening my throat to encourage the safe passage of the two Aspirins I'd popped a few seconds before. Despite the brilliant comfort of the plush bed, I'd slept like shit, tossing and turning worse than a rowboat ripping down some rapids. It was the nightmares. I just couldn't escape them. The continuous foray into the depths of my subconscious was making me a nervous wreck. I had no desire to relieve the past, yet every time I closed my eyes it was there, in full colour, running like an endless movie clip, over and over and over. From Michelle to Brian to Rondell and Pierre; my mind was awash with images, some a vivid recollection, some a figment of my imagination, most a convoluted mishmash of the two.

Clothed only in my boxers, I ventured out to the hotel balcony, hoping the fresh air would offer some clarity to my muddled head. The day was perfect, with the bright sun smiling fondly, shooing away even the slightest bit of cloudy wisps. A couple of cigarettes and a couple of cups of coffee later, I was feeling much better, my headache calmed to a dull roar. Cassandra had wanted me to spend the day with her driving along the coast but I'd already accepted an invitation with Robert King and his yacht. Either way, I was looking forward to being outside enjoying what the day had to offer.

Just after ten am, Robert pulled up in the front of the Beverly Hills Hotel in his flashy white Mercedes convertible, glowing cigar firmly planted in the side of teeth.

"Good day to you Lord Coventry! You're looking well!"

"Thank you Robert," I said ignoring the annoying Lord reference again. "You're looking well yourself." I hopped in the front seat as he held out a cigar. "Oh no thanks. Not much of a cigar smoker but I am partial to my cigarettes!"

Robert turned right onto Hartford Way, then headed south on North Rodeo Drive. Lined with stores like "Tiffany", "Armani", "Gucci", and "Coco Chanel", Rodeo Drive was the most famous shopping district in America, and one of the most expensive blocks of shops in the world. It was the place Hollywood came to shop, and where regular folks came to watch how the rich and celebrated spent their money. Driving down the palm-tree lined street, I marvelled at the beautiful buildings and ridiculously expensive wares in the shop windows. The concentration of wealth and luxury in that three-block radius certainly rivalled, if not exceeded, the best shopping in London and Paris. We had to wait while a long black stretch limousine pulled up in front of the busy Chanel store and two impeccably dressed women got out of the car to a wall of snapping photographers.

"I can't even imagine living like that," I said shaking my head at the spectacle.

"This is Hollywood John…Rodeo Drive," answered Robert. "They know full well the paparazzi are waiting for them. In fact, their publicist probably tipped them off about the appearance. Here any publicity is good publicity. It's all about keeping your name on the edge of everyone's tongue."

"I guess," I laughed. "But I still can't imagine living that way. Actually inviting attention to yourself? I go out of my way to stay unnoticed!"

"And why is that John? I'd think a man of your pedigree and culture would relish time in the spotlight."

I feigned a laugh. "No, no, that's not generally the British way. I'd rather just go about my day and mind my own business."

"You're not going to last long in LA then!" he laughed, exuding a huge puff of smoke. "Good thing you've got me in your corner. Trust me, if you want to make it in America, then you've got to get out there and grip it by the ass! It's yours for the taking!"

He hung a right onto Santa Monica Boulevard, skirting north of Century City, then south on the San Diego Freeway through West Los Angeles and south to the Marina Freeway. It wasn't a long drive but I couldn't believe the number of streets and other major highways we flew by. There was no way I'd ever learn my way around this sprawling metropolis. Unlike London and most of the large European cities I'd been to, Los Angeles was built for cars, more specifically convertibles, and I was quite enjoying the sun on my face, and the wind in my hair as we whizzed closer to the coast.

Stepping out of the parked car, I got my first full view of the glorious Fisherman's Village, one of the largest man-made small boat harbours in the United States. I followed Robert past the rows upon rows of boats moored on the wooden docks, from sailboats to cruising boats to speed boats to some of the largest and most luxurious private yachts I'd ever seen. He stopped in front of a handsome double-decker yacht and held out his arm.

"After you. Just climb on over."

"Wow Robert this boat is spectacular!"

"Yes, it's not half bad if I do say so myself!"

The teak trim juxtaposed against the cream coloured cabin bulkheads gave the boat a lavish but comfortable atmosphere. Robert pointed to bar.

"Help yourself. I just need to go check a few things with the captain before we shove off."

I poured myself a rather large whiskey then headed out for a seat and a smoke on the top deck. I wondered how in the hell the captain was going to manoeuvre the boat out of the slip and into the harbour canal. The place was packed, with little room for error on every side.

"It's quite a sight isn't it," said Robert. "There's something about being on the water that I find so relaxing. How about you?"

"I love the water," I answered. "My family and I spent many summer vacations in the Mediterranean."

"Tell me about your family John," he said tilting back his glass of scotch. "You obviously come from some money. I could tell the moment I met you."

"Well yes my family has done all right in the business world." The less I told Robert about my family and my past the better. He seemed to me the sort of person who enjoyed gathering tidbits of personal information to use at his own discretion in the future. I hardly knew him, and I certainly didn't trust him.

"What sort of business were you in back in England? And on that note, what brings you to Los Angeles?"

The captain steered the boat out of the slip and headed up the canal towards the open sea. "How does he do that? So effortlessly?" I said changing the subject.

Robert laughed. "Money. Money can buy you the best of everything, including sea captains! So you were saying about your family?"

I hadn't been saying anything about my family but Robert was keen to push the subject. "My family owned a customs business in Liverpool. Sim and Coventry was the name. It's changed hands and names now." I figured there was no point in lying about the family business. It's not like that was the family secret.

"So why come to Los Angeles then?"

I polished off my drink with an exaggerated gulp. "I think you said it yourself Robert. Los Angeles is a place for opportunity. I'm young and single. Why the hell not come here? I mean look at this view?" The yacht was now steaming through the open waters of the deep blue Pacific Ocean. "Perpetual sunshine, warm breezes, and whiskey on a fabulous yacht? Is there any better place on earth?"

I knew I was laying it on a little thick, but Robert didn't need to know I'd essentially been blackballed from gainful employment back in England. Apparently reputable companies weren't all that interested in hiring someone with a criminal record.

"I worked in Finance," I lied. "Handling the money end of customs transactions and such."

"Oh splendid!" he answered. "I'd love to introduce you to some people I know. Very well connected in the business world."

"I'd like that Robert, thank you."

Seeing my empty drink, he motioned for me to go back downstairs, refill and bring up the bottle. I didn't know that much about the man but he certainly seemed generous. The conversation drifted into small talk as Robert gave me a rundown on the Marina and surrounding coastline. I was shocked and delighted when he pointed out a small pod of dolphins swimming off the starboard side of the boat, diving and dancing across the sparkling waters like a well-rehearsed recital. While in South Africa with Michelle, I'd glimpsed some dreadful sharks in the display tank in Durban, and they definitely were not as playful as these seemingly similar but non-related aquatic friends.

"So let me ask you a question John," said Robert filling his own glass. "Why don't you have a title, like Lord or Count or something like that?"

"Well not everyone in England has a title," I laughed.

"But you should." The crease on his forehead deepened as he inhaled deeply on his cigar. "Titles are very important in the United States. They can open a lot of doors and get you places the common man isn't welcome."

"That's all well and good but it's not like I can just knock on the door to Buckingham Palace and ask if they'd be so kind to grant me a Lordship!"

Robert smirked. "What would you say if I told you I've already taken care of it?"

"What are you talking about?"

Robert reached for a file folder of papers tucked in the side of the empty chair. "I've told you before John, or should I say Count Coventry of Rozel, money can buy you anything!" He handed me the file folder.

After flipping through and studying the pages, much to my utter amazement I was now legally and officially Count Coventry of Rozel. I was stunned.

"How did you do this?" I said laughing.

"It's just a $100 title," he answered. "On the surface it means nothing, but trust me…in the long run it will help us both.

I took another long gulp from my drink. "Where on earth is Rozel?" The absurdity of it astounded me.

Robert chuckled. "Rozel? I just made that up! But it sounds damn good doesn't it!" He roared with laughter, the cigar smoke shooting out his nose. "You can pay me back with a drink sometime!"

Finishing off my glass and refilling another, I wondered why Robert would buy me a title. What did he want from me? I knew he didn't do it out of the goodness of his heart. He wanted something. Men like him always did. But what? I couldn't quite put my finger on it. No harm in playing along and seeing where it all might lead. I had to admit, the whole thing was rather amusing. Me? Lord Coventry of Rozel? I suppose it couldn't hurt my credibility, after all, there was nothing illegal about it and it actually might add to my cover. I had to hand to Robert, he didn't dick around. And if he was trying to impress me with the title and the day on the yacht, he did.

We toured around the open sea and up the coast towards Malibu. Robert handed me a pair of high-powered binoculars as he pointed out the tip of the Channel Islands just visible on the horizon. I'd come five thousand miles in an attempt to distance myself from the past and my memories, yet once again, a name and an image threw me right back. My mind immediately journeyed to the wonderful time I'd spent with Michelle in Jersey, one of the Channel Islands off the coast of France. We were like two teenagers, lost in our love, without a care in the world. It's crazy how things change. Now I'm in Los Angeles and Michelle's ashes lie scattered in St. Brelards Bay. Sometimes I couldn't even wrap my head around the concept.

Scanning the water with the binoculars, I noticed a smaller type of boat, not a yacht, but more of a speed boat sitting about two hundred meters off the portside. With a zoom of the lens, I saw two men standing in the boat. One of the men had a pair of binoculars pointed our way.

"What the hell?" I mumbled.

"What's that?" said Robert.

"Maybe it's just me but I think these guys are watching us? Here, take a look."

Robert peered through the lenses. "Well they don't look like photographers now do they?" He laughed. "And I've never quite seen boaters out for an afternoon cruise wearing suits and ties! That's really quite odd. I don't recognize them but I wouldn't worry John. Probably just some gossip mongers out trying to rustle up a story. Happens all the time."

I was worried. The more I thought about it, the more those men on the boat rattled my nerves. Why were they out there? What did they want? Were they watching me or Robert? I tipped back the remainder of my drink, then took another look. The boat was gone, heading back along the shore. I'm sure Robert was right. No big deal. Maybe the toxic combination of the hot sun and the near empty bottle of whisky had my imagination running on full throttle. I was feeling rather lightheaded and more than a little drunk. I chocked it up to old fears, cast from a different time and in a vastly different place. But still, I couldn't help but wonder.

Robert King was a wonderful host and despite my apprehensions about the man, I'd thoroughly enjoyed my day on the yacht. I'm not sure how much credence I'd give to the development of a true friendship, but he seemed to like me, and was definitely the sort of man you wanted on your side. Right now, that's all I wanted, to make a few acquaintances, set up some business connections, and perhaps have a wee bit of fun. So far so good.

I blamed my wobbly legs on the sea and not the booze as I stumbled behind Robert back to the car. He'd suggested we meet up for a late dinner at the Polo Lounge but I had to decline. All I wanted was a sandwich from the Fountain Coffee Room at the hotel, a nice long hot shower and some television in bed. Hopefully tonight I would just sleep. No dreams, no nightmares, no recollections of anything whatsoever. Just sleep. That would be a welcome reprieve.

CHAPTER FIVE

Rondell shifted Pierre's heavy, sleep-laden head from the crook of her arm and arched her aching back, sending a staccato of cracks down her spine. Stiff and sore, her body yearned for a relaxing soak in a steaming tub of hot bubbly water. What she wouldn't do for a coffee. She carefully laid the bundled Pierre on the leaves beside her and crawled out of the shelter. The sun was barely peeking through the tree tops, spotlighting a chorus of birds ushering in the morning with a cheerful song. Rondell kneeled at the side of the brook and splashed some cool water on her face, attempting to brush through her tangled hair with her wet fingers. With Pierre still sound asleep, she dug into the knapsack for a pre-packaged meal. It wasn't the tastiest breakfast she'd ever had, but it was enough to keep the barking dogs in her stomach at bay.

After her meal, she readied some food for Pierre. She wanted to hit the road as soon as possible but the sight of his peaceful, even breaths swaying the blanket made her take pause. The little guy had been through so much drama in the last twenty-four hours, the thought of disturbing him made her cringe. Had it really only been twenty-four hours? Rondell straddled her legs over a fallen tree trunk, leaning back against the crux of a branch. Twenty four hours. A mere blip of time in the grand scheme of things, yet to her aching heart, it felt like years. Years since she felt the warmth and security of four walls filled with the laughter and comfort of friends, of Michelle. She longed for the chance to say good bye, to at least have been able to see her infectious smile one last time. Just one more laugh. One more hug. One more word. Goodbye.

Rondell knew the farmhouse had been close to the village of Périers-sur-le-Dan, which was about twenty kilometers or so south of the shores of Juno Beach, one of the five Allied landing spots during the Normandy landings in World War II. From her crude calculations, she judged that the city of Caen was approximately fifteen kilometers south of the village. Of course, that didn't take into consideration how far they had walked yesterday or in what direction. In her panic to escape, she hadn't bothered to worry where they were headed, as long as they were headed away from the farmhouse. She needed to find a road, any road, something that had a sign, something to give her the slightest notion that she knew where the hell they were going.

Bonn, Germany was at least eight hundred kilometers away. If she could steal a car or hop a ride, she could maybe make it in seven or eight hours, otherwise, she was looking at an almost impossible trek on foot, especially with Pierre. But her options were limited. Stealing a car was a huge risk. If she got caught, that would be the end of it, and she would probably never see Pierre again. Besides, car license plates could be tracked. Even if she did make it to Bonn in a stolen car, the police would eventually find the car wherever she ditched it, and would be one step closer to finding her. She would have to find another way.

Feeling anxious and apprehensive, she gently brushed back Pierre's black curls, hoping the slight touch would rouse him from his slumber. They needed to get going. The police would be out looking for them, perhaps setting loose the tracking dogs. It wouldn't take them long to pick up their scent. Pierre yawned as Rondell spoke softly, freeing him from the constraints of the blanket and changing his diaper. She fed him his breakfast and let him play in the leaves while she packed up the knapsack.

"Okay sweetie, it's time to go. Come to..." She hesitated, not sure what to call herself. Circumstances had changed. Was she still Aunt Rondell? Would that raise suspicions? She couldn't use the name Rondell anymore, at least not outside the comfort of her Aunt's home. Pierre's chocolate brown eyes smiled at her indecision, his chubby little arms outstretched, waiting to be held.

"I'm doing this for you," said Rondell holding back the tears. The words barely made it past the lump in her throat. "Come to Mama, Pierre. Come to Mama."

Not knowing the difference, the child scampered into Rondell's arms, just happy for the attention and snuggle.

"Oh my poor child, you have no idea do you?" She hugged Pierre tight, her wet eyes moistening the side of his cheek. "I will never let you forget about your Mama, I promise you that. She will always be a part of your life and right here in your heart." She took the boy's hands and placed them on his chest. "Always in your heart Pierre. Right there." The boy giggled, tilting his head to the side, almost as if he was weighed down by his enormous smile. Rondell couldn't help but laugh. That was the innocence of a child. Everything was in the moment. No worries about the past, no worries about the future, the here and now was all that ever mattered. She wished she could be so carefree.

With a quick kiss on his nose, she saddled him into the pouch and strapped on the knapsack. For some reason, the burden seemed lighter today than it did yesterday. Maybe it was perspective. Yes, she had a long troublesome journey ahead, and yes she wasn't exactly sure how she was going to manage, but she was alive and above all, she had hope. That was Pierre's doing. Just knowing that the incoherent baby babblings coming from his mouth would one day turn into discernable intelligent words, and that his wobbly footsteps would become powerful youthful strides, buoyed her optimism. Life moves on. There was no turning back, only steps forward. Rondell tightened the pack around her waist, checked the direction of the sun and breathed deeply. Somehow, someway, she would make it to Caen.

According to the conversation between her two visitors last night, the road couldn't be too far away. She just had to find a way across the creek. She picked up a rock and tossed it as close to the center of the water as she could. The resounding deep and hollow "kerplunk" echoed water not shallow enough for an easy crossing, especially someone laden with a backpack and a child. She'd have to keep looking. Rondell followed the bank of the creek as it twisted through the branches and undergrowth, randomly throwing in rocks to check the crossing depth. Finally, she happened upon a narrow strip with a large dead log draped three quarters of the way across the water.

"I think this is as good as it's going to get Pierre," she laughed. "Just hold on and hope we don't get wet."

She tightened the straps around the child and climbed onto the edge on the log. With controlled trepidation, she steadied her foot on the decomposing bark, careful to avoid the slimy, green moss creeping up the sides. It's not like she was one hundred feet in the air, crossing the creek on a tightrope or anything, but Rondell didn't want to fall and add wet clothes to their already damp disposition. Seeming to sense the adventure, Pierre babbled non-stop, providing a rambling play-by-play with each step. The sweet sound of his innocent little voice made her smile.

"Oh you think this is funny do you?" she said under her slow and steady breath. "Here I am doing all the work, while you get to sit nice and cozy, just watching the scenery." Pierre twirled a piece of hair in his chubby fingers, paying no attention. "Just what I thought," she laughed. "You have nothing to say for yourself!"

As she neared the end of the log, she surmised how she was going to execute the final jump to dry land without ending up face first on the shore. The distance was more than a step but not quite a leap. Eying a small green patch of moss, she wrapped her left arm around the front of Pierre, took a deep breath, and promptly slipped off the side of the log, falling shin deep into the water.

"Shit! Well that didn't work out the way I'd planned." She hauled herself up the bank, half cursing, and half laughing at her misfortune. "You stupid woman Rondell! All you had to do was jump to the green spot! But no…you have to slip and land in the water." She'd managed to keep Pierre somewhat dry but the thought of having to trudge along in squishy socks and sopping shoes made her wince. "I bet you're just loving this aren't you Pierre?" she said tickling him under his arm, eliciting a playful screech. "You crazy rascal!

The exposed edge of a nearby rock proved to be a worthy chair while she removed her shoes and rung the water out of her socks; a constant stream of angry German phrases muttering from her lips. She twisted each sock around a buckle on her knapsack and gingerly tucked her feet into each shoe. As uncomfortable as bare feet inside her shoes might be, she'd rather risk a few blisters than walk a minute in those socks.

"C'mon Pierre," she said picking up a long piece of wood to use as a walking stick. "We've got to find that road and figure out where the heck we are. Those kids must have been following some sort of path. I just have to find it." She peered around in the underbrush for a minute until she found what appeared to be some trampled growth heading in an easterly direction. "This must be it. In any case, we have nothing to lose do we kid?"

Trudging along a semi-groomed path was much easier than hacking and beating away branches with every step, and Rondell was able to set a much faster pace than she had the day before. The growing intensity of the sun and the lessoning of the shadows told her that she was close to some sort of open space in the forest. She prayed it was a road. Better yet, the road to Caen.

"Okay Pierre," she whispered. "You're going to have to be real quiet okay? Mama just has to take a quick peek and make sure no one is sitting up there waiting for us."

She slowed her step, her senses heightened to any extraneous noise or movement. The path veered to the left, jutting into a small hollow, then out into the opening. Being extra cautious, she crouched low to the underbrush, stepping off the path and sneaking around the other way, so she could get an unimpeded view of the roadway. Convinced the coast was clear, she scampered through the gully and up onto the roadside.

"We did it Pierre! We did it!"

With the sun not quite high in the sky, Rondell figured it was around mid-morning, and if it was around mid-morning that meant the sun shining parallel to the road was still in the eastern sky. With a triumphant smile, she turned to the right and started walking. She had no idea if the road would lead to Caen but at least they were headed south. It was a start.

Rondell stuck close to the side of the gravelly road, unsure if she would dive back into the forest at the first sound of a car or take her chances and maybe hop a ride.

While she moved at a decent pace, the weight of the knapsack, the child, and her anxiety at being picked up by the police, made her feel like she had a load of bricks tied to her legs. There was no way she could walk the entire way to Germany. She needed to get off this road. A ragged looking single woman walking with a young child on a forest-lined road was a sitting duck for the police or any other creep who might happen by. She needed to get to the city and disappear into the crowd. She would figure out the next step from there.

The hot summer sun pounded against them, raising both Rondell's temperature and her ire. Pierre was restless and irritable, whining and whimpering. She tried to soothe him with words and then some water from the bottle, but the child wanted down. She tuned out his cries and pushed on, hoping he might eventually tire and fall asleep. But the cries intensified, forcing Rondell off the road and under the cool shade of a tree for a brief respite and a bite to eat. She couldn't deny the rest felt good on her weary legs.

Pierre eagerly gobbled his snack, then explored his new surroundings on his hands and knees, laughing and giggling with each new discovery. Rondell smiled and wished she shared his enthusiasm. Sweat dripped from her forehead, carving out a winding path as it meandered through the dust caked wrinkles on her weather worn face. Her green eyes, once filled with youthful exuberance for life, for love, and for the 'cause', dimmed with the reality of the farmhouse raid. It wasn't supposed to end this way. They were supposed to be the victorious ones.

She gathered up their things and bundled a reluctant Pierre back into the harness. She felt bad for the child but she just didn't have the strength to carry him in her arms. Besides, with him strapped to her chest, there was no chance they'd become separated if she had to make a run for it. They'd been walking for about fifteen minutes when Rondell heard the sound of tire tracks ripping through the gravel. She had to take a chance. Stepping out into the middle of the lane, she held up her hand, frantically waving it in the air. The car slowed to a stop.

Rondell ran around to the open passenger side window. "Excuse me ma'am but I'm wondering if you can help me out with a ride." The woman lifted her sunglasses. "You see my son and I need to get to Caen as soon as possible. You wouldn't happen to heading that way would you?"

The woman looked at Rondell and smiled. "I don't usually pick up hitchhikers, but you look like you've been through hell and could use a break. Hop in."

Rondell unhooked Pierre from the harness, threw the knapsack over the seat, and climbed in the front. "Thank you so much. You're a lifesaver." She set Pierre on her lap and buckled the seat belt as the woman shifted gears into drive.

"So if you don't mind me asking," said the woman. "What are you and your son doing out here?"

"It's a long story," answered Rondell. "You see my boyfriend...he can get to be a certain way when he starts drinking...and well I just couldn't take it anymore. I had to get out of there. And fast."

"I know the type," said the woman. "My first husband was a bastard. Cheated on me. Liked to knock me around. Like you, there came a time when I said, enough is enough...and I left. Divorced him and left Paris about five years ago. Found myself a nice quiet farmer, got remarried, and couldn't be happier."

Rondell smiled. "Does he have any brothers?"

The two chatted and laughed while they drove, Rondell breathing a huge sigh of relief that the woman seemed to buy her story and didn't probe any deeper.

"I am headed to the market in Caen," said the woman. "Is that close enough to where you need to go?"

"That's perfect," said Rondell. "I can't thank you enough for helping my son and I. We certainly appreciate it!"

"No problem...I'm sorry," she said, "I didn't get your name?"

"Lisette," answered Rondell without hesitation. "And this here is Andre."

"Well my name is Jules and I am pleased to meet the acquaintance of a strong, brave woman like yourself."

Rondell really didn't feel all that strong or all that brave, and she felt horrible for having to lie to Jules about being abused, especially since the woman had actually been through the experience herself. But she needed a sob story, and playing the 'abused woman' card was the best move she had. At this point, getting a ride to Caen was more important than keeping her integrity.

The market was jammed as Jules pulled her car into an empty spot, narrowly avoiding a collision with another parked car. Rondell thanked the woman again as she threw the knapsack over her shoulder and cradled Pierre in her arms.

"Are you sure there isn't anything more I can do to help?" said Jules.

"No, I appreciate your kindness but you've done more than enough."

"Take care of yourself Lisette. And take care of that cute little boy. I wish you the best of luck." Much to Rondell's surprise, the woman reached over and gave her and Pierre a hug. "Stay safe. And get to wherever you need to go as soon as possible."

The soft lingering touch of Jules' hand on her own made Rondell wonder if the woman suspected there was more to her story than an abused boyfriend. News of the farmhouse raid would be all over the papers, radio, and television, and if Jules put two and two together, it wouldn't have been that difficult to place Rondell in the middle of it all.

Not letting down her guard, Rondell smiled. "Next time, I will be sure to pick a better boyfriend!"

The market at Caen was a wonderful sight of colours, smells, and sights. Various vendors selling local fruits and vegetables intermingled with a mix of vendors selling household goods, clothing, and beautiful flower stands. Rondell had been here many times with Michelle, and the memory of their good times filled her with grief. Almost completely destroyed in the Battle of Normandy during World War II, Caen was a tribute to the tenacity of its residents and a triumph of marrying pre-war architecture with post-war modernism.

The first thing Rondell wanted to do was find a washroom with some nice hot water so she could give her face a good scrubbing, and at least attempt to lose the 'woman on the run' appearance. Digging into the knapsack she found the wallet of money, tucked the bills into the front pocket of her pants, then discarded the leather purse into a trash can. Finding a small café, she ordered a coffee and some pastry for herself and a glass of milk and some bread for the child. The waiter pointed out the washrooms and Rondell made haste. She didn't want to linger.

"Oh my God," she said looking at herself in the mirror. "You are a sight!"

She still had traces of black soot everywhere. No wonder Jules was suspicious and the waiter gave her an unsettling look. As Pierre sat on the floor, she quickly found the soap and washed the grunge from her face, arms, and hands. Every bit of exposed skin was given the once over. She ducked her hair under the running tap, working up the soap suds with her strong fingers. Dirty water splashed over the sides and onto the wooden floor. She was making a mess, but at this point, she didn't care. Once she started to cleanse, she couldn't stop. It was like this was her chance to wash away the pain and anguish of the last few days and start fresh.

Finished with herself, she went to work on Pierre. He wasn't pleased about sitting naked in the small sink and voiced his displeasure.

"Oh stop it," Rondell laughed, wiping her soapy hands under his armpit and down his back. "You're going to feel so much better. And you're going to look like a brand new little boy!" Pierre slapped his hands against the side of the sink, sending water droplets shooting up into the air like a rocket. "Okay, we're almost done. Just a few more scrubs between your toes and voila!"

She lifted the boy out of the brown water and hit the button on the automatic hand dryer. Pierre giggled as the warm air tickled his bare skin. With a clean diaper and new set of clothes from the knapsack, no one would ever suspect the hell the boy had been through the past couple of days, and that's just the way Rondell wanted it. She cleaned up the mess as much as possible, and fluffed her hair one last time under the hand dryer. It wasn't pretty, but it would have to do. At least she felt like a human being again, and not some wayward creature roaming the streets.

She tucked Pierre into the highchair, ripped up some pieces of bread and placed the glass of milk to his mouth. He drank heartily, sucking back the goodness with a satisfied lip smack. After existing on dehydrated food, the warm pastry and steaming coffee was manna from heaven to Rondell's senses.

She savoured each bite and ordered a second cup of coffee and Pierre another glass of milk. She knew she needed to get moving; staying in one place for so long wasn't safe, but it had been such a long trip, and such a long time since she'd sat among civilization, that she just couldn't help herself. Besides, Pierre needed the break and his body needed the milk.

Now what? They'd made it safely to Caen but Bonn was still a long way to go. Rondell took a sip of her coffee. She had to think. Walking was out of the question. She could try and find another sympathetic person like Jules who might drive her but that was risky. A long car ride meant conversation, and conversation meant questions that Rondell didn't want to answer. A piece of flying bread snapped her train of thought. Pierre was restless and tired of sitting in the highchair. Rondell paid the bill, strapped on the knapsack and buckled Pierre into the harness. Just as she was going to open the door, a policeman stopped to talk to a shopper, smiling at Pierre through the windowpane. Rondell froze.

Running wasn't an option. It would raise the alarm. She took a deep breath and steadied her hands on the door handle. She could do this. All she had to do was walk out the door and disappear into the marketplace. The officer didn't know who they were and at the moment, he didn't suspect a thing. He was too busy chatting and laughing with the middle-aged woman carrying a satchel of fresh flowers. One more deep breath. She closed her eyes, pulled back the door and stepped right into the path of the oncoming policeman.

"Oh I'm sorry," she said. Her voice quivered.

"My fault madam. Wasn't watching where I was going," the officer answered. "That sure is a cute little boy you have there!"

"Thank-you. Yes he is." Rondell could feel the colour draining from her face and the sweat begin to build along her hairline. She had to get out of there. She smiled at the officer and tried to manoeuvre to the left but his hand was on her arm.

"Is everything okay? You seem rather upset."

"No, no, not upset," laughed Rondell. "Just hot and tired."

The officer removed his hand. "Yes it certainly is a humid one today."

Rondell nodded in agreement and took a few hurried steps forward, doing everything in her power not to run. The officer watched her walk away. Something didn't seem right. By the time he pulled out his notepad, glanced at the description of the possible runaway terrorist, and readied his radio, the woman was gone, vanishing into the crowd with her beaten, smoke-stained knapsack, and her baby. Rondell heard the police whistle crackle through the air and took off running, her heart thumping wildly, Pierre screaming in her ear. The police sirens grew louder as the marketplace streamed with badges, all trying to be the one to catch the fugitive. Dodging through the market stalls, she took off down an alley way, then another, turning left, then right, then left, then right again. She had no idea where she was going.

Rondell slowed to a fast walk as she turned a corner and came upon a large soft-sided container truck parked along the side of the street. The back of the truck was open and piled high with crates marked "Strasbourg" in big black letters. Sneaking a peek around the side of the truck, Rondell saw a heavy-set man with grey hair leaning up against the front of the truck smoking a cigarette and drinking a coffee. The sound of laughter indicated he was not alone. Placing her hand gently over Pierre's mouth, she stole towards the back of the truck, heaving her body onto the metal frame, and up and over the barrier. As quickly and quietly as she could, she struggled through the crates to the front of the truck, finding a bit of an open space to lie down. All she could smell was apples. She'd take apples over dehydrated food any day.

With a massive thud that shook the sides of the truck, the driver closed the two big back doors, throwing Rondell and Pierre into complete darkness. A minute later, the engine growled to life, drowning out the sound of the sirens and whistles. For the first time in ages, Rondell felt safe. She dug into the knapsack and retrieved the flashlight. At least they would have a little light. With Pierre on the floor playing in the blanket, she attempted to move some of the crates to give them a bit more room, but they were too heavy. Not knowing when she'd get another chance, she filled the knapsack with as many apples as she could carry, then settled Pierre in her arms for the long ride.

On the border between France and Germany, Rondell figured it would be about an eight hour drive to Strasbourg, provided the driver didn't stop. It was perfect. A little further south than she wanted to go but at least she'd only have to worry about eluding customs once. This wouldn't be the first time she'd snuck back into Germany. If she'd gone the shorter, more direct route across the top of France, she would have had to cross into Belgium before she hit Germany. That was too many borders and much too risky.

Of course, she had no idea how she was going to get out of the truck without being seen, but she'd deal with that later. Right now, all she wanted to do was sleep. Her body ached with exhaustion. Little Pierre was already sound asleep in her arms, lulled by the rocking motion of the truck speeding down the highway. She kissed the top of his head and wiggled her back into a more comfortable position. Maybe, just maybe, this nightmare would soon be over.

CHAPTER SIX

"Good morning John, it's Cassandra."

"Hello Cassandra. How are you?" I said adjusting the phone against my ear.

"I am very well. You on the other hand don't sound too great."

"Didn't have the best sleep. Again."

"Sorry to hear that. Well maybe this will make you feel better. I have a dinner date tonight with some friends at the home of Vincent Schiavelli…want to come?"

"Sure!" I said happy at the prospect of getting out. "Who is Vincent Schiavelli?"

"You're kidding right?"

"No…I have no idea who he is."

"Ghost with Demi Moore and Patrick Swayze? The subway spirits? Any of this ringing a bell?"

"Again…sorry I never saw the movie."

"What am I going to do with you?" she laughed. "No mind. I'll pick you up at seven."

"That sounds wonderful Cassandra. I'll see you tonight. Looking forward to it."

I couldn't have picked a better first friend to make than Cassandra. She seemed to know all the right people and had invitations to the best dinners and parties. First, it was Barbara

Saberton's blow out gala, now it was off to Vincent Schiavelli's for an intimate dinner. Vincent lived with his wife Carol in a beautiful apartment in Hollywood. I didn't know much about them except what Cassandra told me in the car. She looked gorgeous in a yellow cotton dress that flirted all the way to the tops of her knees. If Cassandra was trying to flaunt her feminine whiles, as a way to capture my attention, it was working.

Vincent was a rather small eccentric man with very sad, droopy eyes, a pronounced Roman nose, and scraggly hair that had the appearance of a recent run-in with an electrical outlet. But those sad eyes were warm, and his demeanour, kind and inviting. He answered the door smoking a deep brown, wood grain tobacco pipe, the kind that curved up to the sky, then down to ground, then back up to the sky, a la Sherlock Holmes. The sitting room, with its antique look and big leather chairs and sofa, reminded me of the old drawing room in my parent's house, complete with a beautiful collection of pipes that were perched on a stunning mahogany rack, not far from a vase chocked full of very large peacock feathers.

Besides Cassandra and I, there were only about five other guests milling about and none that I recognized. After a round of introductions, I took a seat beside a fellow Englishman named Bernard Hill, and I wasn't the least bit surprised when he told me he was an actor.

"I have to be honest Bernard. I haven't seen many movies, so I'm at a loss when I'm introduced to all these actors. I have no idea who played a part in what! I feel so out of place!"

"Nonsense," he answered. "Let me see if I can help you out. I played Captain Edward John Smith in Titanic. Surely, you've seen that movie? It's one of the highest grossing films of all time."

I blushed. "I'm sorry…never got out to see it."

"Well you should! It's a spectacular film...and I'm not just saying that because I happen to be in it!" He laughed. The man had a real laid-back way about him, and I felt like the two of us could have just as easily been sitting back in a London pub having a pint together, as we were sitting in Vincent's home.

"Listen John, I'm having a dinner party tomorrow night at a nice little place in Beverly Hills just off Sunset Boulevard. Nothing special but I'd love for you to come."

"Are you serious?"

"Sure I'm serious," he answered with a smile.

"In that case, I'd be honoured. Thank you so much for the invitation...I really appreciate it. I can't believe how generous everyone has been here. I'm not sure I'll be able to keep up with the schedule!"

"Since you're new here John," chimed Vincent. "C'mon upstairs with me. I want to show you something."

Bernard noticed the quizzical look on my face and whispered, "He means upstairs to the roof mate."

"Oh yes...the roof! Of course!" I hopped off the couch, smiling at Bernard and followed Vincent up the stairs.

"It's my secret hideaway," he said opening the door.

"Vincent it's fantastic!"

A lush garden, full of brilliant flowers, fresh vegetables, herbs and other sorts of vegetation blanketed a large section of the roof. My eyes followed the cobblestone path that led to the middle of the garden, where a scrumptious rack of lamb was inching its way around on a large barbeque spit. The twinkling lights from Hollywood below gave the impression the sky was just an extension of the city, all aglow with a glorious shimmer, while the smell of the lamb hung in the air like droplets, caught in the haze of the warm humid night.

As we were chatting, another couple surfaced from the stairs below.

"John Coventry," said Vincent, "I'd like you to meet John Clark and his wife Lynn Redgrave."

John Clark bounded across the terrace, grabbing my hand for a hearty handshake. "How are you? It's a fine evening up here tonight."

Clark was dressed in a pair of jeans with a brightly coloured shirt that matched his youthful enthusiasm and sense of humour. For a man in his late 60's he looked very young, his crystal blue eyes dancing like stars. Lynn Redgrave was the picture of beauty, and looked as though she'd just stepped off the stage. The Redgrave's were acting legends in Britain, from parents Michael and Rachel, to children Corin, Lynn, Vanessa, and their children. Lynn herself was nominated for both an Academy Award and a Golden Globe Award for her work in the 1963 film, "Georgy Girl". That much of movie history I knew.

A most delightful woman with her reddish hair and bright blue eyes, Redgrave had the smile of a movie star, yet her graciousness and humble nature gave the impression she'd prefer talking with friends over a steaming cup of tea. She glided over and reached for my hand in such a light and majestic way, I felt my heart jump just a little. I wasn't often star-struck but this woman had me in a tizzy.

"So nice to meet you John," she said with her delicate British accent, not letting go of my hand.

"The pleasure is certainly all mine," I replied.

We chatted on the roof, downing drinks and stories, while the lamb turned slowly on the spit. It was a glorious evening and I was thoroughly enjoying myself. Lynn and her husband invited me to visit them in their home in Topanga Canyon, not too far away, but up in the hills. Of course, I couldn't turn down the invitation! Dinner at Lynn Redgrave's house? My former friends in London would be so jealous. Would they still shun me now? I wanted to send them all a picture from one of these little dinner parties.

This seemed to be my life now. Parties, drinking, more parties, more people. It was the kind of lifestyle you could lose yourself in, and probably the exact kind of lifestyle that Michelle abhorred. Wealth, money, estates, caviar, eating lamb off a rooftop barbeque spit. Michelle would see the lamb as a sacrifice made by 'the people' for the comfort of the upper echelons of society. I saw the lamb as a tender piece of meat to be enjoyed with some mint jelly and a good glass of wine. We had our differences - that's for sure.

Cassandra had a later engagement to see a friend performing at a club, and since I wasn't really in the mood for loud music, I declined her invitation and told her I could find my own way back to the hotel. I was quite enjoying my time at the Schiavelli's and was in no hurry to leave. As the party thinned out, Vincent invited me back up to the roof for another drink and a smoke. The two of us sat there for hours, just chatting, smoking, and getting to know one another. I found a very kind soul in the man, almost a kindred spirit. He made me feel comfortable, like I could tell him anything, and the secret would be safe. But as much as I wanted to trust him, I just couldn't tell him the truth about my past. It was still too early, and I still had to be so careful.

As I stepped out of the taxi, I wasn't sure if the alcohol was playing tricks, but I swore the man sitting on the bench outside the Beverly Hills Hotel looked familiar. His dark suit and dark demeanour gave me the creeps, and I could feel his watchful eyes on my back as I paid the cabbie and stumbled along the walkway. I tried to be friendly and said hello but he just turned his head and walked away. Very odd to say the least.

That last scotch with Vincent was a real kicker and I struggled to make it up to my room, the halls like a fun house, widening and narrowing with every step. But it'd been a great night; well worth the headache that would be knocking in my brain tomorrow. For once I slept soundly and late into the morning.   No nightmares, no worrying, no thoughts whatsoever. I could thank the alcohol for that. But I stunk. My stomach was growling, but there was no way I could face people without a shower and some alone time with my toothbrush.

After a solid American style breakfast of bacon and eggs, I found myself wandering around the lobby of The Beverly Hills Hotel. Since arriving in America, I hadn't really taken a day to just walk around and play 'tourist'. With my small digital camera tucked firmly in the pocket of my blazer, I was ready to see the sights and get acclimated with my new surroundings. The hotel lobby itself was a masterpiece of elegance and charm, with a large chandelier inlayed in the centre of a dome in the ceiling. Judging by the ornate detail, the massive 1995 restoration project had spared no expense.

I headed out the main doors and down a small pathway. I was very keen to check out the Hotel's world famous gardens, and send some pictures back to my darling mother in England. We use to spend hours walking through the grounds of 'Townfield' and I knew she would appreciate the beauty and exoticness of this west coast splendour. The morning air had lost the humidity of the night before and the cloudless sky shone a brilliant blue. I wandered through the palms and hidden fountains, snapping pictures and taking in the scenery. It really was a gorgeous sight.

The afternoon was still young, so I decided to continue my tourist trek down to Rodeo Drive. If I timed things right, I'd only be a short cab ride away from my dinner party with

Bernard Hill and his friends. I was looking forward to it. Every night had been a different adventure, meeting all these new fabulous people, and making important connections and friendships.

I strolled down the palm-tree lined street and marvelled at the beautiful buildings and ridiculously expensive wares in the shop windows. Some tea at the Cafe in the Beverly Wilshire Hotel, another old and grand icon, capped my splendid afternoon. Like The Beverly Hills Hotel, the Beverly Wilshire has hosted scores of celebrities, royalty and other people who don't mind dropping more than a few hundred dollars for a night's sleep. My table sat overlooking Rodeo Drive, allowing me to just relax and people watch. America was very different from Britain, and I could see why so many people flocked to California; the blue skies, the cloudless days, and the laid-back sort of attitude.

I hailed a cab to the Beverly Centre, an eight-story building containing a slew of retail stores such as Macy's, Bloomingdale's and Victoria's Secret, as well as several boutiques and restaurants. Totally unfamiliar with the area, I had a bit of trouble locating the restaurant, circling the retail plaza on foot for almost a half an hour before I finally broke down and asked for help.

"I'm so sorry I'm late. I couldn't find my way around this mammoth place."

"No worries John," said Bernard holding out his hand for a shake. "Come and sit down, everyone else is here and we're just enjoying a few cocktails." He pulled out a chair.

"Hello, I'm Francis," said an attractive woman with reddish hair. "And the woman to your right is Kathy."

"Nice to meet you both," I said. "I hope I'm not intruding on your little dinner party but I met Bernard for the first time last night and he insisted that I join you."

"Nonsense," said Kathy. "You're not intruding one bit. Enjoy yourself! We will!"

Both Francis and Kathy were charming, elegant ladies, easy to talk to and a ball of fun. Most of the talk around the table seemed to be about the movie 'Titanic' and the film industry.

"Am I the only person in Beverly Hills who isn't an actor?" I laughed.

"You and the man who parks my car," laughed Francis. "But he's currently auditioning!"

The evening flew by and I was sorry when the maître-de informed Bernard the party had to wrap up because they were closing. I was having such a good time, enjoying the company of my crazy new friends.

"Where are you staying John," asked Kathy.

"At The Beverly Hills Hotel."

"Let me grab your telephone number. Maybe we could meet for lunch sometime."

"That would be splendid," I said giving her the number. "And I'm so sorry...but I didn't catch your last name."

There was a silent pause as everyone looked at each other, trying to repress their laughter.

"Don't worry my dear," said Kathy patting my hand. "The name is Kathy Bates." Her eager anticipation was shut-down by my blank stare.

"You really have no idea do you honey?" laughed Francis. "We're the main cast from the movie 'Titanic'...you know the one we've been talking about all night. The movie that just won eleven Academy Awards?"

"Oh my God," I said full of embarrassment. "I really didn't put two and two together. As you can probably tell, I don't go to the movies much."

"Well you've gotten yourself in with a crew tonight," laughed Francis.

"And I'm the captain aboard this sinking ship!" added Bernard.

The table roared with laughter. They were all very gracious and the laughter put me at ease. I couldn't believe I'd been such an idiot not to figure it out.

"Is there some sort of handbook I can purchase informing me of who the hell all you actors are and what you've starred in?" I laughed. "If so, I'll go home and study it right now! Because at the moment, I feel like an absolute ass!" The entire table laughed again.

Kathy leaned over and whispered in my ear. "I think you're doing fine. I don't remember who the hell half these people are anyway!" I smiled my appreciation. "It's true," Kathy continued. She winked and held up the piece of paper she'd written my number on. "I'm gonna call you."

"I look forward to lunch," I replied. "My treat for not knowing who you were."

I followed the group outside, lingering on the sidewalk, not really wanting the night to end. I waved goodbye one more time and just as I was about to walk away, Francis rushed towards me, planting a big, wonderful goodnight kiss on my lips. I tried to hide my surprise and act cool and nonchalant, but the cheeky grin spreading across my face was a dead giveaway to the boyhood excitement racing from my chest. I was beginning to fall in love with Los Angeles.

The hour was late by the time I got back to the hotel, but I wasn't quite ready to retire to the solitude of my room. An empty seat at the hotel bar sounded so much more inviting. I pounded back a drink, ordered another, then brushed some peanut shells off a newspaper I found lying on the seat next to me. I wasn't really in the mood (or the condition) to be reading, my eyes barely discerning the words from the pictures.

"Such a sad story isn't it?" said the bartender. He set a fresh drink on the black coaster in front of me. "I couldn't imagine not knowing where my kid was."

I pressed my eyelids together in an attempt to wash away the fuzzies and figure out what the hell the guy was talking about. It didn't help. He pointed to a black and white photo. The boy couldn't have been more than five years old.

"He was snatched right from her cart in the middle of the parking lot," he continued. "She turned her head to unlock the car door, and by the time she knew what was going on, the guys took the kid, threw him in the back of their van and drove away. You go to buy groceries and they fucking take your kid? Seriously, sometimes I don't know what this world is coming to."

He shook his head and stared at me like he was waiting for a response. I tried to formulate a sentence but the words just couldn't make it past the growing lump in my throat. How could I possibly convey how I was feeling inside? This boy in the picture was my boy, snatched away from me before I even got the chance to see him, let alone take him grocery shopping. I didn't even know what Pierre looked like. I could only assume he had dark hair. Was he short? Tall? Did he walk like me or talk like me? Over the years I'd tried to put together a picture, but with so many missing pieces, the task proved impossible.

When Rondell came to England and told me that I had a son, I agreed it was best for him to go with her to Germany. What else was I supposed to do? My future with Michelle was dead. My life was a sordid mess and I was in no position to care for a child. I truly thought he'd be better off with Rondell. I knew she loved him and would take care of him, provide him with all those intangible things that I couldn't – like the love of a mother. But what about the love of a father?

My father had been an instrumental part of my life; educating me, supporting me, and above all, just loving me no matter what. Even in death, I felt his spirit guiding me, and the strength of his love carrying me forward. But I was none of those to my son. I wasn't there for his first words, and I didn't get to see him take his first steps. We couldn't chat about life, and I knew nothing of his losses or his heartbreak. And he didn't know about my heartbreak. How every time I saw a young boy in the store or playing in the park, I thought of him. How every time a friend proudly talked about the accomplishments of his son, I thought of him.

For every one of Pierre's 'firsts', I had nothing. I didn't even know the kid's birthday. No memory, no photograph, no sense of belonging to a life I helped create. I only had guilt and wondering. Guilt that I hadn't been there and wondering what could have been. But you can't frame 'guilt and wondering' and hang it on the wall or keep it tucked inside your wallet. No, guilt and wondering lingers like a thick haze, invading happy moments with a shadow of doubt, knowing that something or someone is missing from the celebration. The more time passed, the more I wondered. And the more I wondered, the more I began to realize that maybe I'd been wrong to let him go.

CHAPTER SEVEN

Rondell tugged against the inside ropes that fastened the blue sheeting across the steel bowed roof of the truck. She wasn't sure how long she'd slept and had no clue where they were. If she could just sneak a peek outside, maybe she could reorient herself and develop a plan. Getting to Strasburg was one thing, crossing the German border without getting caught was quite another.

"Damn it! This is too tight!" The top of her hand was red and raw.

Finding the flashlight, she dug into the knapsack to retrieve her small pocket knife. With the flashlight clenched firmly in her teeth, she cut away at one of the ropes, being careful to leave enough slack so she could refasten the rope to another one on the inside of the truck bed. The synthetic rope proved a tough opponent for her dull blade, which slipped along the slick fibres, nicking her flesh as the truck rumbled down the road. Undeterred, she continued to saw away at the tiny microfibers. One by one they sprung back, released from the tension, frayed and frazzled. With a final tug, the rope was free, sending a beam of sunshine streaming through the narrow gap.

Rondell smiled and put away her tools. Sometimes the smallest gains provided the greatest pleasure. Steadying the flapping rope in one hand, she stole a glance, keeping her eyes level with the horizontal wooden slat at the top of the truck bed. Nothing but trees. Air slowly exhaled from her lungs. At least she wasn't peering straight into the eyes of some curious onlooker driving alongside them on the road. They had to be past Paris. She chided herself for not checking her watch before she fell asleep. With all the commotion in the marketplace, she'd lost all sense of time. She held the watch up to the sunlight. It was almost six! No wonder her stomach was grumbling. She guessed they'd been travelling for at least three hours, and were definitely past Paris and probably getting close to Reims. That would explain the trees; the road passes through Parc Naturel regional de la Montagne de Reims. Unfortunately, they still had a long way to go to get to Strasburg.

Rondell tucked the flap under another rope, trying to keep as much light as possible coming in the truck, without making things look suspicious. Settling back into her spot on the floor, she took an apple from the bin and bit in with a noisy crunch. Pierre's food sense must have kicked in because he began to stir and stretch, mumbling a faint whimper. Rondell readied some of the remaining food from the knapsack, so she could feed him before the quiet whimper turned into a full blow wail. The child ate heartily, finishing off a jar of sweet potatoes and a jar of pears. She figured she had enough baby food to last another meal but that was it. They needed to get to Germany.

Rondell sat the boy on her lap for a game of paddy cake. After such a long nap, Pierre was bursting with energy, wanting to explore every nook and cranny of the truck on his hands and knees.

"There you go," she laughed. "Get down and play. I don't think there's too much trouble you can get into back here."

She watched him crawl around, pawing at an errant apple on the floor like a cat. With Pierre occupied, Rondell took the opportunity to stand and stretch her cramped legs. Her body ached. Everywhere. From the nape of her neck to the length of her calf, knotted muscles screamed in anger, pleading for relief. She did her best to soothe the pounding in her shoulders, but her tired, worn fingers just didn't have the strength or the knowhow. All she wanted was a plush mattress with a nice fluffy feather duvet, and a pillow she could snuggle against her chest. Normally, those weren't unrealistic requests. Normally.

Rondell lurched forward, her hip slamming into the corner of a crate, as the truck abruptly slowed. Frightened and unsure, she scooped a bruised Pierre into her arms and dove deep behind the bins just as the truck jolted to a halt.

"Shhh Pierre," she whispered, kissing his arm. "I know it hurts but no crying okay? You must be very, very quiet." Pierre looked at her with sad, watery eyes, seeming to understand, but unable to hold back his tears. The slamming of the driver's side door reverberated against her spine, stimulating every nerve, heightening every sense. Pierre continued to sob. Each heavy footstep pounding across the pavement echoed through her lungs like a cannon, tensing her chest, and sending her heart into wild convulsions. Still Pierre cried. Her hand only muffled the noise. It wasn't enough. The lock rattled against the metal door. She had no choice. Rondell buried the boys' face into the blanket, holding firm against the back of his head.

"Hold on son, hold on," she thought, her eyes wincing as Pierre fought against her, trying to lift his head. "Just stop crying...please just stop crying."

As the metal door slid up, the pungent smell of diesel fuel exploded into the truck, choking out any remaining droplets of fresh oxygen. The driver hauled his strong, stout frame into the back of the truck and began to rifle through one of the bins of apples. Every muscle in her body froze. The seconds seemed like minutes. She didn't know how much longer she could keep Pierre buried in the blanket before he began to suffocate. With a massive crunch, the driver dug his coffee-stained teeth into an apple, grunting with satisfaction.

"Mmm magnifique!"

Throwing another apple in his pocket, the man jumped down from the truck, then reached for the strap to pull down the large metal door. As soon as Rondell heard the crash of the metal against the truck bed, she released a gasping Pierre from her grip.

"I am so sorry my love," she whispered, wiping tears from both their eyes. "I wasn't trying to hurt you…I promise I wasn't."

He eyed her with malcontent, then wiggled from her lap to the freedom of the floor, amusing himself with an apple. Rondell sighed. She had no way of knowing how much Pierre would eventually remember from these last few days, but she hoped it was as little as possible. It was better that way. Rondell stole a peek through the hole in the tarp.

The driver had pulled the truck along the side of the road, about twenty meters from a small diner. Rondell caught the tail end of his green jacket going through the front doors.

"I hope it's just a bathroom break! I'll feel much better when we're in Strasburg."

Thirty long minutes later, the driver slouched across the gravel parking lot, shuffling his feet as he made his way to the truck. Rondell took Pierre in her arms, loosely cupping her hand over his mouth until the diesel engine sprung to life and the truck was motoring down the road. Forgetting his earlier annoyance, Pierre giggled as Rondell ran her fingers through his dark curls, tickling the sensitive skin behind his ears.

"Do you want a lullaby? La petite poule grise?"

His brown eyes glowed with anticipation as Rondell's sweet voice melodically moved through the first few bars before being choked with tears. When the midwife placed the newborn Pierre into her arms, Michelle sang this lullaby to soothe her sons' cries. She sang it to him before every nap, and every bedtime; it was their thing and Rondell felt guilty about intruding on the memory. She kissed his cheek, then switched from the French lullaby to an old German standby, "Brahms's Lullaby", the same lullaby her mother use to sing to her. Pierre didn't seem to notice the change as he nodded his head from side to side.

Rondell ran through her entire repertoire of songs, passing the time, as the spinning wheels on the truck brought them closer and closer to the German border. She still hadn't figured out how she was going to get across the border unnoticed, or how they were even going to get out of the truck for that matter. Perhaps she could risk a call to her Aunt? She'd know what to do, but Rondell didn't want to trouble her any more than she had to. She was just going to have to wait and see, and hope and pray, everything would be okay. The police would still be looking for her, so any kind of a clandestine border crossing was going to be a challenge. With Pierre fast asleep in her arms, Rondell closed her eyes, trying to catch as much rest as she could before the next leg of their journey began. She had a feeling she was going to need it.

The truck slowed, jolting Rondell from her sleep. A quick peek through the tarp told her they'd finally arrived at their destination; a large warehouse somewhere in the middle of Strasbourg. With great speed she gathered up the blanket, strapped a sleeping Pierre into the holster, and tiptoed towards

the metal door. Night had pushed the sun from the sky,
providing ample cover for the fugitives as they moved from
crate to crate. Daring to get as close as she could, Rondell
tucked into a corner and waited for her opportunity.

She didn't have to wait long. The driver unhitched the lock,
threw the door up halfway with a big heave, then walked
towards the lights of the warehouse office. In one deft motion,
Rondell slipped out from behind the crate and carefully
jumped to the ground, one arm firmly guarding her precious
cargo. Wary of watchful eyes, she slinked around the corner
of the truck, hiding in the long shadows of stacked crates and
shipping containers. Silently she moved, aware of each breath,
conscious of every footstep. She could see the guarded gate
about thirty meters away, illuminated by a single metal grate
enclosed light bulb. The guard looked unarmed but she
couldn't tell for sure from where she was standing. She'd have
to tempt her luck.

Rondell reached inside the knapsack and retrieved one of
the apples and a jar of Pierre's baby food. Moving as close to
the edge of the shadows, she tossed the glass jar as far as she
could to the right of the guard station. The guard sprang from
his chair and took off towards the crash. Without hesitation,
Rondell sprinted across the lighted strip and out through the
gate, not stopping until her lungs were begging for mercy. She
found herself on a narrow street lined with old architecture,
the black and white timber-framed buildings reminiscent of
medieval days, with a definite German influence.

Strasbourg, France was a very old city, with deep German
roots dating back before the Holy Roman Empire. The capital
of the Alsace region, it was situated on the Ill River, which
flows into the Rhine River on the border with Germany. The
city had seen its share of destruction through occupation and
war, bombarded relentlessly by Allied aircraft during the

Second World War as they attempted to free the area from German soldiers. Rondell had been to Strasbourg many times and knew the nuances of the city well. She followed the old road down to the docks, where she could rest for a bit in relative safety.

With all the excitement, Pierre was thrashing about in his holster, wailing in anger partly at being woken up mid-sleep, and partly because the poor child was soaked through his pants and desperately needing some food and drink. Rondell calmed him for the moment with a bite of an apple, while she looked for a place to lie him down and change his diaper. A thin fog drooped off the edge of the docks, dipping in and out of the water as it danced to the rhythm of the swaying river. Rondell had been in some precarious situations many times before, and normally the creepiness of the night and the men hanging around the docks wouldn't bother her, but she found her nerves weren't quite what they used to be. Maybe it was watching Michelle die or maybe it was knowing that if anything ever happened to her, Pierre would be all alone. Either way she wanted to get the hell out of there. Lingering wasn't an option.

"Excuse me sir," she said to a tallish man leaning up against the side of a building. "Can you tell me where I might find a pay telephone?"

The man nodded, rings of cigarette smoke blending with his wisps of greying hair. "There's one down around the corner, about half a mile. Do you need any change?"

"No thank-you, I should be good. But thanks for the offer and your help."

"The little guy there looks like he's a bit grumpy." He reached forward and tickled Pierre on the leg, a gesture that made Rondell uncomfortable.

"Well thanks again for your help! You said about half a mile down?"

"Yes, that's right. Would you like me to show you?" he smiled.

"No, no, we're fine…I think we can manage."

Rondell didn't glance back to acknowledge the hungry, gleaming eyes focused on her ass; her strong purposeful steps were intent on finding that telephone booth and calling her aunt. She was tired of being on the run and being afraid. The tragedy at the farmhouse made her long for stability. She still believed in the cause but had decided that maybe it was time to leave the fight up to others. Responsibility to her family, to Pierre, trumped everything now. That was one thing Michelle never understood. She didn't have to die in a shootout, she could have been living happily ever after with Pierre and John in South Africa or even South America, somewhere warm and free from persecution. Sadly for Michelle, happily ever would only be in a fairy tale.

Rondell spotted the phone booth, tensing the muscles in her legs to keep them from shifting to an all-out sprint. Discretion was imperative, especially since the booth was situated about ten meters from a small pub, where several people were milling about. She smiled at the patrons and nonchalantly stepped into the phone booth, like she was just a regular person making a regular phone call. She felt quite safe from the police at the moment, and had no reason to think that anyone here suspected anything, other than she was a transient just passing through on her way to Germany.

"Hello?"

"Auntie, it's me. I'm in some trouble and need your help. You see there was an incident at the farmhouse…"

"Stop talking." Her aunt's voice was stern and sharp; the sort of person you didn't dare disagree with. "Where are you?"

"Strasbourg…in front of a little pub down by the docks."
Rondell glanced up. "Le Chien Qui Aboie".

"Go in there and wait. My people will come for you."

"I have the child," said Rondell.

There was a brief pause and a deepened breath. "Take the
child and go in the pub and wait. Say as little as possible to
anyone. Someone will be there soon."

"How will I know?"

"They will ask if you've ever been to Paris on the train."

"What then?" said Rondell. Her question was interrupted
by a click, then silence, as the line went dead. She hung up the
phone. "Well Pierre I must warn you now, my Aunt was never
one for long conversations." She chuckled as she kissed the
child on the top of the head. "Come on, let's get something
to eat. Anything but apples! Am I right?"

As Rondell swung the heavy wooden slab door open, the
scrumptious smell of grilled meat and fresh bread blasted
through her nostrils, sending her growling stomach into a
frenzied tizzy.

"Oh my God Pierre, do you smell that? I don't care how
much it costs! We will eat like kings tonight!"

She took a seat at a small booth kitty corner to the entrance,
just in case she had to make a mad dash. Pierre relished being
unrestrained, crawling around on the padded bench seat and
playfully whacking his hands on the table. Rondell ordered a
bowl of homemade "pot au feu" and some yogurt, and a boiled
egg and milk for Pierre. Her senses desired something a little
stronger than milk. The schnapps tingled as it flew down her
throat, spreading a comforting warmth throughout her body,
relaxing her just enough to take the edge off.

The pub had a very Old World feel to it with its thick
wooden bar top, handcrafted furniture, and jovial atmosphere.
A middle aged group of men sat in one corner drinking red

wine, the smoke from their cigarettes billowing over like a storm cloud. Rondell smirked when she noticed the old man sitting at the bar, so drunk that the tip of his long unkempt beard kept bobbing in and out of his glass of bourbon. By the looks of the assorted patrons, Rondell had nothing to fear. Nobody gave a shit who she was, nor did they try and strike up a conversation. It was just her, Pierre, and the delectable beef stew. For the moment life seemed almost perfect.

With their bowls emptied and their bellies finally warm and full, Rondell settled a sleepy Pierre in her arms, while she sipped on a coffee and waited for the contact to arrive. A steady stream of customers filed in and out of the doors, but none paid her even the slightest attention. Finally, after about an hour and half and two more cups of coffee, a woman with tightly bound greying hair, wearing a smart navy blue skirt and blazer, strode through the door. Her crystal blue eyes met Rondell's with an icy stare.

"Excuse me," said the woman pulling up a chair, her German accent curt and clipped. "Have you ever been to Paris on the train?" Rondell nodded and went to get up. "No, no. Stay seated. Wait ten minutes then exit the building. Walk around to the north side of the building. Ten minutes."

The woman rose and disappeared through the door. Rondell checked her watch. Ten minutes. She gathered up her knapsack and cradled the sleeping Pierre on her shoulder. The minutes dragged. Now that she had been 'rescued', she just wanted out of there and into the safety of the car. And Rondell knew she'd be safe. The woman may have looked older and unassuming, but underneath Rondell had no doubts she could and would clip someone point blank to the head if they crossed her. Auntie knew people and had connections. Rondell and Pierre were in good hands.

Checking her watch a final time, she threw some money on the table, then casually made her way to the door.

"The north side of the building?" she muttered. "I'm too tired to figure out left from right, let alone north and south!" She took a guess, turned left around the corner and ran straight into a large man urinating against the side of a garbage bin. "Oh my God! I'm so sorry!"

Her apologies were met with a drunken leer and a near miss of some wayward spray as he brazenly flashed his goods. Half disgusted and half laughing, Rondell ignored his advances and stepped past the man and into the darkness of the alley. The lady in the smart blue suit waved Rondell over.

"Hurry, hurry. We must get a move on!"

Two identical black Mercedes sedans were parked lengthwise in the alley, the last with the side back passenger door open, and the woman looking very impatient. Rondell threw the knapsack on the seat and slid in behind it, Pierre tightly clutched in her arms. With a slam, the door closed behind her. The woman was around the front of the car and in the passenger seat before Rondell could even get settled. She nodded to the driver, who then flashed his headlights once, signalling to the lead car that the package was secure and they were ready to leave. With a jar, the small convoy took off into the night, winding through the backstreets, splitting up, then reuniting, then splitting up and reuniting once again, like a choreographed dance.

"So you are a friend of my Aunt's then?" said Rondell breaking the silence.

"It is an honour to help and serve such a patriotic woman. Please rest now. We will be at the German border shortly."

Rondell took that as her cue to shut-up and mind her own business. She was okay with the silence; she really didn't feel much like talking anyway. She wondered how they were going to get her and Pierre across the border and into Germany with no passport, identification, and probably on a watch list. Did her Aunt's connections really run that deep? As they approached the first check point, Rondell found the moisture draining from her mouth and somehow pooling in the palms of her hands. They couldn't come this far and then get caught. Was she right to trust these people? She forced a deep breath of air into her lungs and held it for as long as she could. It was the lack of sleep talking. She just needed to settle down. Calm down and relax.

"Rondell. Please stay in the car with the child and away from the windows. Do not get out of the car no matter what. Is that understood?"

The stringent voice from the front reminded Rondell of her dreaded Grade six school teacher; the one who walked around the classroom with a wooden ruler and a sardonic smile. Rondell nodded and carefully shifted her tired rump and a sleeping Pierre more towards the middle of the seat. Not knowing what to expect, she set the knapsack on her lap, hiding the gun firmly clasped in her hand.

Rondell watched between the seats as the first Mercedes pulled up to the guarded check-point, and a man in his mid-forties got out of the car and walked over to talk to the Custom's Officer. At first, the Customs Officer seemed intent on ushering the man back to the car, angry that he even got out, but as the conversation continued, Rondell could sense a shift in power. The Custom's Officer took a clipped step back, and Rondell could have sworn he raised his hand almost in a salute to the suited man.

The man returned to the Mercedes and drove off through the crossing without incident. The Custom's Officer waved the second car through, without so much as asking the driver to roll down the window. After a long and arduous journey,

Rondell and Pierre had finally made it to Germany. There were many times over the past few days that she'd wondered if they were going to make it there alive and in one piece. So many close calls, so many twists of fate, yet here they were, zooming along the highway, embraced in the comforts of the Fatherland.

"It will still be a few hours before we reach your Aunt's house. Why don't you try and get some rest. You look tired," said the woman, surprising Rondell with a hint of empathy.

"I am tired," she replied. "And thank you for everything. I'm not sure we would have made it the entire way on our own."

A semi-smile pushed its way through her grim demeanour. "If you are anything like your Aunt, I have no doubt you would have found a way. Does the child need anything?"

"No," answered Rondell. "I think he'll be fine until we get there."

The plush leather of the high-backed seat cradled her head like a mould, allowing her tired neck and shoulder muscles to finally relax. Within minutes, she was sound asleep, shutting out every thought, dream, and picture that even attempted to cross the threshold of her subconscious. She didn't want to think about the past, she didn't want to think about the future. For now, she was just the passenger in the back seat of a shiny black Mercedes, content to let someone else drive for a while. When she woke up, she'd be in a different time and a different place – ready to take the wheel and begin a new chapter.

CHAPTER EIGHT

Erika Zschape smoothed a strand of her stubborn, wiry grey hair and pulled back the corner of the heavy velvet curtain. She was not the type of woman who worried about anything, but this slight delay was admittedly causing her grief. The cars should have returned by now. Was there unseen trouble at the border? She let the curtain fall, and sunk deep into her favorite plush high-back chair, the once blood red cloth tattered and worn to a ruddy pink. All she could do was wait. She swirled the remaining shrivels of ice in her glass as she sipped away at her second serving of schnapps. Ever since Rondell called, she hadn't been able to sleep or even relax. With no children of her own and her husband long since passed away, her niece was all she had left. She would do whatever it took to help keep her safe.

Erika glanced above the fireplace at the large hand-painted portrait of her beloved husband wearing his distinguished military hat, the thick braid across the peak signaling his rank as an officer. His impeccably tailored black uniform framed his broad shoulders, the lapels of the jacket dipping low, proudly displaying the twin-lightening SS insignia patch on the right, and his rank of Captain on the left. Screaming out against the backdrop of black was the red swastika armband, the universal symbol of Nazi Germany. She had met her mentor, Adolf Hitler, at a small party gathering in 1940, shortly after he had given the orders to advance upon France. It was such a glorious time in the Reich. Germany was at the height of her power and on top of the world. The fight wasn't just about restoring the Fatherland to great and rightful glory for the near future; it was about entrenching the Third Reich for the next one thousand years.

Her heart longed for the old days, and she loathed the sad sack post-war 'illegitimate government' of the 'New Germany' as she called it. They had no real plan for the nation, just capitulations to the Americans and the Russians. The idea made her sick. But she was, and had been, doing everything she could to keep the Nazi spirit and objective alive. After the war, there were whispers of her involvement in the secretive ODESSA, otherwise known as the "Organization of Former Members of the SS". The ODESSA was designed to help members of the SS and other Nazis, especially the members of the notorious "Death Squads" escape Germany to the relative safety of South America and Spain. They'd planned their getaways well before the war even ended; hoarding stockpiles of gold to offshore accounts, and setting up exit routes and overseas connections.

With the Allied forces advancing, the Nazi's knew they needed to transfer or hide Germany's assets, lest they fall into enemy hands. The fact that much of this wealth was acquired from the nations it had plundered and murdered during the war was of no consequence. It was in German hands now and in German hands it must remain. Less prominent and visual party leaders were employed as 'technical experts' in various German industries to help set up Nazi funded networks for these industries abroad. With a well-organized and well-financed operation in place, ODESSA assisted scores of fleeing Nazis escape justice, and begin new lives. One by one, influential Nazis vanished from the country, smuggled through one of many intricate underground routes such as 'Die Spinne' or 'The Spider', which made their way through the unpatrolled Swiss mountains into Italy. Once in Italy, with new papers and new identities, they were safe to sail to any port in the world.

Still many Nazis chose not to leave, so ODESSA helped them erase the past, and find new identities as 'regular Germans'. Erika smiled at the thought of how many Nazi members she'd helped infiltrate into the 'New German' establishment. They had to be careful and move slowly, but when the time was right, and everything was in place, they would rise again to their former glory. Only this time, it would be forever. While the years may have withered her face and slowed her step, they didn't diminish her passion or determination. After ODESSA operations died down, Ericka headed a group called 'Kameradschaft', which promoted and financed various Nazi extremist groups throughout Germany. The name itself, meaning a 'bond between soldiers', signified the intense feelings of camaraderie these Nazis still had for the cause and for one another.

Well respected and well protected, Erika worked secretly and tirelessly to re-affirm Nazi ties and strengthen the various networks. She was the bridge linking the past to the expectations of the future. A new Nazi regime, the Fourth Reich, would rise from the ashes, maybe not today or tomorrow, but sometime soon. The seeds were planted, and she was one of many loyal gardeners charged with tending and watching the many branches of the movement grow. The German Badder Meinhoff group was a promising start, with their deep connections within the whole Euro-terrorism network, stretching from the Irish Republican Army (IRA) from Ireland, the Euskadi Ta Askatasuna (ETA) from Spain, the Brigate Rosse (BR) from Italy, to the Action Directe (AD) from France.

Each of these groups had their own reasons for fighting, most of which Erika cared nothing about, since minds and causes could easily be manipulated and changed. Their true value lay in the established supply lines, volatile anti-government attitudes, and contacts with other nations, especially in the Arabic world. After the war, many Nazis were welcomed to Arabic nations, sharing a hatred of Jews and minds bent on revenge. When the time came for Germany to rise again, these channels would prove to be an invaluable resource. With Rondell, an active member of the Badder Meinhoff Gang, acting as a trusted go-between, Erika was able to track the inner developments in the network, especially of the French Action Directe. She really had no time for the French, calling them cowards for surrendering so quickly to the Nazi onslaught during the war. Not that she minded the victory, but it showed weakness, and weakness had no part in the Fourth Reich.

Nonetheless, the Action Directe seemed to be making some progress and showed great enthusiasm for the cause, so she would at least give them the benefit of the doubt. Besides, Rondell had befriended the French girl Michelle, and now was apparently bringing her child home to live with them. Erika had met Michelle once and thought she was a nice girl, dedicated and strong, almost reminding her of herself when she'd been younger. Except of course, for the relationship with the English man John Coventry; Erika would have never done something so foolish. Who was this Coventry? What did he know and more importantly what had Michelle told him? She made a mental note to have her people look into his past and investigate his acquaintances. Rondell had suggested he was harmless, but if his child was to become part of her family, she needed to know every detail of his father's life and whereabouts. Erika didn't like surprises.

The bang of a car door slamming jarred her from the silence of her thoughts.

"Finally! Marta!" The old woman straightened the sleeves of her wool sweater and centered the iron cross necklace hanging down her chest. She didn't want to give her niece any indication she'd been even the slightest bit concerned at their delay. A small, stout, middle aged lady entered the room.

"Marta, I believe they are here. Here take this," said Erika thrusting the empty glass into her hand. "Is the room ready for the child? I am sure he will be tired. Both of them will."

"Yes Ma'am, the rooms are ready and I've laid out fresh towels."

"Good good. We can figure out what supplies the child will need in the morning. Perhaps you should prepare some sort of snack in case they are hungry?"

"Yes Ma'am. Can I get anything else for you?"

"No Marta, thank you I'm fine."

The minute Marta left the room Erika made her way to the window and pulled back the curtain. She was anxious to see her niece and to find out what happened at the farmhouse.

Rondell smiled at the familiar sight of her Aunt's large stone and plank board villa. It was good to be home. Just being within the confines of the tall black cast-iron gates, made her feel safe and protected, something she hadn't felt since the morning of the raid, and she knew she'd made the right choice in coming here.

"You take the child and I'll gather your things," said the woman in the front seat. Several times on the trip Rondell had tried to strike up a conversation and exchange pleasantries but she wouldn't bite.

"That sounds good. Thanks."

Rondell carefully laid the sleeping child over her shoulder. He'd been such a good boy on the ride, only stirring once or twice for a bit of water to quench his dry throat. His soft cheek, warm against the coolness of the night, pressed against hers, filling her with an intimate realization of love, deeper than she'd ever felt before. This child was now hers. Hers to raise and hers to love. She didn't mean for the tear to escape down the side of her face, then again, she didn't do anything to stop it. This was her new reality. And that was just fine by her.

"Rondell, it's so good to see you again," said Marta opening the front door, relief etched in the crevices of her tanned and wind-worn skin. "We've been worried."

"We've?" answered Rondell.

"More than you know dear. She's in the front room. Would you like me to take the child?"

"No that's okay," said Rondell. "He's fine where he is and I don't want to wake him."

Marta smiled. "He looks good on your shoulder like that. I always thought you should have a child."

"Yes but not this way," Rondell sighed. "Too much pain."

The woman nodded her head. "You'd best not keep her waiting any longer. I'll make sure your things get taken up to your room."

"Thank you Marta," Rondell answered with a half hug around the woman's broad shoulders. "It is good to be home again."

Marta had been with her Aunt Ericka for as long as Rondell could remember. The two of them made an odd couple, Marta's warmth and sheer good-natured personality juxtaposed with Erika's steely constitution and no-nonsense attitude. While Erika was the supreme matriarch of the household, it was Marta who made sure the cupboards were stocked and the clothes were ironed. Erika didn't have time or much concern for such trivial matters. When Rondell was younger, Marta was the one who buttoned her school coat and pulled her scarf tight against the brisk north German winds. There was a time when Marta was quite fearful of Erika and the power she wielded, but time and the death of her beloved husband had softened the older lady, and her threats of 'banishment' now rang hollow, unable to penetrate Marta's engaging laugh.

Rondell hesitated before she entered the front room, feeling an unaccustomed nervousness. She'd only spoken to her aunt for a few minutes on the telephone and wondered what she really thought about her bringing a child home, not that she even had a choice. Aunt Erika would understand, but she liked things a certain way and Rondell knew throwing a baby into the mix complicated her regimented lifestyle. She needn't have worried.

"Rondell! My dear! There you are!" said Erika with relief.

"Thank you so much Auntie for sending someone to get us so quickly. I wasn't exactly sure how I was going to make it across the border, especially with Pierre here. The normal routes would have been impossible."

"Ah yes," said Erika glancing at the child. "He sleeps so soundly for so much excitement."

"He's a good boy Auntie, you'll see...and he's been through so much. Far too much for someone his size."

Erika smiled. "His hair is so curly and his little hands so pudgy. It's been a long time since there's been a child around here. Might do us all some good to have that youthful enthusiasm for a change."

"So you're okay with me bringing him here then?"

"Of course Rondell. Don't be foolish! You had no other choice! He is safe here. You are both safe here. Although I'm sure authorities will be looking for him. I know they are looking for you."

"What have you heard?"

Erika noted the oversized clock on the side wall. "It is late my dear and you and our little friend look exhausted. We will talk more in the morning. Marta has made up your beds. I hope the provisions for the child will be sufficient for now."

"As long as there is a soft mattress and a warm blanket, we'll both be fine," answered Rondell. "And a hot shower. God I could use a hot shower."

Erika surprised Rondell with a soft kiss on her forehead. "Sleep late my child. Do not worry about a thing."

"But I do worry Auntie."

"Not tonight you don't," she answered softly, gently ran her fingers through the back of Pierre's hair. "Such curls!"

"Thank you."

"No thanks needed. Now go. These old bones of mine need to go to bed!"

As the hot water pounded against her naked skin, she could feel the tightrope of knots in her back begin to unravel. Aunt Erika was right. For the first time in ages she could relax. Marta had offered to sit with Pierre in case he woke up disoriented and crying, so Rondell was free to take as long as she liked, relaxing and unwinding, scrubbing off the stubborn remnants of her perilous journey with her favorite vanilla bean flavor soap. Bless Marta for picking up a fresh bottle.

She wrapped one plush towel around her body and wound her hair up inside another. She felt like a new woman. Being home would do her good. The stability, the routine, and a chance to build a life, a new life, a solid life. Maybe she could find a job? Or explore some hobbies. She always liked to draw and paint or write. Maybe it was time to channel her energy into something positive, or at least something that didn't turn out in tragedy. She'd always have a strong sense of commitment to the cause, it was ingrained in her soul, but the time had come to move on, let those younger and more enthusiastic pick up the torch. She'd had enough playing with fire. She just hoped her aunt would understand.

Rondell owed her aunt her life. She'd given her everything she'd ever wanted, and instilled in her a sense of pride and commitment that was hard to explain. Aunt Erika still held such a firm grip on her beliefs, that the past would rise again to glory, but Rondell wasn't so sure anymore. Living on the run and in constant chaos wasn't all that it was cracked up to be. You went in with guns blazing and a solitary focus. No fear. No remorse. Your life wasn't really your life and the choices you made, weren't really your choices. For the longest time, Rondell believed she was part of this destiny, a higher calling that was far greater than anything she could ever accomplish on her own. And while outwardly she would never go against her aunt, her allegiance to the cause suffered a fatal blow the minute the first bullet exploded into Michelle. That life was over. It was time to begin again. Right now, sleep was all that mattered.

Rondell threw on her housecoat and wandered downstairs, her nose following the wondrous scent of freshly brewed coffee. She'd slept well. And late.

"I knew the coffee would get you!" laughed Marta.

"Where is…"

Marta interrupted. "He's right here playing with some blocks. He's all bathed, changed and has a full belly. He's quite a happy young fellow!" Rondell instinctively went to pick him up and out of Marta's way. "Leave him be. He's fine and we've been getting to know each other."

"Are you sure? I don't want him to cause you any trouble or extra work. I fully plan on taking care of him, you know? This morning was an exception…"

Marta laughed and set a steaming mug of coffee on the table. "Sit down and enjoy your coffee. I don't think I've been this excited in a long time! If I want to get up in the morning, give the child a bath and some breakfast, then I'm going to get up in the morning and give the child a bath and some breakfast…and you miss, aren't going to stop me!"

"You're the best Marta," Rondell laughed taking a long luxurious sip of coffee. "I'm not sure what we'd do without you."

"Well for one thing, you'd starve!" she said placing a plate of pancakes down. "Now eat!"

Rondell shoved a thick wedge of pancakes in her mouth, letting the syrup dribble down the side of her lip. "Auntie still out for her walk?"

"Yes. God bless her, she never misses a morning you know? Rain, snow, blazing sunshine…she's out there marching around the grounds like she's twenty years old."

"Marching is a good way to put it," laughed Rondell. "She was never one for a leisurely walk. I remember the days she would meet me at school and walk me home…. 'Straighten your back and walk with a purpose Rondell' she'd say."

"Well you were always walking with such a slouch," said Erika entering the kitchen. "It drove me crazy! And do you walk with a slouch now? No. See. I did you a favour." The three women laughed as Marta set another mug of coffee on the table. "Did you have a good sleep?"

"Yes, wonderful thank you," answered Rondell. "My back was thankful for something softer than a few branches or the back floor of a truck."

"Tell me," said Erika, her tone turning serious. "What happened at the farmhouse? How did you and the child make it out alive?"

Rondell took a deep breath and started at the beginning. The memories were painful and raw, each one tearing at the scar on her heart until it burst open, unleashing the full magnitude of her anguish.

"I can't go back to that life anymore Auntie Erika," she sobbed. "I just can't. It's too hard and I have Pierre now."

Erika handed her a tissue and smiled. "Then you won't. I only want you to be happy Rondell, I hope you know that. And you are right, that type of life is no place for a child. Your friend Michelle, was she planning on leaving the Action Directe? How was she managing?"

"Michelle give up the fight?" Rondell shook her head. "That would never have happened. If only she'd listened to John. He pleaded and pleaded with her to go away somewhere safe with him but she wouldn't listen…and that was before Pierre."

"John. The boy's father" said Erika.

"Yes, John Coventry, he's an Englishman. She met him while she was in England for business with Brian and the IRA. He's a nice man. Poor guy doesn't even know he's a father, and I'm sure he has no idea that Michelle is dead. For the most part, she kept him out of her world. He has no idea how to contact her."

"Probably for the best," said Erika. "Those English are a hard bunch to read sometimes. Perhaps we just put this all behind us and move on? If he truly is a gentleman like you say, then his association with Michelle will only put him in danger. The less he knows the better."

"I have to tell him Auntie. He has to know about Michelle and Pierre. It's only right."

Erika poured herself another coffee. "Okay then, he shouldn't be too hard to track down I imagine. We'll send a letter of some sort…posted from elsewhere. Leave it with me. I'll take care of it."

"No," answered Rondell. "I want to tell him in person. He deserves that much."

"I don't like the idea Rondell. What if the police know more than we think and they are watching him?" She paused and sipped at her coffee. "It's too risky. A letter will be sufficient."

"And when Uncle died, would a letter have been a sufficient way to break the news to you?" Rondell pleaded.

"Let me think about it," Erika answered. "Nothing is going to happen today anyway. It's nice and sunny out, why don't you take Pierre outside and let him play in the warm grass. It will do you both some good."

By the tone of her aunt's voice, Rondell knew the subject was closed for the time being. But she wasn't going to let it rest. John had done nothing wrong and was just as much a victim in this whole mess as Pierre. He fell in love with a woman he couldn't have. There was no shame in that, only hopeless romanticism. For her part, Erika wasn't about to let her niece go traipsing off to England to meet with a man she knew nothing about. Rondell didn't know that she'd already made a few phone calls that morning. At this very moment, her sources were digging for any sort of information they could find. For his own sake, Erika hoped John Coventry had nothing to hide.

CHAPTER NINE

I pulled the covers up over my head, trying to ward off the intense stream of daylight searing through the gap in the curtains, taunting me with its morbid promise of optimism. I had become a creature of the night, fueled by alcohol and a never-ending quest for the best and most exclusive party. Nights drifted into days, which drifted into weeks, which drifted into months. All so new and exciting, I had trouble pulling myself away, and instead got sucked into the lifestyle, a perfect escape from the past and the perfect way to avoid the future. I lived in the moment, my one way ticket for the fast lane stamped so full, the destination was illegible.

On one of my many hot spot jaunts around Los Angeles and area, I met an interesting man named Dr. Mark Saginor. At the time, I had no idea his patients called him 'Dr. Feelgood' or that he had his own issues with drug addiction. Apparently the ink in his pen never ran dry when it came to prescribing Quaaludes, Xanax, and other 'important' medicines for himself and others. I had only met him at a party and when we seemed to hit it off, he invited me up to the home of one of patients for another get together. HrHe He didn't mention right away that his patient happened to be Hugh Hefner and the 'get-together' was at the infamous Playboy Mansion.

Back in England, Hefner's name didn't quite have the 'royal ring' as it did here in America and I'd only really heard about the man in passing. The more Mark described Hefner and his habit of throwing ridiculously huge parties with A-List Hollywood stars and half-naked 'bunnies', the more I was of course delighted to accept the invitation, especially since this particular party just happened to be the annual 'Valentine Ball'. While there is always a party going on at the mansion, Hefner throws several big bashes each year like the Valentine Ball, the Midsummers Ball, the Independence Day Ball (with its huge display of fireworks), and the Halloween Ball. For Halloween, the entire estate becomes haunted and scary as hell, with the front gardens morphing into a graveyard, and paid actors roaming the grounds in spooky costumes, ready to jump you from behind until you scream bloody murder. Rounding out the spectacles was the fantastic New Year's Eve bash, complete with champagne, delicious food, and bouncing bunnies at midnight. Really, what wasn't there not to love about a party at the Playboy Mansion?

Because the Valentine's Ball was such a special event, we had to meet at a specific location in Beverly Hills and then be bussed up to the Mansion.

"Make sure you wear pajamas or you're not getting in," said Mark on the telephone the night before.

"You're kidding right?" I answered.

"You really don't know a thing about Hef and the Playboy Mansion do you?" he laughed.

"What can I say?" I said smiling, "I'm a naïve Brit unaccustomed to your wild American ways."

Mark's laugh bellowed through the phone. "Well it seems to me, you're catching on quite quickly!"

The parking lot resembled an upscale car lot, with BMWs, Mercedes, Lexus', and Cadillac's row on row and sparkling against the fading sunlight. I managed to find Mark quite quickly through the throngs of pyjama wearers, although I'm not sure you could adequately describe many of the female outfits as pyjamas. With nary a sign of a solid patch of cotton or flannel, the pyjamas were more like strings with tiny bits of lace attached, and no one seemed to mind that the tiny bits of lace really didn't do an adequate job of covering much of anything. We made our way into the long queue for the mini buses and it seemed that Mark was quite a popular fellow, and knew just about everyone, especially the ladies. I tried to be polite and carry on a pleasant conversation with my new acquaintances but those damn little pieces of lace were very distracting.

Security was tight and before we boarded the bus, a private guard checked our identification against an invitation list. I felt foolish having to pull out my passport but it was the only identification I had!

"Your hand sir," said the security guard.

"My hand?" I answered. "What on earth do you need my hand for?"

"So I can stamp it sir." Stupidly, I held out my palm. "No the back of your hand please." I could tell he was getting rather frustrated with my lack of Mansion etiquette and the growing line behind me.

"Here you go," I said flipping my hand over, not having the slightest idea what the man was going to do.

He placed his palm under mine, and then stamped the top of my hand with some sort of ink contraption, leaving a black bunny imprinted on my skin. I was stunned and didn't quite know what to say. I'd never been stamped before.

"That's how we do things here," Mark laughed. "Don't worry, it washes off. Eventually."

Still staring at the funny little bunny, I climbed aboard the bus and settled into a seat right behind the driver. The night had already been one of the most bizarre experiences I'd ever had, and we still hadn't even left the parking lot. Americans could be an odd bunch and I wasn't sure what to expect next.

"So are you excited?" said Mark sliding in beside me.

"I am. I have a feeling I'm going to remember this night for a very long time!"

With all its passengers stamped and settled, the bus took off out of the parking lot on its short ride through Beverly Hills and up into the Holmby Hills area. Holmby Hills is home to some of the most prestigious properties in the LA area, if not the United States. People such as Frank Sinatra, Humphrey Bogart, Lucille Ball, Bing Crosby, Elvis Presley, Michael Jackson, and Marilyn Monroe have all lived in the Hills, making it a much desired and exclusive neighbourhood. Hugh Hefner's Playboy Mansion was just one of several landmark buildings in the area, dwarfed in size by Aaron Spelling's one hundred and twenty-five room mega mansion next door.

The bus turned up a driveway and slowed towards a set of closed iron gates. Mark nudged my arm.

"Watch the rock."

"What rock," I said peering out the window.

"That rock," he said pointing just over the driver's left hand shoulder to a large sandstone boulder right near the curb.

The driver opened his window and said something I couldn't quite hear in the direction of the rock. All I could think about was how crazy these Americans were talking to a rock. Until of course, it talked back.

"Isn't that fantastic?" said Mark.

"Quite unbelievable actually."

"See...the rock has a hidden intercom and video surveillance system in it, allowing security in the house to see who's coming and going. As you're about to find out, the Playboy Mansion is a very popular place!"

The iron gates swung open and the bus chugged through and up the winding path. My eyes were amazed at the beauty of the lawns and the meticulousness of the hedges that scoped along the right side. I laughed at the yellow sign staked in the ground on one of the lawns, 'Beware Bunnies Playing'. I loved this man's sense of humour. The bus crawled under a large archway, then stopped in the front courtyard area to free its cargo of pajama-passengers. The night air was fresh and still, a perfect night for a Valentine celebration. As the bus disappeared through the opposite archway, I marveled at the splendour of the water gleaming in the underground lights of the beautiful fountain that centered the courtyard.

Built in 1927, the 22,000 square foot Playboy house was sprawled over almost five and a half acres of lush green lawn and tall trees, which keep the celebrity seekers at bay. The architecture of the house looked like a mix between Gothic and Tutor styles, with two large wings bookmarking the large front oak door. Thick walls of ivy clung to the brick and snaked their way above the door and across the facings, creeping up the edge of the windows like curtains against prying eyes. The whole area sparkled with white fairy lights, which glowed against the darkness of the setting sun, igniting a spirit of magic and mystery.

As I followed Mark towards the entrance, I saw two large peacocks just sitting on one of the lower branches of a nearby tree. They just stared at all the people, not moving, not making a sound, like seeing hundreds of people all dressed in pyjamas was just an everyday occurrence. Trying to keep sight of Mark, I maneuverer through the mob of guests bottled up between the magnificent hallway beams that stretched to an impossibly high ceiling. Huge portraits of Hefner hung everywhere, his boyish grin illuminated against the masculine darkness of the walls and heavy wood trim, solidifying his reign as the Playboy king.

"C'mon John," said Mark with a wave. "This way."

The minute I set foot into the backyard, my eyes exploded with the kaleidoscope of colours and pageantry. A massive white marquee, the largest I'd ever seen, stretched across a huge garden, and over the famous Playboy Mansion pool. The pool was lit with these magnificent flaming torches that danced against the water, bouncing flashes of yellow and orange off the outcroppings of rock. Jutting up from the middle of the pool was this exotic island, complete with flora, fauna, and two half naked gorgeous blond 'mermaids', waving and splashing their tails in the waterfall. Waiters swarmed like little worker bees, zipping in and out between the guests, trays of canapés with caviar, oysters, prawn, crab and foie gras, balanced expertly on their fingertips.

Drinks flowed as freely as the waterfall, and as I reached for a glass of wine from one of the waiters, I had to hold back a gasp when I realized that besides a few splashes of well-placed body paint, she wasn't wearing a thing! She just smiled at my surprise and handed me a second glass. There was no sense of inhibition whatsoever, from her, or any of the other absolutely stunning women parading around the grounds. And as I stared at the myriad of boobs and ass cheeks, I knew for certain, I wasn't in England any longer.

Armed with my liquid courage, I decided to strike up a conversation with a brunette woman standing near the edge of the dance floor. She seemed a little lonely, so I thought what the hell! Her slim, tanned body didn't seem like it could possibly be strong enough to counter the weight of her chest, which was absolutely overflowing her tiny floral bikini top.

"Is that a diamond in your belly?" I said unable to take my eyes away from her glittering mid-section.

"You sound shocked," she laughed.

"I am! I've never seen a diamond in someone's belly button before." I found my fingers reaching out. "Can I touch it? I know that must seem odd but..."

"It's not odd at all," she laughed. "Go ahead."

Sure as hell, there was a real diamond nailed in this girls' belly. "Why may I ask would you do such a thing? Don't get me wrong, it's beautiful, but it looks like it must have hurt!"

"Only for a second really," she answered, twirling the diamond in her fingers until I thought I was going to be sick. I could hardly stomach a woman playing with her pierced earrings, let alone a pierced belly button. "I want to be a Playboy Bunny, you know in the magazine, and thought maybe this would help give me an edge up on some of the other girls."

I wanted to tell her that most men probably weren't going to be looking at her diamond belly stud, seeing as her breasts could pretty much pop the lens out of the camera.

"That's fascinating!" I said, not knowing what else to say.

"Yeah, I'm so excited!" She took a sip of wine, leaving a bright red imprint of her lips on the rim. "One of Hef's people saw me at a hockey game on the big screen. I had no idea they were even there or saw me until they came over to my seat and asked if we could talk! Hef paid for my flight and everything. I have my photo shoot tomorrow, so hopefully Hef likes what he sees!"

"Oh I'm sure he will," I answered. "So you're not from around here then?"

"No, I'm from Vancouver."

"Ah, a Canadian I see! I've never been to Canada myself," I said, "but I've heard it's a really nice place."

"John! Hey John!" said Mark grabbing my elbow. "C'mon I want to introduce you."

"Well it was so nice to meet you," I said placing my hand on the young woman's arm. "Good luck tomorrow. He'd be a fool not to pick you!"

"She's a nice one," winked Mark. "You could get lost in those tits! Did you get her number?"

"No," I laughed. "Didn't even think of asking."

Mark stopped. "John. There are hundreds of fantastically beautiful women here tonight. There is no reason a man needs to be lonely."

"Who said I was lonely?"

"When's the last time you've been laid?"

I scooped another glass of wine from a waitress and downed it in a single gulp. "Fine. Point taken."

Mark pulled me through the crowd of people towards the front of the dance floor. The one side of the tent was lined with these massive pillows and cushions, reminding me of the Arabian harem tents I'd seen in books and on the television. Sitting at the front of the dance floor in an oversized white arm chair sat the harem leader himself, while his three young girlfriends occupied smaller chairs off to the side. I had no idea what to expect. Hefner was like a God to these party goers; the ultimate symbol of a man who started with nothing, yet was able to build a fortune off the notion that men liked to look at pictures of naked women. But it was more than that I think. Whether they wanted to admit it or not, every man envied Hugh Hefner in some way or another. Whether it was penchant for non-committed relationships with multiple women, his old-school sense of style, or the whole playboy 'I can get away with whatever I want' attitude, Hefner was the man. Hell after being at this party, I wanted to be Hefner, if only for an hour! He had it all and just seemed so calm and cool, sitting there in his black silk pyjama bottoms and famous scarlet red smoking jacket. What other guy in America could get away with wearing pyjamas to work every day? No one. Because they aren't Hugh Hefner.

Hef grinned and stood up when he saw his good friend Mark. "How are you? Glad you could make it."

"I'm fine Hef," answered Mark. "I'd like you to meet a friend of mine, John Coventry."

Hef reached for my hand. "So nice to meet you John."

"It's an honour to meet you," I replied returning his warm handshake and smile. "I want to thank you so much for having me to your party. I'm delighted to be here."

"You're very welcome," Hef answered returning to the comfort of his throne. "You're from England? We must talk more sometime."

And with that, the interview was over and Hef resumed his conversation with one of his blond acquaintances. I had this innate feeling that I should bow or walk away backwards, like I was in the presence of greatness, but I have to say he wasn't at all what I expected. His smile was warm and gracious, his nature genuine and unpretentious. Eccentric? Sure, but in a most enjoyable way. In my experience, he was a true gentleman, quite extraordinary actually.

The party continued late into the night and there was nary a person not laughing or having fun. I mean how could you not? Free booze, free food and half naked (and in some cases completely naked) women? It was almost too good to be true. Desperately needing a cigarette, I found a chair in the 'designated smoking tent', a small tent off to the side of the main tent. Not that the smoking tent was anything less luxurious than the main tent, with its plush chairs, space heaters to ward off the night chill, and of course the constant presence of waitresses with food and drink. I could have sat there all night just smoking my Dunhill's and watching the people.

Young, old, nobody seemed to care about the difference. So many people coming and going, a conversation here and a conversation there, it was hard to keep up with all the names and faces, some I recognized, many I did not. I exchanged a flirty glance with Paris Hilton, who was looking rather delicious in a most provocative and skimpy nightie. She was sharing drinks with a friend and quite enjoying the male attention.

"My brother sure knows how to throw a party doesn't he?" said a man plopping into the chair beside mine, his wild curly grey hair bouncing as he moved. "Keith Hefner. Hugh's younger brother."

I held out my hand. "So pleased to meet you! John Coventry. And yes…this party is nothing short of spectacular."

We chatted for the longest time and I found him to be a pleasant, kind man, much like his famous brother. He told me some history of the mansion and recounted with a wide smirk some of the previous parties.

"Honestly, just when I think I've seen everything…and let me tell you, I've seen my fair share," he laughed. "Something else happens that just makes me shake my head."

His complexion was much darker than his brother's but the smile and wrinkles around the mouth were the same. Like most in Beverly Hills, he dabbled in acting, and was a songwriter and composer, but his main claim to fame was of course being the younger brother of the American playboy. I guess he came by his 'Heath the Hearthrob' and 'Kissin' Keith' nicknames honestly. Cassandra told me later of a rumour running around from back in the 1950s that Keith, his wife

Rae, and Hugh and his wife at the time, Millie, had a foursome one night.

"I guess Millie backed out from having sex with Keith but Hef did sleep with his sister-in-law," she laughed.

Cassandra couldn't confirm the accuracy, but after seeing what I saw at the Valentine's Ball, I came to my own sordid conclusions. It really did seem like anything goes in this neighbourhood.

After Keith had moved on, Mark found me and offered to show me around the Mansion. I couldn't say no, even though the amount of alcohol flowing through my veins made walking any great distance very problematic.

"Have you seen the grotto yet?"

I shook my head no.

"Oh my God, it's amazing," said Mark with the enthusiasm of a school boy. "Hef had the thing built when he bought the place back in the 1970s. See the waterfall in the pool there? Well to get to the grotto, you have to swim under the falls."

"I didn't bring my bathing suit," I laughed. "Not that it seems they are needed."

Mark smiled. "No worries, there's another entrance around the side." He led me down this back path through rocks and shrubs. "You're going to die when you see this."

He was right. I couldn't believe it. It's like I'd stepped into this great underwater world, a hidden paradise tucked away right in the middle of Beverly Hills. People were chilling in the various hot tubs, drinking, laughing, and exploring each other, while water lapped up against the mammoth amounts of rock. One area of the large cave was devoted to 'dry-land' activity and had couches and cushions to relax against, while smaller caves jutted off from the main room. The whole thing lit up with these lights built into the sides of the rock. I was spellbound.

"Those smaller caves," I said. "Where do they go?"

A mischievous grin darted across Mark's face. "I'm sure one of these lovely ladies here would love to take you on a more personal and in-depth tour if you'd like".

"Are they change rooms for after the pool?"

"If that's what you'd like to call them," he snickered. "Here, come take a look."

As soon as he opened the door, and saw the bedroom suite, I knew what I fool I'd been. I didn't even know what I could say to make me look like less of an idiot, so I just kept my blundering mouth shut and took in the atmosphere. The windowless room was dark and sexy, with just a small dim light on the night stand alongside a box of tissues. Wanting to show me more, he tried the doors on a couple of the other rooms only to find them locked. He just smiled, and I just kept the thoughts that were running rampant through my head from formulating into words.

"The property has more than just the pool and the grotto," said Mark as we walked along another path. "There's a wine cellar, tennis courts, zoo, and the games room."

"A zoo?"

"Oh don't worry. We'll go there after I show you the game room."

"But really…a zoo? Here at the Mansion?"

"Yep! Hef spares no expense when there's something he wants. Like this," he said pointing to a big star cemented into the sidewalk. "It's a replica of the star he has on the Hollywood Walk of Fame."

The replica Hollywood star seemed pitiful compared to the idea of the zoo. I just couldn't move past the idea of one man having a private zoo on his property. The games room, actually a separate house and not just a room, was situated on the north side of the property. Once again, I wasn't disappointed. Scores of old-school arcade video games like Pac Man, Frogger, and Donkey Kong, along with various 'Playboy' themed pinball machines were lined up against the wooden planked walls, with a full-sized billiard table centered beneath the dark stained cabin-like beams of the roof. The blue-green plaid carpet was the perfect juxtaposition against the leather couches, giving the room a very homey yet masculine feel. There was even a god damn vintage coin-operated Orchestrions player-piano with gorgeous stained-glassed panels on the front. The blaring music had trouble competing with the raucous group of men flying around the foosball table, flipping the bars in a symphony of chaos. A huge black and white caricature drawing of young Hefner dressed in a tuxedo with a bow tie and smoking a pipe hung above the row of windows on the far end of the room. It was the perfect touch to cap off the perfect room.

"I can only guess that hallway leads to other types of games rooms," I laughed.

"Now you're catching on Coventry!" He knocked and opened the first door. "This here is the Red Room for obvious reasons." A red silky-type bedspread tickled the tips of a scarlet red plush carpet. "I think the red phone is a nice touch, don't you?" I could only laugh and nod my head in agreement. "This room is…"

"Let me guess," I interrupted, "the Blue Room."

"Right you are!"

"I don't even want to fathom a guess as to the name of this room," I said as Mark opened another door.

"This, my friend, is the Round Room. Take off your shoes and go step on the floor." The man was almost giddy.

I slipped off my loafers and cautiously stepped forward. I had no idea what to expect. "It bounces!"

"Yes! Yes!" cried Mark. "The floor is squishy and bounces like a trampoline."

"Amazing. The abundance of mirrors makes me nervous though," I laughed. "What if I bounced too hard and they all came crashing down?"

"Then I'd say you were probably having one fucking good time!"

We both roared. "So be honest…a place like this has to have some secret rooms. I know my old family estate in England had tunnels leading to secret locations. I can't imagine there isn't a few in this place."

"Well I don't know about hidden tunnels but there are a few rooms that are off limits to the public, even to the most esteemed guests."

"Really?"

"See Hef is a big Elvis Presley fan and one night in the early seventies, Elvis was over, and Hef let him use one of the suites…you know 'cause Elvis wanted to have some fun. Well Elvis, god love him, he spent the night in that suite with no fewer than eight women! Ever since then, it's been known as the 'Elvis Suite' and no one…and I mean no one…has stayed in it since. It's not for lack of trying. All the big boys want to use it."

"Big boys?"

"The celebrities, the CEO's, the who's who of the who's who. But Hef always says no. I think it's out of respect from one king to another you know?"

"King is right," I said. "The man amazes me."

"Who? Elvis?"

"No. Hefner!"

"He is something isn't he? I'm his doctor and sometimes I don't even know how he keeps up!"

"Just out of curiosity," I said. "How many girlfriends does the man have?"

"Well, at the moment," answered Mark leading us back out along the path, "his main girlfriend is Holly Madison…but Bridget and Kendra live in the Mansion as well, so technically it's three. His ex-wife Kimberly lives in the mansion next door. It's like a mini Playboy Mansion, without all the…well Playboy…"

"Three girlfriends? And all so young…"

"And energetic," Mark laughed. "Hef wouldn't have it any other way!"

Mark weaved his way through the labyrinth of lit gardens and paths until we came upon another building. The minute I stepped inside, I felt like I'd be transported to the deepest of Africa. Different animals, all screeching and hollering, pissing mad at being disturbed from their sleep so late at night.

"Hef's got some cranes, flamingos, trumpeters, waterfowl and peafowl. And those things you hear screeching are the spider monkeys and the red-handed Tamarins."

"What are those?"

"Another kind of monkey."

The zoo was incredible, and had the same sort of feel as the grotto – minus the sex and abundance of water. Many of the animal enclosures were built into these stone walls, giving a very exotic yet natural habitat for the animals. There were monkeys swinging about in their cages, and an illuminated fish tank set back beneath a crook in the wall. The lizard (or whatever the hell that creature was) that was crawling around on his dead log scared the shit out of me, and the splendid parrots wouldn't stop yapping their talk. Everything seemed so authentic. I was completely blown away. As I walked, the ferns and greenery growing from the ceiling brushed against the top of my head, sending a creepy chill down my spine. Just please dear god no snakes.

From beginning to end, my night at the Playboy Mansion was one of the most intoxicating, unimaginable, experiences in my life. I spent the night in ecstasy, full of drink, lobster, and the best tasting oysters and caviar. Hefner amazed me. Long after some of the younger set had retired to bed or at least a cozy spot on the lawn, he was up on the dance floor, dancing away, his girlfriends never far from his side. I had no idea how I even got home, and could only imagine what a fool I looked like, walking into the prestigious Beverley Hills Hotel in my pajama pants and nothing else. I seemed to remember starting the night wearing a shirt. Oh well, I guess shit happens, especially when it's at the Playboy Mansion.

As I was sleeping off my hangover the next afternoon, the telephone rang. The lady introduced herself as Hef's private assistant and said I'd been put on the list. I had no idea what list she was talking about and despite her assurances that we'd met the night before, I had no recollection.

"I was blond, with blue eyes and was wearing the little black teddy? You remember?" she said.

Oh sure because a blond haired, blue-eyed woman wearing a skimpy black teddy stands out at a Playboy party. Where did Hef find these girls?

"Hef would like you to join him on Wednesday's and Sunday's for a small private dinner and then a movie in his theatre at the Mansion."

"You're kidding right?"

"Of course not," she answered with a high-pitched laugh. "And Hef always shows the best movies. Can you make it for Wednesday?"

I had to deliberate for a minute. Let's see, free dinner made by an executive chef, drinks served by scantily clad Playboy

Bunnies, and a movie and conversation with the Playboy god himself?

"I think I can probably manage that," I answered. "What time should I arrive?"

I hung up the phone and smiled. Could this really be my life?

CHAPTER TEN

"I have something to give you," said Erika handing Rondell a wooden container about the size of a shoe box. "I've had it for a while now but I wanted to wait to give it to you until you were ready."

"Until I was ready?" said Rondell taking the box. "I don't understand"

They were sitting on the large stone slab bench overlooking the back pond, the warm spring breeze finally chipping away at the last of the winter ice. Throughout the long cold, winter months, Rondell had often found herself alone on the bench, just peering out onto the white snow laden grounds, thinking and wondering. Her heart ached constantly for Michelle, the loss and loneliness far greater than she would have ever imagined. Rondell missed Michelle's craziness and fun. The way she tilted her head back and laughed from the tips of her toes, never caring who was around or what others thought. She had a deep strength, an unspoken confidence about her that Rondell had always admired and looked to when she needed a boost. Marta was a great companion, and did her best to keep Rondell occupied, but she was more like a mother than a best friend.

"You have mourned long enough," said Erika. "It is time to move forward. I see you moping around and sitting out here on the bench. No more. It is time to put the past in the past. We cannot achieve our goals if we are not moving forward!"

Rondell wanted to tell her that she didn't really give a shit about her goals. She was thankful for the safety of her Aunt's compound but just like when she was little, she was resentful of the control and manipulation. Things were done Aunt Erika's way or they weren't done at all.

"So what's in the box," asked Rondell. "Is this instantly going to make all of the pain go away? Do you not still grieve for Uncle? You must. Memories of him are everywhere in this house and on these grounds. I see the way you look at his photo and I know you're remembering…why can't I be afforded the same consideration?"

"That is different," snapped Erika. "You are talking about my husband, a great and courageous man who gave everything he had to the cause."

"And Michelle didn't?"

"Michelle was just a girl Rondell. Yes, she died for the cause, but she was not destined for greatness! Not like your Uncle!"

"She was my friend Auntie, my best friend!" cried Rondell. "And I watched her get her guts blown out by bullets! I'm sorry if that takes a little bit of time to get over! Don't you understand that?"

Erika's voice calmed. "You seem to think I am this unkind and uncaring old fool."

"No, no, Auntie…"

"Let me finish. I know that I was never the one you went to for hugs and kisses, or when you scraped your knee or got stung by a bee. That was Marta…you always wanted Marta. She just knew how to comfort you in a way that I didn't. But that doesn't mean I don't love you and care for you."

"I know that Auntie…"

"I'm not finished," Erika scolded. "I wanted you to become a strong and independent woman, and you have…and maybe I was wrong to not give you the outward affection you craved, but that doesn't mean I didn't come in your room at night, after you'd been asleep for hours, and kiss you goodnight or sing you a lullaby." Erika smiled. "You were always such a light sleeper and I was always afraid that I would wake you or scare you and you'd scream for Marta. But your little face showed such innocence. We live in a dangerous world Rondell, I know you know that. You'd already lost your parents at such a young age…I guess I didn't want to risk getting too close." A small chunk of ice met its demise under the heel of her black boot. "Maybe that was to protect me, more than it was to protect you." She placed her hands on top of the wooden box. "Open it."

Rondell lifted the latch and found a small sea-shell green coloured glass container cradled in wood chips. "It's lovely Auntie, but I still don't understand."

"It is an urn Rondell. These are the ashes of your friend Michelle."

Letting the tears fall freely down her cheeks, Rondell took the urn out of the wooden box and cradled it in her hands. "How did you get this? My God Auntie…"

"As you know, I have many friends in many places. Someone had to claim the body at the morgue now didn't they?"

"I still don't see how you could have gotten these…" Rondell sobbed. "All the security. The police must have been waiting…"

A small smile crept across Erika's face. "There are always ways to circumnavigate security my dear and your Auntie just happens to be an expert!"

Rondell wiped her tears with the sleeve of her blue cotton sweater and smiled. "You have no idea how much this means to me." She paused, taking a deep breath to regain her composure. "But I can't keep these ashes in the urn. I must set them free."

"Sprinkle them in the pond. That would be nice."

"No, no," said Rondell. "This place has no meaning for Michelle…it has to be somewhere special…somewhere Michelle loved. It must be in Jersey. St. Brelades Bay."

"The Channel Islands?" said Erika, the terseness in her voice reappearing. "Rondell, that is much too much out of the way. Find a nice spot on the estate and be done with it."

"And be done with it? Really?" Rondell shook her head in disgust. "I don't care what you say, one way or the other I'm taking these ashes and sprinkling them in the water of St. Brelades Bay. It's what Michelle would have wanted. It's the least I can do for her and her son."

"You will go even if I forbid it?"

"Yes I will."

"Then I will make the arrangements and we will go together."

"I want Pierre to come."

"Rondell, I don't think that is such a good idea. He is just a small child."

"I want him to be there," said Rondell. "He needs to be there, to share in that moment."

"He will never remember."

"You don't know that," said Rondell. "One day I will tell him the truth…that I am not his mother, and I need to be able to tell him the story of how we all travelled to Jersey to scatter her ashes, and how much that meant."

"The child would be better off if he never knew the truth," said Erika. "It will only do him harm in the long run."

"And what do I say when he wonders why he looks nothing like me? How do I explain that?"

"Lots of children do not resemble their parents," scoffed Erika. "You're making a big deal out of nothing."

Rondell stared at the urn. "After Jersey, I want to go to England and tell John. He must be going crazy wondering why Michelle hasn't contacted him."

"If you must," answered Erika.

Rondell was surprised her Aunt gave in so easily. "Then I can truly move forward Aunt Erika. I just need to do these things…for myself and for Pierre."

"I understand. I will make the arrangements. You can telephone this Mr. Coventry before we leave and set up a time and place to meet. Preferably somewhere public. You will say as little as possible and be quick. I'm not all that sure how much I trust the man Rondell. I have done some digging and there are certain things about him that do not add up."

"That could be said about all of us Auntie."

Erika ignored the comment. "When the child gets older, you will tell him his father is dead. Killed in a car crash. He was the last of his family. Is that understood? I don't want the child to get curious and start wondering about brothers and sisters or aunts and uncles."

"Whatever you say," said Rondell to placate her Aunt. She would tell Pierre the truth one day, whether her Aunt liked it or not. Pierre was her son now, and she had the responsibility to do what was right.

A few weeks later, Erika gave Rondell the word that the plans were complete, and they would leave in the morning for Jersey. The small piece of paper wavered in her nervous sweaty hand. She didn't want to give John any indication on the phone that there was anything wrong. She took a deep breath, steadied her voice and dialed.

"Hello."

"John, hi it's Rondell. How are you?"

"I'm fine! How are you?"

"I'm coming to Liverpool in a few days," she said her voice cracking ever so slightly. "Can we meet?"

"Of course we can," John answered. "Just tell me where and when."

"The Atlantic Tower Hotel, say at two pm, day after tomorrow."

"I'll be there and I look forward to seeing you. I have so many questions."

Rondell hung up the phone before he could start asking any of those questions. His voice was filled with so much relief and anticipation, and it broke Rondell's heart knowing how he was going to react to the news.

"It's done. We're meeting on Thursday at two pm."

"At the Atlantic Tower Hotel in Liverpool?"

"Yes," she said turning toward her Aunt. "I followed your instructions exactly."

"Splendid Rondell. I will have a few people milling about just to be safe."

"Nothing is going to happen," said Rondell. "John isn't like that."

"You know I don't like to take chances." Erika retrieved her purse from the kitchen countertop. "Marta has already strapped the child in the car. They're waiting."

Rondell settled into the back seat of the Mercedes. Not wanting to talk, she stared out the window as the car made its way to the private air strip, some thirty minutes out of town. Erika had commandeered a private plan to fly them to the French coast, where they would then take a small boat out to Jersey in the Channel Islands, avoiding French Customs. The next morning, they would scatter the ashes, then Marta, Pierre and Erika would return to Germany, while she made her way to Liverpool. A night crossing of the busy English Channel, with all its tankers and ferries, was problematic at the best of times, so Rondell had no issues agreeing to leave Pierre with her Aunt. Not that she had much choice.

Besides Pierre throwing his bowl of oatmeal on the plane, the trip to the French Coast was uneventful. The cloudy sky revealed only glimpses of the beautiful patchwork of French farms below, their colourful fields seemingly sewn together in perfect rectangles. Rondell missed France, and the long walks she and Michelle used to take through the woods and meadows of wildflowers. The plane landed at a small private airstrip, and as expected, there was a black Mercedes waiting to pick them up and drive them to the dock. Rondell knew her Aunt had a deep connection of contacts, but sometimes, even she was surprised at what the older woman could pull off.

After a quick bite to eat at an out of the way roadside diner, the group boarded the mid-sized fishing vessel and took off for Jersey. As the choppy water sent the boat swaying, Rondell found her recently consumed meal creeping up her throat.

"I'm going to take Pierre below deck," she said to her Aunt. "Hopefully the waves don't upset his stomach."

"Or yours," smiled Erika. "You look pale my dear. Go below with Martha and make some tea."

"Would you like a cup?"

"I'll be down in a bit," answered Erika. "It's been awhile since I felt the sting of saltwater on my face. Invigorates the soul and makes me feel young again."

Rondell laughed at Erika standing at the rails, eyes closed and her stern face jutting out into the wind with a smile as big as the sky. Every now and then, her Aunt would drop her guard, revealing snippets of a woman Rondell barely knew – a woman who laughed at playful rabbits chasing each other through the thickets, or who shouted with glee at the rainbow after a powerful thunderstorm. It didn't happen often, and Rondell was careful to never make a big deal, but she liked seeing her Aunt smile. It gave her hope that buried deep beneath that shield of propriety and austerity, was a woman who at one time, believed in living just for the sake of living, with no ultimate purpose or end goal; just pure enjoyment of life.

Arriving well past the setting of the sun, the group spent the night in a small cabin the owner of the boat rented out to vacationers. It wasn't the Taj Mahal, but after a long day of travel, nobody complained about the soft mattresses or worn blankets. Rondell brushed her fingers through Pierre's mop of curls, as he lay tucked beneath her chin on their shared mattress. Groggy but not yet asleep, the child giggled, sporadically kicking out his left leg, prolonging slumber as long as he could.

"You are such a sweet little boy. Always laughing and smiling…never giving mama any trouble. I don't know how much you'll remember about tomorrow, but I promise you now, that one day when you are older and can understand, I will bring you back here and tell you all about it."

Pierre yawned and smiled. "Mamamamama."

"Yes," Rondell laughed. "Mama is here. Now go to sleep my son. Go to sleep." She kissed the top of his forehead, then tucked the blanket up under his chin, content to let the crashing waves crashing, sing them both to sleep.

With Pierre in one arm and Michelle's urn in the other, Rondell looked out over the bay, the grey rain clouds matching her sober mood. The enormity of this moment had kept her tossing and turning in her bed all night. She missed her friend dearly and the finality of this goodbye was almost too much for her fragile heart to take. She was almost glad Pierre was too young to understand, especially since she didn't even understand it herself. The urn felt cold in her hand. This was not her friend. Her friend was too vivacious and alive to be contained in a small metallic casing. Her throat burned with the fire of indignation.

Rondell placed a soft kiss on his cheek, as Marta took Pierre from her arms, but staying close by her side. Standing by the side of the car, Erika flipped the large collar of her black wool coat, shielding the dampness and hiding her indifference. This whole scenario was needless. Rondell should have just sprinkled the ashes in the garden and be done with it. The girl had been dead for months now, and having this 'ceremony' wasn't a productive use of time or resources. But she loved her niece and if being here at this bay was going to help her move forward, then it had to be done.

"You stay here," said Rondell turning toward Marta. "I'm going to walk further out on the rocks."

"Be careful, my dear."

Slick with spray and moss, Rondell cautiously navigated the rocky path jutting out from the shore near the inland hollow. Her hands trembled. She could sense her Aunt's piercing glare, and wanted to be far enough from the shore and the old woman's impeccable hearing, to say her goodbye in peace. Rondell smiled as a slight rain began to fall.

"You would send rain now wouldn't you?" She said holding up the urn. "Always had to have the last laugh! And you know how curly my hair gets in the rain!"

Anchoring herself at the edge of the final rock, she closed her eyes and let the rain mingle with her tears.

"My dear, dear friend Michelle. I cannot tell you how much I miss you or how much my heart aches. I miss your smile, I miss your enthusiasm, I miss your silly sense of humour, and the way you used to make me laugh. Oh you used to make me laugh! It didn't seem to matter where we were, or what we were doing…you could be so serious one minute and then have me in stiches the next. I miss the laughter. I will always miss the laughter. Pierre laughs just like you, you know? From the bottom of his toes, right through his belly." Rondell softly chuckled. "He is such a good little boy Michelle…and I promise you, I will do my best to raise him right, and to love him even more than humanly possible…I already do. It makes me sad to think of all the times that you won't be there. His first real words, the first day of school, the day he comes home and says he's met the love of his life! Oh God help us all then!" Her laugher trailed off into the crashing of the waves.

"I know I am not you and I can never pretend to be even half the person you were…but I will give Pierre everything I have. He will lead a peaceful life. None of this craziness anymore Michelle…it has to stop. For me, it has stopped… And I guess for you too. Sometimes I still can't believe that day. And I can see the pain in your face as the bullet…." Rondell couldn't say the words. She felt the anger and resentment overpowering the sorrow.

"Why did you have to run out? You could have run for safety, and the three of us could have gotten out alive? But no…there you were…guns blazing…going down in glory while I sat there and watched…" Rondell sobbed. "God damn you Michelle!"

She felt the warmth of a comforting hand on her shoulder. Turning around, she expected to see Marta, but Marta was still on the shore holding Pierre. Rondell smiled.

"I see that I am not alone my friend. Here you are comforting me. Even in death, you give me strength." She unscrewed the lid of the urn and stretched her arm outwards over the water. "It is time to set you free, my wild and crazy friend. You will forever be in my heart and in my soul. You always had a saying, 'until we meet again, someday with the wind'. This is not a goodbye, this is just a separation. We will meet again soon Michelle…someday with the wind."

The moment Rondell tipped the urn, the wind swooped in and caught the ashes, sending them forth on an unwritten adventure over land and sea, and spreading the life-force of a woman whose spirit would never be forgotten. Screwing the lid back on the urn, Rondell reached back and tossed it as far as she could out into the water. With the rain dotting the bay, she watched the urn bob and weave with the waves, finally drifting out of sight.

"May you find peace my friend. May you find peace."

"Are you sure you must go to England?" said Erika as Rondell joined them in the car. "A hand delivered note from one of my people would certainly suffice."

Rondell didn't want to argue but she wasn't changing her mind either. "I'm going to England."

"All right then. Franz is going to drop us off at the airstrip and then drive you to the north coast. A boat is waiting. With this weather, the crossing is not going to be pleasant."

"I've crossed in worse."

"Suit yourself. I just think it's a silly idea."

"I'll be fine," snapped Rondell. "I owe John at least the courtesy of telling him in person. He must be going insane with worry and wonder."

"Oh he's doing just fine, I can assure you."

"You're having him watched?"

"Of course Rondell. I need to know exactly what this man knows. I'm not sure he was totally honest with Michelle about who he was."

"And I can be totally sure that Michelle was never totally honest with him either."

Rondell was tired of talking. At this moment, she didn't care what secrets John Coventry had or didn't have. He deserved to know about Michelle and above all about Pierre.

"What if he says he wants the child?" said Erika.

"He won't," answered Rondell. "I'm just going to tell him that Pierre is living with me. End of story. He'll understand and he'll agree."

"Are you sure?"

"Why so many questions? I told you I'd stick to the plan and I will." Rondell was becoming annoyed with her Aunt's constant need to micromanage. "John will be so upset about Michelle that he won't even think about asking for Pierre. And by the time he does, I'll be gone."

"I have no worries Rondell. There are ways to make sure he doesn't come snooping around."

"Please leave him alone Aunt Erika. He's done nothing wrong. His only crime was falling in love with a woman who couldn't and wouldn't love him back the way he needed her to."

"Maybe…and maybe not," she answered. "Only time will tell." Erika had no intention of pushing the issue of John Coventry off the table. Something just didn't seem to fit. Just a feeling she had, and when she had those feelings, she was more often than not right.

Rondell watched the plane take off down the runway. While she was sad to leave Pierre, she was glad to finally have some time to herself. She didn't want to admit it in front of her aunt, but she was a little worried about crossing the English Channel at night in this weather. When she did it before, she'd only had herself to worry about. Things had changed. A small boat dodging in and around merchant ships, coupled with a choppy sea didn't always make the most comfortable ride.

She wondered if her Aunt really did know something about John and just wasn't telling her. It wouldn't be the first time. Erika liked to have control over everything and everyone. Still, it made her think. If John was just a nobody, a regular gent like he always said he was, then there shouldn't be an issue, but what if he wasn't? Rondell dismissed the idea. Michelle would have caught on to him long ago if something was awry. The woman had a sixth sense about people, and trusted no one until she was absolutely sure she could. Michelle trusted John enough to form an intimate relationship, and Rondell had no real reason to challenge her judgment.

"As usual, Aunt Erika is just being paranoid," she thought. "But I guess that's better than being unprepared."

"How long until we get to the coast?"

"A couple of hours or so ma'am," answered the driver.

Rondell stretched her legs out under the back seat, and tucked the collar of her coat up around her face. All she wanted to do was shut down and not have to think about anything. Seeing John was going to be emotional, she knew that, and she wanted to be prepared, but in her heart she knew that nothing could prepare her for the grief and anguish she was about to bestow on another human being. It almost made her sick.

By the time the cabin cruiser journeyed through the rough Channel waters, Rondell was feeling sick. She had planned on sleeping during the crossing, but the constant thrashing of the waves against the hull tossed the boat around like a toy. But at least they'd been able to circumnavigate the Customs Officials. Rondell waved goodbye to the Captain and ducked into the waiting Mercedes for the long drive north to Liverpool. Tired and nauseous, she just wanted the day to be over. The sooner they got to Liverpool, the better.

Arriving early at the Tower Hotel, Rondell found a seat in the corner of the lobby and waited for John. She'd tried to sleep on the way, but with every mile, she became more anxious, her mind racing in circles with her heart. How would John react? Would he make a scene? Despite feeling quite safe and inconspicuous, Rondell didn't need any extra special attention pointed her way. She keenly scanned the room for anything or anybody out of the ordinary. Although she didn't recognize them, she knew her aunt would have the area 'protected'. Rondell checked her watch, five minutes to two. John would be here any minute. She took a deep breath, trying to control the emotions that were already lurking in the pit of her stomach.

"Rondell!" said John from across the lobby. He gave a wave and a big smile.

Rondell walked over and put her arms around his waist. She could hardly look him in the eye. "I'm so sorry. I'm so, so sorry."

John didn't seem to understand. "Sorry about what?"

"I'm just so sorry John. So, so, sorry." She was rambling, just repeating the phrase over and over and over.

John pulled back from the embrace. "Rondell. What's wrong? Where's Michelle? I thought she'd be here with you."

"Michelle is dead."

"She's dead?"

"She's dead John, she's dead." The words were barely audible through her sobs.

"How did it happen?"

"She was shot."

"Where? When?"

"At the farmhouse."

"I don't understand." His face was pale, his voice a whisper."

Sensing his need for her strength, Rondell swallowed hard. "Let's find a seat and talk for a bit."

She ordered two cups of coffee and two pieces of pie, not that either of them remotely felt like eating. Rondell told John as much as she could about that day, changing details and sticking to the story she and Erika had concocted. It was best if he didn't know the whole truth.

"Unfortunately John…that's not all. Oh my God I don't even know how to tell you this."

"Tell me what? Rondell…please…just tell me…whatever it is."

"She had a baby...a son…your son. His name is Pierre."

"What? A baby?" John could hardly breathe.

"I'm so, so sorry. I begged her to tell you but she would have none of it."

"Why? Why didn't she not want me to know?"

"I don't know…I honestly don't know. Michelle was like my sister and I loved her dearly…but something changed after our trip to see you in South Africa. She became so distant and distracted…not the Michelle I knew. I don't know if it was the hormones from the pregnancy, or just the years of stress catching up to her, but she became increasingly odd. She spent most of her time alone in her bedroom at the farmhouse, drawing on the walls with coloured rocks she found on her walks through the woods. As time went by, her mood got worse and she became lazy and violent. She'd draw a knife or gun on anyone who even slightly annoyed her…and that included me. I kept trying to get through to her…to find out what was wrong…but I couldn't. She wouldn't talk about it."

"She had such a difficult pregnancy John," continued Rondell. "Bleeding, cramping, and a lot of pain. There were several times Michelle thought she was going to miscarry, but little Pierre hung in there. She used to hold her stomach and walk around her room just repeating your name over and over."

"My God Rondell, I could have been there for her…why didn't she contact me. I would have come to France right away. My God, my God, my God…"

"That's exactly what she didn't want…you coming to France. It was too dangerous and she knew you'd come."

"Damn her! I feel so angry at being kept in the dark. I feel betrayed".

"Pierre was born in her bedroom at the farmhouse."

"No hospital?"

"Oh God no John, she couldn't risk going to a hospital. She would have been arrested for sure. She did have help from a sympathetic midwife, and the birth went quite well considering…I asked Michelle again after Pierre was born if she wanted me to contact you directly, and her face went white with anger. Under no circumstance were you to be told about Pierre."

John buried his face in his hands. Rondell could see the pain in his tensing of his shoulders. "Don't think that she forgot about you though John. After she found out you left South Africa and went back to England she did everything she could to find out what had happened to you. It's just all so complicated…you have to understand that."

"I do Rondell…I do understand. It just makes me sick to think she had to go through all of this on her own. I know she had you…and thank God she did but I could have been there."

"So how did she die?" I asked. "I mean you said she was shot. Was it by the police? How did it happen?"

"Soon after the baby was born, Michelle was downstairs with a bunch of us, just sitting around. The birth of Pierre didn't seem to change her mood any. Yes, she loved the baby but she was still having these real 'dark' moments that she didn't seem to be able to overcome. I remember she was playing with a gun…just clicking it on and off with the safety latch on. There was a sudden unexpected bang outside the farmhouse and everybody rushed outside with weapons drawn thinking it was the police or god knows who else. I lost sight of Michelle as we all scattered to take cover. Poor Pierre was still upstairs asleep. I made for the cover of the bushes and just lay as flat and as still as I could. I heard several gunshots ring off then silence. I waited until I saw some of the guys reappear before walking back towards the farmhouse. I looked for Michelle but I couldn't see her anywhere. She was the only one missing from the group. The guys found her lying just off the clearing with several bullet wounds. She was unconscious but still alive. They carried her back to the house and we tried to tend to her, but there wasn't a thing we could do. There was just so much blood. I tried to bind the wounds but it was just too difficult. I couldn't stop the bleeding. God knows I tried but she'd been shot too many times. She never regained consciousness and died a few hours later in my arms. It was horrible. I didn't even have anything to give her for the pain."

Rondell hated lying to him but it was the only way. The less he knew about the farmhouse raid, the safer we would be.

"Was it the police?" he asked.

"I don't know for sure. Whoever was there killed Michelle and then took off."

"You'd think the police would have raided the farmhouse and not just killed Michelle."

"John, who knows who it was…honestly…it could have been anyone. Michelle certainly had her share of enemies that wanted her dead."

"I guess they got their wish."

"After her death, we drove to the nearest hospital and quickly dumped her body by one of the exits."

"You what?"

"It was the only way John," she pleaded.

"Doesn't seem right. You don't just drop a body off at the hospital like it's a sack of garbage."

"Michelle would have done the same thing…in fact she had done the same thing before." All John could do was shake his head in disbelief. "I called a few hours later pretending I was a relative and they said that she was indeed dead and the police were investigating. Eventually they released the body to me." There was no way Rondell could mention her aunt's role in any of this.

"So what did you do then," he said bitterly. "Bury her out behind the shed at the farmhouse?"

"Please John, this is hard for me too you know?" She was crying.

"I know Rondell…and I'm sorry."

She gathered herself and continued talking. "Her body was cremated. I pretended to be her next of kin, so I got her ashes, took them to the Channel Islands, and scattered them in the water at St. Brelards Bay in Jersey. That's what Michelle would have wanted. She made me promise if anything were ever to happen to her, I would find you and tell you as soon as I could."

"I do appreciate you making the effort Rondell. I hadn't heard anything in so long…I was beginning to wonder if I'd ever see her again. Oh God, I'm going to miss her." His eyelashes glistened with tears.

"I miss her everyday…every time I look at Pierre."

"What about Pierre? How is he?"

"He's fine. He's still too young and will never remember anything."

"That's probably a good thing." John paused to collect his thoughts. "So what are your plans now? What are you going to do?"

"I'm going to live with my Aunt in Bonn, Germany. It's a nice place, safe and secure. A good place to start again and raise Pierre."

"Start a new life Rondell and take care of my son."

"I will John, I will. Well it's getting late," she said standing to leave. "I'd better get going." John stood to say his goodbyes when suddenly she sat down and beckoned him to do the same. "I don't think we should see each other again." She paused and leaned in close. "In fact, we should not."

"Okay," he said nodding, not really knowing how to respond. "If you say so."

"I do. It's for the best. Good luck to you my friend." Rondell forced a smile, rose from her chair, then gave John a kiss on the cheek, and walked away. She didn't dare look back. She couldn't look back. She knew he was crying. She had just destroyed this man's life. The weight of the moment, the weight of the last few days, came crashing down like a thundering falls. Her legs weakened and her eyes blurred. She only had to make it a few more steps to the Mercedes, and then…darkness.

CHAPTER ELEVEN

Pierre tilted his head and let the enormous rain drops splat on his sun-kissed cheeks. He relished the moments he was able to sneak away undetected, and just be a twelve year old boy, enjoying the rain storm. He knew he'd catch hell from his Aunt Erika, especially since he hadn't quite completed the drill sheet on quadratic equations, but he didn't really care. The lure of the thunder cracking through the clouds, and bullets of warm summer rain firing at the Koi fish in the pond, were just too much distraction for a naturally curious boy with a penchant for puddles. His playful brown eyes stole a quick glance up towards the main house, and with the coast clear, he rifled a pebble off the side of the stone bridge, the ricochet pinging the top of the clay planter hanging from the gazebo. His face exploded in fear. Aunt Erika had very strict rules and breaking one of her planters with an errant rock would not go over well. He ducked into the gazebo to survey the damage.

"Oh good," he sighed. "Just a little chip off the top." He took some dirt from the pot and smeared it around the edge, expertly concealing the evidence. "Hopefully she won't even notice." Pierre knew he was only fooling himself. Aunt Erika noticed anything and everything. It drove him crazy.

"Things have their place, and you mustn't touch or disturb anything that isn't yours," she'd tell him.

He remembered a time when his mother Rondell use to stand up to Aunt Erika or at least assert some independence, but these days she seemed to be more content to wither away the days reading or working in the garden. Pierre didn't fault his mother for giving in; despite her age and rather fragile looking appearance, Aunt Ericka was not a woman who took kindly to someone challenging her authority. Giving in was less painful than the beaded stares and disapproving tirades. From a very young age, Pierre sensed an unforgiving hostility in his Aunt. She was always talking about the 'old days' when things were perfect, and how ashamed she was at the current crop of Germans.

"These people have no pride and no soul Pierre. They let Germany be split in two for no reason. They are weak and disjointed. But there will be a time when we all will fulfill our destiny."

And so went the daily rant. For as long as he could remember, every evening from six to seven was spent listening to his Aunt reminisce and lecture, while his bottom fell asleep sitting on the hard wooden stool.

"Sit up and pay attention Pierre! No slouching!"

He tried to pay attention as best he could, but oftentimes the monotony was too much, and he would nod off for the briefest of seconds. Punishment was always the same; no dessert for a week, and an extra hour spent in the 'dungeon' with Claudia, his teacher. Wary that outside distractions might affect his concentration, Erika had one of the rooms in the basement of the manor converted into a windowless classroom for Pierre and his private tutor. Rondell had pleaded to send Pierre to the local village school so that he might meet some friends and fit in, but Erika thought it was inappropriate for a boy of his stature to be taught by uneducated heathens, who knew nothing about his future.

"He's just a boy!" said Rondell. "Let him go to school, learn, and have some fun!"

"He is not just a boy as you put it Rondell," Erika sneered. "I have plans for him. You remember our agreement don't you? You can stay here for as long as you wish, doing as you please, without having to worry about a single thing…and in return I get to make decisions for the boy and educate him as I see fit. That was the deal."

"Deal? You gave me no choice. Where was I supposed to go? What was I supposed to do? He was a baby! I have every right to be involved in the decision making! I am, after all, his mother!"

Erika scoffed. "Really? Are you sure about that?"

Rondell eyed the old woman with disbelief. "You are the one who insists on keeping his true identity a secret! One day he will start asking questions and I will tell him the truth! About everything!"

Erika's boney finger jackknifed to an inch of Rondell's cheek. "You will do no such thing! I have raised you and kept you safe your entire life. You owe me. Pierre was brought to us for a reason. We both know that. And I am going to make sure that the child fulfills his destiny!"

Rondell knew there was no point in arguing with her any longer. In her twisted mind, Erika believed Pierre was a gift, sent by those who had come before her; the son she never had, whom she could bend and mold like clay into the perfect Nazi protégé. Rondell's heart ached for her him, but she was powerless against the raging force of her aunt's propaganda and rhetoric. Erika was right, Rondell had nowhere to go. Still on police wanted lists, Rondell depended on the protection her aunt provided. Life was about choices and sacrifices, and in choosing personal security, she was forced to sacrifice the only thing in her life that really mattered - Pierre.

That's why the moments they did spend together were so special and cherished. A walk in the garden, a long afternoon lunch (while Erika napped), or stolen moments snuggling in bed or playing cards, long after Erika had retired for the night to her bedroom or study. Rondell knew she only had short snippets of time with her son, and in that time she tried to teach him the lessons she wished she had learnt when she was younger. While she loved her Aunt dearly, Rondell no longer espoused Erika's acrimonious aspirations, and somewhat resented the old woman force-feeding these same views to an unsuspecting and naïve Pierre. So Rondell did her best to secretly undue some of the more stringent teachings in his daily lesson plans, and give him some semblance of a childhood.

"Why does Auntie hate so many people?" Pierre and Rondell were strolling through the quaint village square on their usual Sunday afternoon outing.

"Your Auntie doesn't hate people Pierre. She just has different opinions than most."

"No," he said honestly. "She told how much she hated the Jews, the blacks, gay people…"

Rondell cut him off and bent down, her eyes level with his. "You should never hate anyone Pierre. I know that's what your Auntie believes, but it's just not true. You should never hate a person because of the colour of their skin or their beliefs. I thought the same way once because I just didn't know any better. I've watched friends die…and so many people get hurt. It's not worth it. Your Aunt is an old woman Pierre, and she still believes in old ideas and things that will never happen. Always remember that." She kissed the top of his forehead. "And always remember…you are your own person and have the right to believe in whatever you want to believe in." Pierre's big brown eyes smiled, melting her heart. "Oh and one last thing. Always remember that I love you!"

"Well I know that!" he giggled. "You tell me every day!"

Rondell smiled and grasped the young boy's hand. "Well it's true! And, I love you are three words you should never grow tired of hearing…especially from your mother!"

Plagued with guilt and insecurities, Rondell took every opportunity to reiterate her feelings for Pierre. She knew one day the full truth would come out, and the fear of his reaction and possible rejection haunted her more than she cared to believe. She fended off those fears with love, hoping that a strong bond forged with that love and affection might only bend, and not fully break under the weight of a Pandora's Box of secrets. To keep him from asking too many questions, Pierre was told his father had been killed in a car accident, not long after he was born. Of course, Pierre wondered why there were never any newborn pictures of him and his father, or him and his mother for that matter. Rondell only half lied when she told him they were destroyed in a house fire, conveniently leaving out the part about the police starting the fire, and the bullets that ripped through the chest of his mother. But she was truthful when she explained how much his mother and father had loved each other, a love that even death did not diminish. Witnessing the devastating hurt in John's eyes and the pain in his voice were proof enough to Rondell that he lost a part of his heart when Michelle died. She saw that raw agony that keeps a person from completely forgetting and moving on. She knew his pain because she lived the same pain day after day. Pierre's doe eyes were not the eyes of his mother, they were the eyes of his father, and Rondell often wondered if those eyes held secrets of their own.

Rondell's heart ached for John. She knew the years since his time with Michelle had not been easy. Erika had spared no expense in learning all she could about Pierre's father, and kept a tail on his every move. Everywhere he went, and everyone he saw, was carefully relayed back through her deep network of contacts in Britain, France, and Germany. She knew that he'd been in jail, and that the Irish Republican Army had twice tried to kill him while he was in prison. And while she hadn't been able to quite establish a definite confirmation, Erika suspected that John had been a British plant, sent to infiltrate the IRA. Why else would they have wanted him dead? But if he was a plant, then why was he still living at his parent's home with no protection whatsoever? The IRA had ample opportunity to murder him; in fact, it was a scenario Erika contemplated many, many times herself.

With John dead, there would be no chance he'd ever come looking for his son. But while she had done many ruthless things in her time, without even a second thought, Erika just couldn't bring herself to give the order to kill the man responsible for creating her prized pupil. She had plans for Pierre, plans that would change the course of history, and she wouldn't jeopardize that. She couldn't. Too much was at stake, and the child already had too much of a soft spot for the father he'd never met and thought already dead. If Pierre ever found out that Erika had murdered his father, all her hard work and planning would be lost, and that was a risk she was not willing to take.

Pierre was already asking too many questions, and probably knew too much for his own good. More than once he'd questioned his aunt about the long meetings she held with 'those men' in her study. He was still too young to understand that building an empire required much preparation and legwork, and that all those meetings were for his future benefit. Erika was almost giddy with the thought.

"Finally, we will restore our country and our people to the greatness we deserve. No one is going to spoil this opportunity for me. Pierre is the next one, the chosen one. I've waited over forty years for this, and no one is going to stop me, or get in my way, especially not a silly Brit like John Coventry! I will not kill him but I will keep him close. He must never be allowed to find Pierre. Never."

The latest information suggested that the British government was also keeping tabs on Coventry, which somehow contradicted the idea of him working for them.

"If they were in contact, then why did they need to tail him?" she wondered. "What was their interest in this man now? Clearly he hadn't been involved in any IRA activity in years, otherwise I would have known about it. Did they know about his relationship with Michelle? Were they after Pierre?"

These questions kept the old woman pacing in her study at odd hours of the night, her sanity slowly slipping away with each step and perceived threat. She trusted no one, not even Rondell. Rondell was the only other person who knew the full truth, and Erika saw her as a very weak link. She had changed since the farmhouse. Once a vibrant young woman, full of vigour and conviction, Rondell was now, in her aunt's eyes, a lost cause; caring more about the tulips in her garden, than the fight for freedom and historical righteousness. Erika thought she had everything and everyone under control, meticulously covering all the angles, silencing those who needed to be silenced with threats and consequences. The longer she could keep Pierre from asking questions about his past, the better. What she didn't know was that the questions had already begun.

The brilliant afternoon sun was gently fading behind the showpiece evergreens that lined the outskirts of the Zschape estate three deep. Erika had been gone all afternoon leaving Pierre and Rondell to do as they pleased. Pierre loved to take the German Shepherds out for a good run, with both child and dogs enjoying their time off the leash. Spread out on a blanket, her knees tucked under her arms, Rondell watched the action, happiness etched into every inch of her suntanned face.

"Be careful Pierre! Don't run so fast! The dogs are going to trip you and send you flat on your bottom!" Pierre just smiled, turned hard to the left, the dogs still hot on his trail, tongues panting and tails wagging. Expertly, he zig zagged through the trees attempting to outwit the pups, but they were too smart to follow, and instead cut him off at the turn. Innocent laughter erupted from his heaving chest as he bent down to catch his breath.

"You boys got me that time didn't you," he said plopping down beside Rondell on the blanket, his dark hair glistening with sweat. "Did you see what they did to me Mom?"

Rondell handed the boy a drink of water from her jug. "Yes I saw."

"I mean these guys can really run! I think I almost stopped breathing!"

Rondell laughed at his exaggeration. "Well I think you've worn them out. Look at them. Here, pour some of this water into the lid and let them have a drink."

"Do you think my Dad liked dogs?"

"Excuse me?" said Rondell struggling to find her own breath.

"My Dad. Did he like dogs?"

"I suppose so. I mean who doesn't like dogs?" Rondell was floundering and she knew it. "We never really discussed the topic."

Pierre paused for another drink, scratching one of the pups behind the ears. Rondell braced for another question.

"Where did you meet him?"

"Who? The dog?" Rondell laughed nervously, doing anything she could to change the subject but Pierre persisted.

"No silly! My father!"

"I can't remember exactly where we met," she lied. "I do remember that we were introduced by a friend. Was it at a party? Or just a get together? I seem to be so forgetful these days."

"I don't believe you," he answered, his eyes intense on hers.

"What do you mean you don't believe me?"

"Because you have that same look now you had when you told Auntie that you were the one who broke her favorite mug, when really it was me. You get it when you're being dishonest with Auntie, and you have it now."

"Little observant bugger," she thought. "He can see right through me."

"Well?"

"Well what?" she answered.

"Why do you have that look?"

"You're really not going to let this go are you?"

"No I'm not," he answered. "I'm almost a teenager now and the only thing I know about my father is that he's dead. I think I deserve to know what kind of a person he was, don't you?"

"Of course I do Pierre," she sighed. "It's just that it's much more complicated than you think. If your Auntie ever found out…"

"What does she have to do with my father?" he interrupted.

Smoothing the errant hairs from her now sweaty forehead, Rondell took a deep breath, trying to ward off the sick feeling building in her stomach. "Come and sit right here Pierre," she said patting the spot beside her. "I will tell you more about your father but you have to promise me that you will keep what I tell you a secret, especially from your Auntie. She can never know we talked about this okay?"

"Okay, I promise."

"I'm not kidding around here Pierre," she said clutching his hand.

"I know Mom and I promise. I really, really promise. Please, you're hurting my hand!"

"Oh sorry!" Rondell reached over and gave him a hug. "I know you do, and I trust you to keep our little secret."

"Of course I will."

"You know how much I love you right?"

"You're stalling Mom," he smiled.

"I know I am. Just give me a minute. This is hard for me to talk about and brings back many memories, both good and bad."

But Rondell's hesitation had more to do with the consequences of disobeying her aunt than reliving the past. The anger and power of her aunt frightened her, so much so that she almost abandoned the idea of telling Pierre anything. Yet the child was right. At twelve years old he deserved to know at least a few details about his father. And as much as she wanted to tell him the whole truth about his father and his mother, she knew he was still too young to understand why she made the choices and decisions she did. That time would come, it just wouldn't be today.

"Your   father   was   an   Englishman…"
"An Englishman?" said the boy, his eyes as round as the sun. "I bet Auntie didn't like that, did she?"

Rondell chuckled. "Actually, your Auntie never met your father in person. I was living in France at the time of your birth, and she didn't even know you existed until we showed up here one day on her doorstep." She was trying to be as truthful as possible. "He was a good man, your father. Kind and loving, a genuinely good soul." She paused, taking a minute to brush back Pierre's sweaty locks with her fingers. "You look very much like him, with your dark eyes and dark hair."

"I do?" He could hardly contain his enthusiasm.

"Yes you do."

"Oh I wish you had a picture. Are you sure you don't?"

"I'm sorry Pierre…I don't have a single one."

"That's okay I guess. I just wanted to see what he looked like…even if it was for a minute."

The disappointment in his voice tugged hard at Rondell's heart. She knew how unfair it was to continually perpetuate the lie of his father's death, especially when the child yearned for some sort of connection. The poor boy didn't even have a decent father-figure in his life, and she often wondered how this might affect his maturation as a man. John would have been a good father, he would have added an enrichment and dimension to Pierre's life that neither she nor Erika could offer. Rondell always held out hope that one day, somewhere, somehow, Pierre would get a chance to see his father face to face, and in that reconciliation, she hoped that while a son gained a father, a mother would not lose her son.

"What did he do?" said Pierre.

"He was a businessman," Rondell answered, not knowing whether it was fact or fiction.

"Maybe I will be businessman when I grow up."

"I have no doubt that you will be whatever you want to be my son!"

A sudden twitch and perking of the ears from the pup curled up against her leg, alerted Rondell to the sound of the chauffeured golf cart Erika used to navigate the outer reaches of the estate.

"Pierre," she said trying to keep her voice steady and calm. "Your aunt is coming. Remember what you promised. You must tell no one what we talked about!" An intense pounding echoed in her chest, invoking memories of a terrified young girl about to feel the wrath of a disapproving elder.

Pierre was the voice of calm. "Don't worry Mom. There's no way she knows what we were talking about. The cart isn't even over the bridge yet."

"You're right," said Rondell inhaling deeply. "Sorry…I just know how your Aunt can be."

"Believe me," laughed Pierre, "so do I".

As the cart raced across the grass, Rondell used her nervous energy to fold up the blanket and pack away the snacks.

"Can I just quickly ask you one more question?" Pierre whispered as the golf cart slowed to a stop a short distance away.

Rondell nodded. "Quickly."

"What was his name?"

"Oh Pierre…your Aunt would have a fit!"

"Please Mom please!"

"John. Your father's name was John."

CHAPTER TWELVE

While the constant barrage of Playboy bunnies, ritzy parties, and general 'late to bed, late to rise' schedule seemed like a charmed life, I knew I was floundering in some sort of no man's land; neither here nor there, existing with no real purpose or direction. I had come to Los Angeles to forget my past, yet it hung around my neck like a chain, pulling me further and further down into oblivion. And the oblivion wasn't kind. A few Friday flings begat a few short-term superficial relationships, whose failure, for the most part, could be blamed on my inability to look in the mirror and see the reality of a man lost and wandering. It seemed like nothing in my life was sustainable. I had no roots, no solid foundation, nothing to build on. Every step I took was in quick sand, sucking me deeper and deeper, and the more I flailed, the tighter the dense muck of my life closed in around me. The suffocation was my death knell.

Reaching out for help seemed ludicrous. I wasn't someone who talked about my problems, and especially not since they involved a highly secretive and criminal past. I hadn't even told my parents the full truth about Michelle, and nobody knew about my son Pierre. My son. I found his image percolating in my mind almost daily now, although I had no real idea what that image was. My mind just sort of patched together bits and pieces; sometimes his eyes would be brown like mine, other times they would be Michelle's sea green. His hair was always thick and dark, and his mischievous smile was always Michelle's, the one she would give me when she had a devilish idea up her sleeve, the one that always melted my heart. He was always a boy about eight or nine, with scratches on his knees from climbing trees, and bruises on his elbows from the slight clumsiness he inherited from me. I thought of the wonderful times my brother and I had spent climbing the ancient trees at 'Townfield' the family home and wondered if Rondell had ever married and had children of her own. Perhaps Pierre had a little brother or sister? I hoped he did. I could hear their laughter now, and it made my own loneliness seem a little less lonely.

Friends and acquaintances were certainly not hard to come by in Los Angeles, and I did find myself surrounded by a very kind, loving and wonderful group of people. The hesitation to share my life was my issue, not theirs. I knew most of my friends would be very open and supportive, and I knew I wasn't the only one hiding some deep dark secrets. Still, I hesitated, unable to fully commit myself to trusting anyone, and unable to shake the undeterminable feeling that I was being followed. I saw faces everywhere. In the shops, in the restaurants, on the street corners. Faces I didn't recognize yet that seemed oddly familiar. I had no clue who would continue to spend the time, energy, and concern on my life. I didn't have any 'top secret' information, at least nothing that the British government didn't already know about. It had been years and years since my stint in jail, and I couldn't believe that the Irish Republican Army still gave a rat's ass about my betrayal. If they did, I'd probably already be dead. Nothing made sense or added up. I was a nobody, a playboy sleepwalking through the jungles of Los Angeles, yet the footsteps I heard over my shoulder made me wonder if I was still someone's prey.

I took to walking the streets of Beverly Hills during the day, stopping in the shops to browse and the cafés to people watch. Los Angeles was such a different place than London or France. Here, I could drop dead in the middle of the sidewalk of a heart attack, and I'm quite sure people would have just stepped over me to continue on their way. No one just stopped to say hello or exchange pleasantries, everyone was always in such a hurry to get wherever the hell they needed to go. But maybe that was my problem; I had nowhere to go and nothing to do. In my younger days, a slothful lifestyle would have been a welcome change from the hustle of my corporate work at Sim and Coventry, but now it just seemed like my days were a waste, and I was wasting away with them. I needed a purpose, something to get me up in the morning, and something to knock the cobwebs out of my brain. I needed to find my son.

I'd always wondered if he knew I even existed. I mean, I wouldn't be surprised if he didn't, since that would have only complicated things for Rondell, and I'm sure the situation was hard enough as it was. But the situation was hard on me as well. At first, I tried putting all thoughts of him out of my head. I guess I was just too busy grieving for Michelle, and it was just easier to forget we'd created this little being. Or at least I thought it was. Before Pierre, I never really took notice of children, but now, every child I saw was a stark reminder of the child I'd never met. Was I being selfish? I'm sure he had this wonderful life, and that Rondell was a wonderful mother, and I knew deep down that giving him up had been the right decision at the time. And that was a sticking point. How long does the right decision stay the right decision, before it starts becoming the wrong decision? Is there a statute of limitations?

I fully admit I couldn't have taken care of him as a baby or young child. I didn't have the maturity to deal with my own issues, let alone the needs of a young one, and I would have never burdened my mother with such a task. Even now, I worried about what she might think, knowing that I've kept Michelle and Pierre a secret for all these years. I hated keeping that secret from her especially. She was my rock, my sounding board, and my trusted confident, yet for some reason I couldn't share two of the most important details of my life. I knew she would understand; she always did. Maybe I thought I was protecting her from the pain, when really, I was just trying to protect myself. But maybe it was time I stopped protecting myself and opened up. Maybe by truly experiencing the pain and reliving the moments, I could finally begin to heal. No more hiding behind the booze or getting lost in the parties. Until I reconciled the past, I would never be able to look forward to the future, and my life would consist only of a stagnant present, and that was no life at all.

"You look troubled my friend." Vincent and I were sitting in his rooftop oasis having an early evening drink.

"I haven't been sleeping all that well," I answered. "Lots on my mind."

"Ahhh…it's that cute little blond woman you've been seeing lately isn't it?" He raised the tuft of his wild eyebrow.

"I wish it were that simple," I laughed, watching a small sandpiper dance in the remnants of a rare California afternoon rain.

"You know…people tell me I'm a good listener. I think it's because of my rather large ears."

The door was open. It was up to me to decide whether I wanted to step through.

"I have a son you know."

"What? Really? You've never mentioned him before John. Does he live in England?"

"I suppose he could be living in England. I really don't know at this point."

"I don't quite understand," said Vincent.

"Well the truth is I've never met him."

"Oh my God John, I'm so sorry. Is this something you've just recently discovered?"

"No. I've known for years now. His mother is dead. Murdered in a gunfight."

"Whoa, whoa, whoa!" said Vincent sliding to the front of his chair. "Slow down my friend. Murdered?"

"I never saw it happen. I was back in England at time."

"Where was she?"

"She was in France…fighting for the cause as she liked to call it."

"Okay John, I don't mean to be rude but you've completely lost me here."

"I'm sorry Vincent. I really just shouldn't have said anything…I don't know what I was thinking…and I don't mean to burden you with any of this."

"Burden? It's no burden to me but it's obviously a burden to you! You're white as a ghost!"

"Am I?" I instinctively placed the back side of palm across my cheek to feel for a fever.

"Are you feeling all right? Perhaps some water or another drink?"

"Both if you don't mind." I was suddenly feeling a little off. The water would put some moisture back in my mouth and the drink would hopefully give me some courage to continue.

Vincent walked over to the wooden handcrafted bar and poured another glass of whiskey and a tumbler of water. The pause in our conversation gave me time to reconsider. He handed me the whiskey.

"You look like you could use this one first." His droopy cheeks spread into a warm smile, almost like they were being pulled by marionette strings.

"Thank you," I said swirling the liquid in the glass before depositing it in the back of my throat.

A puff of smoke curled from the end of Vincent's pipe. "I'm ready when you are."

Once I started talking, I just couldn't stop. It was like someone pressed play and this whole intricate and unbelievable movie came flooding out, except it wasn't a movie, it was my life. At times, I felt completely detached from what I was saying and the people I was taking about. I told him about Andy and Craig and the scheme to defraud the government, and I told him about Barrington and the secret hole in his kitchen wall. I didn't hold back when I described Brian and how much the bastard scared the shit out of me, even now. I described how I still sometimes get a shooting pain through my shoulder when I turn suddenly or twist the wrong way. I told him a few batteries in the end of tube sock were responsible for that, and my sinus issues. I went on and on and on, and he just sat there smoking his pipe taking it all in, his eyebrows rising and falling with the ebb of the story. And I told him how patient and wonderful my parents were throughout, and how the sting of my father's death still ached like a fresh wound.

"It sounds like your father was a great man," he smiled.

"He was," I answered. "I miss him dearly. Sometimes I feel bad that I couldn't be totally honest with him and my mother. They were always so open and honest with me, but I just couldn't tell them about Michelle…I just couldn't. I never expected to fall in love with her…it all happened so fast. And you know in a way I regret Michelle not knowing the full truth about me either. I'm sure she suspected that I wasn't exactly who I said I was, but telling her I was a British spy...well that would have only made things even more confusing."

"Yes I can see how that little bit of information might have caused a few problems here and there," he laughed.

I had to smile. He did have a point. "I would have told her eventually. I know I would have. If she just would have left that whole mess behind, the two of us could have gone off together and had a wonderful life. But she just wouldn't do it! Nothing I could say or do would make her change her mind. I guess maybe I loved her more than she loved me."

"You can't think of it that way John." He paused and took a long, deep inhale. "I'm sure she loved you as much as she could under the circumstances. Think of it from her perspective. I'm sure she didn't expect to fall in love with the dashing young Brit, but she did, and it complicated things for her."

"It sounds like you're taking her side," I laughed.

"No no my friend! Just trying to be objective. I mean, here you have this woman, as you've described, who has dedicated her entire life to her cause." He gestured wildly with his hands and rolled his eyes. "And now she's faced with the decision to give it all up for love? The answer should have probably been clear to you from the very beginning. She was never going to change her mind. She was married to the cause, and you John were the mistress, always asking and hoping she would leave the marriage and run away with you to live happily ever after. I think we all know by now that happily ever after is just a myth...something dreamed up in fairy tales and played out daily on television and in the movies. Look at Hollywood John! The land of happily ever after! It's all a big lie...especially when it comes to love." The rim of his glass touched his lips, then dropped. "Look at me. I thought my first wife and I were going to live happily ever after. And for three years we did! After that…not so much." His shrugged shoulders reached up to touch the tips of his broad smile.

"But you're happily remarried now?"

"Oh yes of course!"

"So then how can you say you don't believe in happily ever after?" I laughed.

"Okay, okay," he laughed. "Well maybe I believe in it sometimes, depending on the situation. I think when it comes to the case of the beautiful French terrorist and the suave British spy that happily ever after was never an option. Geez. You need to write a book about all this someday John. Would make a great story. I mean amazing! I just keep wondering though, why couldn't you have fallen in love with the desk clerk at the British Embassy or something?"

"Ha ha ha ha! But that wouldn't have been as interesting now would it have been my friend!" I finished off the last of mouthful of drink and lit a fresh cigarette. "You're right though. I think I always knew deep down that she would never choose me. I just never wanted to believe it you know? A little hard for the ego to take. I guess in a way her death sort of freed me from the 'mistress' trap as you eloquently called it. No one had to be the bad guy, and I could go on convincing myself that our happily ever after was just around the corner."

"Maybe it is? I mean obviously not with Michelle but maybe your happily ever after is something different."

"I don't quite follow your meaning," I said looking at the empty bottle of whiskey, then reaching for the vodka.

"I realize it's late and we're both a little drunk, but hear me out. I think there's something more for you out there John. In fact, I know there is. You just have to go find him."

It took me a minute to register the words through my alcohol haze. "Him?"

"Your son John. Maybe he's your happily ever after."

"But I made a promise…"

"So what? That was years ago and you were in a state of shock when you made it. In my books, that doesn't count. Besides, no one has the right to keep you away from him. You're his father John. He is your son."

"I know. And I can't tell you how much I've been thinking about him lately. It's like I want to put the past behind me but I just can't. And it's not all about Michelle. Yes I love her…I will always love her but I know she's gone…I do think one day I can and will find love again…maybe not the same kind of love, but love just the same. She'll never be a regret. But Pierre? I think about what my life would have been like if I'd just been strong enough, and brave enough, to tell Rondell no…that I wanted to be the one to raise my son."

"Don't be so hard on yourself John. It seems to me that you were in no position to raise a child, and like you said, your parents had no idea."

"But still. I wonder."

"Yes I suppose it's only natural."

"I think it would have been fun. We could have gone sailing and played in the park. I think I would have liked being a father."

"Why are you speaking in past tense? It's not over by any means John!"

"I abandoned him Vincent. How does one ask for forgiveness for something like that?"

"Well I don't quite agree that you abandoned him. I think that is the vodka talking. You did what you thought was best at the time. And now you have to do what's best at this time.

Only you can decide what that is…although I have some good ideas."

"Hmmm I don't know what to do." The pain of thinking made my head spin.

"Look, I'm only trying to help and offer you the best advice I can. You seem unhappy. Maybe not unhappy per se…but sad…a little blue you know? And I know I haven't known you for forever but I'm very observant with these sorts of things. Just ask my wife."

I really didn't have any response to what Vincent was saying. I was down. I was feeling blue and I didn't exactly know how I was going to get myself out of this deep rut. Cross excessive partying and blindly drinking into oblivion off the list. I'd tried both, and all they'd gotten me was dark circles under my eyes and the loss of a few brain cells.

"Go find him John." Vincent's voice snapped me out of my self-pity tantrum. "Go back to England or France, or wherever you need to go, and find him. Find your son. You need him and he needs you. That my friend, will be your happily ever after."

He was right. I needed to find my son. One month later, I said goodbye to my great Los Angeles friends and boarded a plane for France. Somewhere, somehow I was going to find him, and France seemed like the best place to start looking. I'd taken all of Vincent's advice to heart, and realized that I couldn't keep punishing myself for the mistakes I'd made in the past. Pierre would just have to understand why I made the decision I did. I'd make him understand. I just had to. I'd also spent a great deal of time thinking about Vincent's suggestion to write this crazy life of mine down in a book, if not for my own catharsis, then as a record for Pierre. Maybe if he read it, and felt my intense honesty, he would forgive me. I felt a great sense of calm as I strapped myself into the chair and waited for the engines of the big bird to crank up for take-off. In the front pocket of my jacket I'd tucked a small but detailed 'to-do' list:

1. Find Pierre
2. Write my memoir
3. Live my happily ever after

I didn't see it as a challenge, only as a commitment to myself, and to a life of love and happiness with my son. From here on in, that's all I really wanted.

CHAPTER THIRTEEN

Rondell's hand washed against her face, trying to rub out the deepening lines of exasperation. "Does he have to go?"

"Yes," said Erika. "It will be good for him and it help with his training."

"His training?" Rondell's eyes rolled in disgust. "He's only fourteen years old. Half the time he can't even remember where he left his shoes, but yet you're ready to send him off with a bunch of strangers for the summer? And to learn about what?"

"You went to the same camp don't you remember?"

"Of course I remember, but that was a long time ago, and things are different these days Aunt Erika. Much, much different."

"But they don't have to be Rondell. The new world will once again be the old world. Pierre must be prepared."

Rondell laughed sarcastically. "The days of Hitler and Nazi rule are done Aunt Erika! They aren't coming back. Can't you see that? It's all stupidity!"

"You disappoint me Rondell," said Erika slowly lifting the tumbler to her faded lips and taking a sip of drink. "You once had conviction and strength. A real belief in change. Now all I see is a frumpy woman who is content to sit in the garden and watch the birds all day long. Look at you! Look at what

you've become? You don't even care about yourself anymore!
Odd because at one time you cared so much."

Rondell turned away and let the old woman's words sink
in. She was tired. Tired of living in this house. Tired of being
under someone else's rule. And tired of all this fucking talk
about the rise of the new Reich. If it wasn't for Pierre, she
would have left long ago and forged a new life somewhere far
away from the stale and antique air of her Aunt's unwavering
breath. She did care. She probably cared more now than she
had ever cared in her life. But love for the cause had been
supplanted by a different kind of love, and at the moment, she
wasn't all that pleased about that love going off to some Nazi
indoctrination summer camp.

"You know I am powerless against you Aunt Erika. No
matter how hard I try, no matter what I do, I will never be able
to live up to your glorious standards.   It's always been that
way." Rondell paused, controlling her words. "And you're
right, I no longer care about the cause, I really don't. We
fought and fought and fought, and for what? Did the Baader
Meinhof Group make any strides? No. What about the Action
Directe? Last time I checked France was still a democracy…so
the answer there would be no as well."

Her shaking hand found strength cupped against the back
of the red tapestry chair; her sullen temper swollen with
indignation.

"I gave everything I had to the cause and all it ever gave me
was pain and grief. All of my friends dead. All of my hopes
shattered. This life is not the life I expected to be living but
yet…here I am. And now you expect me to be excited and
jumping for joy because you want to send my son down the
same path? I know I can't do a thing to stop you, but that
doesn't mean I have to like it." Rondell bore deep into her
Aunt's icy eyes.   "When he is killed fighting for your

Godforsaken cause, the blood will be on your hands! Yours alone! I hope you can live with that!"

Erika's cold laugh ripped through the heat of Rondell's pulsing heart. "He leaves tomorrow at dawn. I suggest you say your farewell's tonight. Once he's gone, there will be no contact until he returns in August for school."

"Well then, I guess that leaves out the fun family vacation I was planning to the ruins of the burned out Fuhrer-bunker! That would have been such fun to reminiscence about the good old days for us pure stock Germans. Oh wait? Slight problem. Your golden Nazi boy Pierre isn't even German! How convenient that you always seem to forget that. But I'm sure Hitler and the old boys would be proud to have a half French and half English boy running the show! Not one single ounce of German blood runs through those veins of his. Who knows? Maybe there's even a Jew or two in his background? And you call yourself a nationalist? I'd say you were more of a hypocrite…but that's just me. Now if you'll excuse me, I think I hear the birds calling." Rondell could barely hide her pleasure at the look of horror on her Aunt's face. Satisfied she had made her point; she turned from the old woman and strode out of the room, her shoulders high and square, just like a good German girls' should be.

"I'm going to miss you Mom," said Pierre climbing into bed.

"I know you will and I'm going to miss you too…so very much." She tucked the covers around his arm and kissed her forehead.

"Mom stop," said Pierre laughing. "I'm not a baby anymore."

"You will always be my baby, so stop your complaining and let me snuggle you. It's a mother's right."

"Aunt Erika says the camp is really cool…and we go up in the mountains and everything!"

"Yes you do. The scenery is quite spectacular. You will love the camping and the outdoors." Rondell paused. "But it isn't going to be all fun Pierre."

"What do you mean? Aunt Erika said it was going to be lots of fun and that I would have a great time?"

"There is school and lessons to be had. Every day. Every minute of every day actually. And if you don't do what they say, there are severe punishments. So take my advice and do what they say, even if you maybe don't want to or don't believe what they are telling you. And it's okay not to believe in the same things they do or that your Aunt does…it doesn't mean you're bad or wrong…it just means you have a different opinion and that's a good thing."

"Are you saying you don't believe in the same things that Aunt Erika believes in? About the world and the Jews and all the people that are spoiling Germany?"

"I'm saying keep an open mind about everything Pierre, that's all." With her stores of courage running near empty after her afternoon altercation with Erika, Rondell didn't have the nerve to come right out and defy her Aunt to Pierre. "Just know that you have the right to your own opinion. But, and this is a big but…keep that opinion to yourself while you're at the camp. The people there don't necessarily think that being open-minded is a good thing. Get what I'm saying?"

"Ya, I get it. So like when Aunt Erika whips me for not remembering my lessons…"

"You can expect the same and probably much worse my son," said Rondell. "So be on your best behaviour. Promise me!"

"I will! I promise."

She kissed his cheek once more and brushed aside an errant curl from his messy hair. "You'd better get to sleep. Dawn will be shooting up over those trees before you know it. And always remember how much I love you and that I'll be waiting right here when you get home."

"I love you too Mom."

Pierre shuffled uneasily in his seat, the neatly hemmed cuffs of his khaki shorts sliding midway up his thigh, exposing his skin to the cracked faux leather covering of the bench. He'd never really been away from home for more than a few days at a time, and the thought of spending the entire summer with strangers in a strange place wasn't very appealing. Still, being free from his Aunt's wrath for a few months would be a welcome relief. He'd begun to resent 'his daily lessons' and his lack of freedom. Her eyes were everywhere. Always watching, always following, never a moment's peace, and it seemed to get worse the older he got. Everything had gotten worse. His backside still ached from stinging tip of her bodyguard's whip. The beatings were now more frequent and severe. She said she was teaching him to be strong and brave, and it was just a part of growing up, but Pierre wasn't so sure anymore. Aunt Erika had this power over people, and could make them do whatever she pleased, and while she was scary as hell, the idea of having that much power exhilarated him. He put up with all the shit because he knew that she had some sort of plan for him, and if that plan meant having power, he was willing to gut it out and see where it all led.

The bus pulled up to a little roadside market just outside of Bonn and stopped. Besides Pierre, there were only three other kids and a tall blonde man on the bus.

"We will be stopping here for a moment to pick up some other children," said the man. "If you have to use the washroom, go now because we won't be stopping again before we reach Munich."

"Munich?" said Pierre. "I thought we were going to a summer camp in the mountains?"

"You make it sound so fun and peaceful," the man laughed sarcastically. "We stop in Munich first. Now, no more questions."

Pierre leaned his sleepy head against the window and watched the blonde haired man greet each new boy with an almost violent hand shake before they stepped aboard the bus.

A tall skinny boy threw his knapsack onto the seat in front of Pierre. "How are you?" he smiled. "I'm Harold." He held out his hand for Pierre.

"Pierre."

"Nice to meet you Pierre! Beautiful day isn't it?"

The boy's early morning vibrancy made Pierre laugh. "I guess so, if you like being up at five am."

"I'm up at four thirty every morning."

"Four thirty? Are you nuts man?"

"Well my parents own a farm and my Dad is pretty strict about us all getting up and doing our exercises and drills before morning chores. I've been doing it for as long as I can remember, so it isn't really a big deal."

"Do you go to a normal school?"

"No," answered the boy. "We have a private tutor that comes around for a couple hours a day. He's okay but he isn't much fun. His father was in Hitler's SS during the war, so he knows a lot and has some pretty good stories."

"Cool…"

"Enough talking!" boomed the blond haired man. "I am Gunther Birker and I will be your group leader for the duration of your stay. There are several rules that you will obey. Consequences for disobeying will be swift and severe. Is that understood?" Twenty heads nodded in unison. "Rule number one. There will be no electronics allowed. No cell phones, no video games, no music players, nothing. If you are caught with one, it will be confiscated and you will be punished. Rule number two…"

By rule number ten, Pierre had tuned out the voice and was concentrating instead on a small fly that kept buzzing incessantly around the back of Harold's head. From years of listening to his Aunt's steely voice, he had mastered the art of tuning out while still looking interested. It was a great skill and he took pride in his abilities.

"You heard what he said," whispered Harold. "Sit up and no slouching. Quick he's coming."

Pierre bolted upright and held the pose until Gunther had completed his inspections and returned to his front seat.

"This is going to be a long ride."

"Did you say something?" said Harold.

"Nope," answered Pierre. "Nothing at all."

The bus clanked on for hours as it made its way through the German countryside, southward to the old Bavarian city of Munich. Munich being the 'birthplace of Nazism' was a common subject of Aunt Erika's, and Pierre knew all about its storied landmarks and historical events. Erika had promised to take him there someday, but only when his 'mind was ripe for the understanding'. Pierre never really knew what the hell she meant by it, and like so many other sayings and rules that came out of her mouth, he just chalked it up to old age and senility.

"Have you ever been to Munich," said Harold leaning across the seat.

"No this will be my first trip."

"Really?" Harold's eyebrows rose in disbelief. "Our family visits every November 9th and 10th to celebrate the

Kristallnacht and the Beer Hall Putch! We've never missed a celebration!"

"I didn't know they even had a public ceremony to celebrate The Night of Broken Glass?"

"Well it's not an official public celebration of course," Harold smirked. "People are so sensitive these days with all this fucking political correctness and shit. I say we round up the remaining fucking Jews again and let loose!"

Pierre remembered the story well. It was one of his Aunt's favourites. On the night of November 9, 1938 and into the morning hours of November 10, German rioters spurred on by the SA and Hitler Youth took to the streets and burned and looted Jewish buildings and communities throughout Germany, Austria and the Sudetenland. Over two hundred and fifty synagogues were destroyed, and thousands upon thousands of Jewish-owned businesses had their glass smashed and their stores looted. Many Jews were forced into performing acts of public humiliation, while others were rounded up and jailed, or simply murdered in cold blood. Jewish women not only had to face the emotional terror of the German rampage, but the physical terror of being sexually assaulted and raped. The night marked the true turning point in the National Socialist anti-Jewish policy. When the majority of Germans stood back and watched it all happen with a passive stare, the Nazi regime knew they had the green light to radically intensify their plans to remove all Jews from Germany.

Besides his Aunt Erika, Harold was one of the most fervent Nazi sympathizers Pierre had ever met. He knew every story about every event, and could re-create important battle scenes and strategies from World War II like he'd been on the field himself. When he talked, the large vein in his neck pulsed like a beacon, fascinating Pierre to the point he no longer heard or cared what the boy was saying, only how the blood in his neck moved.

"You hear what I'm saying Pierre? I mean, it's crazy how all these immigrants have come into our country and are fucking things up. Makes me sick! I think we need to beat the hell out of all of them."

"Ya kill them all!" answered Pierre with a joking laugh.

"I'm serious Pierre. They need to die. They are ruining everything. Don't you see that?"

Pierre didn't quite know how to respond. He heard the words of his mother echo in his head...

"It's okay not to believe in the same things they do or that your Aunt does...it doesn't mean you're bad or wrong...it just means you have a different opinion and that's a good thing. Just know that you have the right to your own opinion. But and this is a big but...keep that opinion to yourself while you're at the camp. The people there don't necessarily think that being open-minded is a good thing. Get what I'm saying?"

"Of course I do Harold," he answered with a smile. "I was just bugging you...trying to get you worked up a little. I know exactly what you mean and I totally agree! Kill all the immigrant fuckers!" Pierre didn't exactly believe what he was saying, but the icy blue of Harold's eyes told him he'd be better off not disagreeing.

By the time the bus rolled into Munich, the sun was high in the sky and blistering hot. Gunther instructed the boys to leave their belongings on the bus and form a line in pairs. Pierre fell in beside Harold.

"Eyes front! And stand up straight!" Gunther yelled as he paced beside the row. "Before we head into camp we will be conducting a walking tour of the most important buildings in Munich. You will pay attention to everything you see and hear on the tour, as there will be a test and consequences for those that fail. Unruly behaviour will not be tolerated. Is that understood?" The boys nodded. "This is Ingrid and she will be your guide for the tour." Gunther pointed to a tall woman with stunning cheekbones and blond hair tucked neatly back in a tight ponytail.

"Welcome to Munich boys." Pierre didn't hear a thing she said after that, he was too mesmerized by the perfection of her lips as they formed the words. He had never seen anyone so beautiful before in his life, and as he watched her chest heave with every breath, he felt an intense and immediate hardening in his pants. Like any young teenage boy, Pierre was accustomed to the workings of his penis, but this erection was so quick and powerful, it sucked the breath from his lungs like a vacuum.

"Are you coming?" said Harold.

"What are you talking about?" snapped Pierre, his face flush with embarrassment.

"The tour…it's started. We have to start walking."

"Right, right, of course…the tour." Pierre stuck his left hand deep into his pocket, tugging his penis to the side. "Oh my God." He bit hard on his bottom lip, refocusing his mind on the pain in his lip and not in his pants.

Gretchen led them through the streets of Munich, pointing out the legendary 'Hofbräuhausbeer' hall where Hitler held many of his meetings, and the 'Bürgerbräukeller', where the famous failed Beer Hall Putsch occurred. All the while, Harold provided a running commentary of superfluous information that kept Pierre's focus off the tour guide.

"Did you know that it was while Hitler was in prison for the failed Putsch that he wrote the glorious Mein Kampf? Have you read it?" said Harold.

Pierre nodded. It was the part of his daily lessons with his Aunt that he hated the most. The book was long and boring, full of politics, ideals, and words he didn't understand. Maybe he would appreciate it more when his mind was 'ripe for understanding'. But at fourteen years old, Mein Kampf was an abhorrent slog of a read and he dreaded every minute of it.

"I've read it so many times I can't even count," bragged Harold. He really was quite the keener. Pierre made a mental note to never introduce the boy to Aunt Erika in fear her expectations for himself and his own training would soar.

The tour went on and on, past the 'Verwaltungsbau' or Nazi Party Headquarters, the 'Feldherrnhalle on the Odeonsplatz' and every point in between. It was all very interesting, especially seeing how many of the prized Nazi buildings had survived the intense shelling during the war, but Pierre was increasingly grumpy, tired from the walking, his hungry stomach screaming bloody murder. The quick bowl of oatmeal in the morning, and small sandwich and apple on the bus, hadn't been enough to sustain this much exercise. Harold's constant chatter had been tuned out long ago, and Pierre was desperately wishing he was home, sipping a drink by the Koi Pond in silence.

Finally, after another hour of walking, the group turned a corner and Pierre spotted the bus.

"Thank God," he mumbled.

Pierre collapsed into his seat and groaned. He wasn't the only one. Even Harold seemed a bit spent. Gunther passed around a bag of various sandwiches, cans of cold juice, and some fruit. They rode out of the city in silence, content with their food, and absorbing the events from the day. It was official. Pierre's summer of Nazi indoctrination had begun.

CHAPTER FOURTEEN

Rondell paced anxiously through the kitchen, stopping to peer through the curtains every few minutes.

"Where is that boy? He was supposed to be home hours ago?" She lifted the sleeve back on her purple housecoat, checked her watch and sighed. "I am getting so sick and tired of this waiting and worrying!" The slow creeping of tires along the gravel path caught her attention. "It's about time."

Pulling back the kitchen curtain, her blood boiled as she watched her son stumble from the back seat of the pristine white Volkswagen, his lips attached to those of a young blond woman. She'd just about had enough of his late nights and constant carousing. She waited for him in silence, shadowed in the darkness of the room.

"Where have you been?" Rondell's icy voice pierced the fog in Pierre's brain.

"Out. I told you I was going out."

"It is three-thirty in the morning Pierre. Where have you been?"

"What does it matter?" he answered sharply. "I'm home now. You needn't worry. I'm not a child anymore."

"You are only sixteen year's old Pierre! You are most definitely still a child! I told you to be home by eleven."

"Auntie Erika said I could stay out as long as I wanted. She trusts me and lets me live my life." The smugness in his voice made Rondell want to slap him. He'd become very good at pitting the two ladies against each other, and used Erika's hold over his mother to his complete advantage.

"Did she also give you permission to be out drinking? You smell ridiculous!"

"Like I said, she lets me live my life."

"Let's you live your life...I see...and you think this behaviour tonight is acceptable? Do you have any idea how worried I was tonight? How worried I am every night? Of course you don't because all you care about is yourself and your 'new friends'. And I get it, I was young once too, and yes your Aunt Erika filled my head with lots of crazy ideas too. Ideas that made me feel like I could take on the world and nothing would ever stop me. They are lies Pierre!"

Pierre's eyes surged with rage. "They are not lies! You are just too stupid and weak to understand!"

"Stupid and weak?" Rondell laughed sarcastically. "Stupid and weak. So tell me what you really think about me?"

Pierre stuttered out an apology, desperately trying to take the words back, but Rondell shut him down, her shoulders stiff with resolve.

"It's fine Pierre. Don't think you need to apologize for treating your mother like a piece of shit. It seems to be the pattern with you these days. You want to call me stupid? You want to call me weak? Fine, I can handle your criticisms. But just remember this, strength and intelligence don't come by blindly believing in what someone tells you to believe in, they come from being able to look at those beliefs and form an opinion of your own. You think you know everything. So smart and confident aren't you? Well standing here looking at your drunk, dishevelled self, I'd say you have a long way to go before you amount to much of anything, let alone strong and intelligent. Now get out of my sight."

"Mom...I..."

Rondell dismissed her son with a flippant back of the hand. "I am done talking. Leave me be."

The boy's attempt at a sorrowful puppy dog eyed look was met with a blank unwavering stare. He wasn't going to win this battle and he knew it. Slowly he turned from his mother and clomped down the hall, his alcohol infused brain short circuiting his limbs, causing a ruckus. In the darkness of the kitchen Rondell smiled. Aunt Erika was not going to be pleased at being awakened at such a late hour, and Pierre was going to catch hell in the morning.

"Serves her right, the old bitch. Serves them both right. If he would rather listen to her nonsense, then so be it."

This feeling of helplessness had intensified since Pierre's return from his first turn at 'summer camp' a couple of years ago. She'd noticed the change in him the minute he stepped out of the car and onto the laneway. Sure he gave her a welcome home hug but it was more formality than heartfelt, and she knew right away that her motherly grip on the boy was slipping furiously away. Consumed with reading or playing on his computer, and talking with his new friends, Rondell had been relegated to the bottom of the pile, and it hurt her deeply. Pierre was always too busy to join her in the garden or take their long walks around the property anymore, preferring to stay holed up in the living room or Aunt Erika's office listening to her ramble on about the old glory days. She filled the boys' head with complete garbage and he ate it up with ravenous interest.

Rondell had been shut out, left behind, and spent much of her time alone brooding over past decisions. She should have never given in and let Erika send him to the camp in the first place, and while she didn't know the specifics of his particular camp experience, she remembered her own with a shudder. Nazi this and Nazi that. Hate these people simply because they are a different. We have been wronged and only you, the youth and future of our pure Germany, can save us! It was bullshit then and it's all bullshit now. Unfortunately, once the idealistic claws were in, it was very difficult to break free. Seeing the innate similarities between Pierre and Michelle terrified Rondell, and she had this sickening sensation that fate might lead them down the same path. In the months following his return from the camp, Rondell had done everything she could to dispel the indoctrination, but her unwelcome words buzzed around the child's ear like an annoying fly, swatted away with fierce determination. He wanted nothing to do with her speeches or with her. While Rondell was lost and lonely, Pierre had suddenly found his way.

It hadn't happened all at once. The first few nights at the camp were horrendous, and Pierre would have given anything to hitch a ride out of there. After their tour of Munich, the boys arrived at a makeshift outpost just on the outskirts of the Bavarian Alps. Exhausted from the early morning and hectic day, Pierre barely had enough energy to crawl into his sleeping bag and zip the side closed.

"Everybody up this instant!" Gunther stormed through the maze of sleeping boys, waving a flashlight and whacking the bags with a long stick. "It seems as though some of you think I wasn't serious when I went over the rules." The stick pounded hard across the small of Pierre's back.

"Get your lazy ass up!" Gunther's displeasure bounced off the side of the mountain, shooting back at the boys like a piercing arrow. Scared shitless, Pierre scrambled from his sleeping bag, standing half naked in just his underwear and socks. Gunther's hot breath bore down on Pierre's neck.

"Was it you?"

"I have no idea what you're talking about sir. Honest," answered Pierre, his words barely making it through his tense mouth.

"Honest?" laughed Gunther. "Like by you saying honest, I'm supposed to believe that you're not a fucking liar? Well I think you're a fucking liar! Where is it?"

"I don't know what you mean!" The ripping pain of the stick against the back of his legs sent him flying forward, his throat straight into the v-grip of Gunther's massive hand.

"I don't know what you mean sir!" said Gunther lifting Pierre up by the throat. "Say it!"

"I don't know what you mean sir!" A slight breeze whistled in the gap between his feet and the uneven ground. "Please! I beg you! Let me down! I can't breathe!"

Gunther sneered, then dropped the boy to the ground in a heap of gasps and gags.

"Lesson number one," he said addressing the group, "Is about power and how you exert that power over others. Look at this boy, sitting here in his piss filled underwear on the ground, too scared to move." Gunther laughed and paced around the humiliated Pierre, randomly poking him with the point of the stick. "I have complete power over him. He is under my control. He will do whatever I say. From here on in, I own him. You will learn how to have this sort of power, and how to use it."

"I am not a liar sir!" interrupted Pierre, his shallow voice filled with weak defiance, "And I still have no idea what you mean! Sir!"

Gunther stopped dead. "Get up."

Pierre climbed to his feet and stood straight as a soldier. When the next blow came, he'd be ready. It's not like he hadn't been on the other end of a beating before; it was one of Aunt Erika's favourite chores. She said she was making him a man.

"You have spunk," said Gunther, his voice somewhat softening. "I like that. You will do well here."

A rush of blood coloured Pierre's cheeks, giving him his own sense of pride and power. "Thank you sir."

Gunther nodded, then turned back towards the other boys. "You may go back to bed now. Except for you!" His hand shot out and grabbed a small blond-haired boy about five sleeping bags down from Pierre. "I thought I explained quite clearly on the bus that there were to be no electronics on this trip?" Pierre could see the boys' silhouette shaking in the shadow of the flashlight. "Yet I hear music coming from your sleeping bag?"

The boy stammered, unsure of how to respond. "I have trouble falling asleep without music. I didn't mean to disobey."

"Give it to me," said Gunther.

The boy reached into his sleeping bag, retrieved a small MP3 player and handed it to Gunther. "I'm sorry."

Gunther ignored the apology. "Come with me. The rest of you get back in your sleeping bags."

As Pierre nestled his ears further down into the blankets, trying to drown out the cries of Gunther's victim, he became painfully aware that this wasn't going to be just another summer camp.

Under Gunther's tutelage, Pierre became the model camper, always at the front of the pack, always an eager and enthusiastic student. He learned hand to hand combat, survival techniques, and embraced Gunther's definition of power. He became strong and fit, full of energy, and full of himself. The group had daily lessons in politics, learning which races to hate, which races to tolerate, and which races must die.

He learned that it was okay to use a woman, especially one of 'other' breed strictly for pleasure, even if she said no. Force was power, and power was the ultimate goal. As his innocence waned, Pierre lost the ability to think for himself, or the ability to question the questionable. He became a child of the Reich, and Erika couldn't have been more pleased.

"You sounded beautiful. Sing it again Pierre."

"But I've already sung it three times," he laughed.

"Just one more time."

"For you, Auntie Erika, I'll do it."

> The rotten bones are trembling,
> Of the World before the War.
> We have smashed this terror,
> For us a great victory.

> We will continue to march,
> Even if everything shatters;
> Because today Germany hears us,
> And tomorrow, the whole World.

> And because of the Great War
> The World lies in ruins,
> But devil may care;
> We build it up again.

> We will continue to march,
> Even if everything shatters;
> Because today Germany hears us,
> And tomorrow, the whole World.

> And the elders may chide,
> So just let them scream and cry,

And if the World decides to fight us,
We will still be the victors.

We will continue to march,
Even if everything shatters;
Because today Germany hears us,
And tomorrow, the whole World.

They don't want to understand this song,
They think of slavery and war.
Meanwhile our acres ripen,
Flag of freedom, fly!

We will continue to march,
Even if everything shatters;
Freedom rose in Germany,
And tomorrow the world belongs to it.

Much to the annoyance of his mother, for almost three months after his return from the camp, Pierre insisted on starting each day with a rousing rendition of 'Es zittern die morschen Knochen' the official song of the Hitler Youth. While his enthusiasm for singing may have waned over the following years, his convictions about the lyrics grew stronger. He believed in the words, and he believed in his own ability to create change. His naivety precluded him from seeing that his passion was fuelled by misplaced hatred, and nurtured by the wrinkled yet wicked hands of an old woman, who by her own admission, wouldn't hesitate to put the boy in danger if it furthered her agenda. Some profession of love.

"Fuck…I caught hell for last night man!" Pierre laughed into his phone. "The old lady went fucking nuts on my ass for waking her up in the middle of the night. Apparently, I was a little too noisy?" A roar of laughter shot through the phone. "I know…too funny."

"What about this weekend?"

"I don't know yet," answered Pierre. "I don't want to push it. I might just have to lay low for a bit and let this blow over."

"Are you still in for Berlin?"

"Of course," said Pierre. "I just have to think of a good lie to get there."

Pierre and his buddies had been planning a weekend trip to Berlin to celebrate his recent sixteenth birthday, and everything would have been fine if he hadn't got caught drinking last night. Aunt Erika was furious with him, not just for waking her up, but for drinking so much.

"Alcohol and drugs cloud your mind Pierre! One drink or so for relaxation is fine but what you displayed last night is unacceptable behaviour and I will not tolerate that in my house! You are no use to anyone if you are always drunk! And no relation of mine will been seen as a drunk hooligan. This will not happen again."

"No Ma'am it will not," he lied.

He took his whacks from her switch and carried on with his day. The punishment no longer fazed him, and he was more than willing to risk the consequences to further his pleasure. When it came time to leave for Berlin, he just flat out lied to both his Aunt and his Mother, telling them he was off to a rally in Bonn for the weekend with some of his camp friends. By the time Erika could verify the rally, he was gone, squished into the backseat of the same white Volkswagen, between Lars and Gregor, an open bottle of vodka perched between his legs.

"Boys! We are going to fuck some shit up this weekend!" yelled Tomas.

"Yes we are my man!" answered Markus. "So looking forward to it!"

A couple of years older than Pierre, Markus was the guy who had all the connections and knew all the right people, whether it was getting booze or getting into the best parties, he was the man. His closely cropped brown hair accented a set of massive hazel eyes that seemed to be on the verge of popping out of his head at any given moment. At first they scared the shit out Pierre, and he had trouble looking the guy straight in the eyes, but he was used to them now, and loved how Markus could amp up his intimidation factor. The man never lost a staring contest.

By the time the group hit Berlin, Pierre was juiced and ready to really party. Markus knew a guy who owned a small flat in the Lichtenberg area of the city, so the boys threw their stuff in his place, and then headed out for some action. Pounding the asphalt with his black jeans tucked into his high laced black combat boots, Pierre had never felt so free or so powerful. For the first time, he truly understood what Gunther meant about controlling and using power. The way passerby's would quickly dash off to the side of the street, or turn their heads to avoid eye contact, made him walk even taller and curl the snarl on his boyish face even more. That sense of invincibility was an elixir for his sense of adventure, and Pierre was determined to get the most out of his experience.

The first night was a blur; his lungs clogged with the haze of cigarette and marijuana residue. Somehow they found their way back to the flat in Lichtenberg, with Markus picking up some scrap of a woman along the way to keep him company.

"What are you doing man?" said Pierre. "She's fucking black?"

"So what?" said Markus, "I'm not going to marry her. I'm just going to fuck her. Women like her are meant to be used

Pierre. They like it. They expect it. They want it all the time. Hard and nasty...that's how they like it. I hate the nigger bitches but they do know how to fuck."

With Lars and Gregor laying claim to the bedroom, and Tomas crashing on the couch, Pierre spent an uncomfortable night curled up on the living room floor, in full view of Markus and his 'whore' only a few feet away on a pull-out couch. There were no blankets to shield the full fury of his thrusts against the woman's full hips, her cries both of pleasure and of pain. When it was over, Markus collapsed onto the mattress, a stupidly sick smile on his face, his limbs limp and spent. The woman slid her legs to the side of the mattress, her soft dark eyes catching Pierre staring at her free and dangling breasts.

"You like them?" she smiled.

Embarrassed, Pierre quickly closed his eyes and pretended to be asleep.

"Don't be shy," she continued. "I know you're not sleeping over there. Open your eyes and have a real good look."

She stood up, the full length of her shinning black body only an arm's length away from the boy's anxious touch. He couldn't speak. His invincibility turned to vulnerability. His power drained by the increasing bulge in his pants. The woman reached out, took the boy's shaking hand, and placed it between her legs, pushing his index finger deep into the cavity of her body. The heat torched through his body as she rocked from her heels to her toes with Pierre too dumbfounded to move. With his finger still inside, she dropped to her knees and reached for the zipper on his pants, purposely swaying her breasts past his wide-open mouth.

"Grab them man. With your mouth," said Markus, watching intently from the mattress, his own hand firmly wrapped around his dick.

Unsure of himself and not welcoming the audience, Pierre clumsily managed to catch a nipple with the bottom of his lip and draw it into his mouth. The hardness of the nipple excited him, and he began to ferociously suck, forgetting to breathe until his head spun with dizziness.

"Fuck boy, slow down," said the woman laughing, "I ain't your mamma's titty." While he was sucking, she dropped his drawers down around his knees, his dick shooting out straight like a spring board. The woman pushed his head back from her chest and laid down on the floor, her legs wide open and ready. As Pierre rolled on top of her, a drool of salvia from his over-active mouth dropped onto her stomach. His body was shaking. Lifting her torso up, she grabbed the boy by the ass cheeks and positioned him perfectly.

"Now just shove that mother-fucker in Pierre," groaned Markus. "Hard as you can."

Pierre reared back, took a deep breath and thrust forward with all his strength.

"Ha! Ha! Ha! The useless little bastard missed!" she screamed. "And he just gizzed all over my stomach! What the fuck?"

A laughing Markus pushed Pierre off the woman and mounted her himself. "Shame to waste a good pussy. Let me show you how it's done amateur."

Anger and humiliation filled every inch of Pierre's half naked body as Markus made him sit there and watch them fuck. He wanted to kill that black bitch for laughing at him, and he vowed to never, ever let a woman treat him that way again. The next night, he found his very own whore and fucked her in a dark and dirty back alley until she cried. Gunther was right. Power is invincibility.

CHAPTER FIFTEEN

I ventured out from underneath the wool blanket to throw another log on the old stone fireplace. I didn't mind the cold so much. The crisp air gave me clarity, and at the moment I needed all the clarity I could get. I'd spent a lot of time over the past few months thinking about my life, and mustering the courage to start searching for my son. I had no idea what to expect, and instead had created this vision of a studious young man, with dashing good looks, and good English manners. He liked sports, maybe didn't excel, but still enjoyed participating and engaging his competitive streak. I knew he'd have his mother's spark and fire, he just had to, but I also hoped he'd inherited some of my own mother's softness and sensitivity. I guess I just wanted him to have a good heart, and a kind and happy soul. Of course, I wasn't naïve enough to actually believe my own vision, yet if the reality could fall somewhere in between, I'd be a happy man.

I stoked the fire with the long metal poker and tossed on a couple more logs, sending sparks perilously close to the handcrafted wooden floor. This old farmhouse in the wilds of Normandy France was sure a far cry from my life at the Beverly Hills Hotel. No room service, no pool, and definitely no mini bar. I was lucky to find the place on such short notice. Truthfully, I was enjoying the peace and tranquillity of the

French countryside, even if winter seemed to have set in a little earlier than expected. I had taken Vincent up on his suggestion to write down the details of my life journey. I had no idea what those details would become or if I would ever share them with anyone else. Still, sitting down at the computer and actually typing out the words made me realize what a crazy, mixed up life I had led.

Clarity, that's what I needed. To figure out where I'd been, where I was going, and just how the hell I was going to get there. California was great, and I'd met some of the most wonderful people, yet somehow I still felt like I didn't quite fit in. I wasn't an actor, I wasn't a producer, I was just a guy who lived in a hotel and went to fantastic parties. I'm sure my place at the table had already been filled, and that was okay, I'd had my fun while I was there, and now it was time to move on.

Writing my story was much more difficult than I could have ever imagined. Nobody likes holding a mirror up to every decision they've ever made, and I was no exception. I tried to look back on the events with an open mind, and at first I even saw my actions in a much romanticized way. The fraud, working undercover for the government, South Africa, jail - I'd survived them all. The wounds had healed. Or had they? I poured myself another cup of coffee and wrapped the blanket back around my legs. If I'd really survived them, and the wounds were fully healed, then what the hell was I doing out in the middle of France, with a dumb four-legged ass as my only friend?

Still, I'd had some very good times, and I took full blame for every decision I made, stupid or not. In the past I'd had trouble owning up to my mistakes; it was easier to shift blame and just run the hell away. Running only works until your body starts cramping up, twisting and turning your innards into a knotted mess. There's no eating, no sleeping, no relaxing. The only way to ever find a semblance of peace was to stop running. And I did. I stopped running, and I paid my debt to society, yet somehow, I still felt as though I owed somebody something. I just didn't know who or what.

I'd arrived in France just as the last bits of summer drifted off for another season. Warm days gave way to chilly nights, and the countryside was full of dairy cows lazily packing away the last of the lush green grass. Before I'd left Los Angeles, I'd made a few phone calls back to England, and managed to find an old friend, who had another friend, who knew a guy who was looking to rent out his small farm for the off season. The only stipulation was that I take care of his donkey. It was the perfect place to find my solitude and find myself.

It didn't take me long to get into groove of country living. Morning coffees were enjoyed on the back terrace, watching the birds fight for the last of the seeds I'd thrown out the night before. After I'd fed the donkey and let him out in the field, I usually enjoyed a long walk down one of the many well-worn paths. I especially loved the path that led to the neighbouring property's orchard. The ripe apples bursting off the limbs reminded me of the old orchard at my parent's home, and I couldn't help but store a few of these beauties in the bowels of my jacket for the walk home. By mid-morning, I was at my computer table with a fresh cup of coffee, willing the words to find their way out of the jumbled mess in my brain.

Life fell into this little routine, day in and day out. I found the farmhouse inspiring with its ancient stone foundation and timber-beamed walls. The south side window provided plenty of natural light and a spectacular view of the surrounding countryside. If only these walls could talk. After the Normandy invasion during the Second World War, Allied troops had been stationed all around these parts, and had used the farmhouse as a stopover shelter on their march towards

Berlin. Sitting at my desk looking out the window I could only imagine how different the countryside must have looked during the war. At one of the properties down the road, the farmer had unearthed a couple of old German army helmets when he was digging up a portion of his pasture to plant some trees. When the October breeze whistled through the fields at night, it sounded like a thousand tiny voices calling out, sharing their secrets from a time long ago, wanting us to remember, and begging us to never forget.

Sometimes the solitude got to me, especially as the weather turned colder, and the sun gave up even trying to fend off the dark and ominous rain clouds. One day as I was headed back from the paddock I found a silver-haired scraggly cat sitting calmly by the back door. I'd seen him around a few times before and had even left out some food, but this was the first time he'd actually come within petting distance.

"Hey little guy," I said bending down and slowly reaching out my hand. "You look a little cold and hungry. I know this weather is the shits, isn't it?" The cat tilted his head slightly as if to say, 'you've got that right'. I moved a little closer, letting him become comfortable with my smell and my voice.

"It's okay…I'm not going to hurt you." The cat let out a soft meow and took a slight step forward. "That's it little guy, c'mer." With a little more coaxing I was able to get close enough to rub my hand across his back. "That's right. Doesn't that feel good? You look like a Simon to me? How about I call you Simon? Would that be okay?"

Our bonding session was rudely interrupted by an outpouring of fury from the sky, and the cat took off like a rocket.

"God damnit!"

Dismayed and downcast, I hung my wet jacket on the back hook and made a fresh pot of coffee. At the moment, coffee and cigarettes were the best friends I had. For the next couple of days the weather was relentless. I kept my eye out for Simon and continued to leave some food by the back door but it went untouched, and my heart sank. I was so hoping for a little companionship, just to take the edge off the loneliness. On the morning of the fourth day, I opened the back door to put out some garbage, and there he was, just sitting there waiting. Without hesitation, I invited him in, poured him a drink of milk, and asked if he'd like to stay a while as my house guest.

"I think we're going to get along famously, you and I."

The way he curled up into the crook of my arm, reminded me of my cat Bobby, who was currently living with my mother in England. As much as I wanted to bring Bobby with me to Los Angeles, he was old and I didn't think he'd adjust too kindly to being uprooted from his quiet and pampered English life. He just wasn't an L.A. sort of feline. Besides, he was good company for my aging mother, and I knew he was loved and well-cared for. That's all that mattered.

I hadn't been home to England since my return from North America, but being just across the Channel and not the 'big pond' made communication much easier. With an eight hour time difference from England to Los Angeles, it had been somewhat difficult to schedule regular telephone calls with my mother. Thank God for email; it had been nice waking up most mornings to a friendly hello and message from my mother. Originally, the plan had been to go home for a visit before I went to France but in order to secure the cottage, I had to move in right away, so my visit was placed on the backburner.

I thought about home and what it meant to me. Was it a physical place, with a roof and walls and a bed? I had a roof, and walls, and a bed here at the farmhouse and it still didn't feel like home. Or was home where you laid your roots? Grew up? I'd always felt a sense of peace and relaxation when I was at my childhood home 'Townfield', but since my father's passing, my mother had sold the property and moved into a smaller place not too far away. Someone else was now living in my 'home'. Maybe home was all about people and had nothing to do with bricks and mortar. I finally decided that home was a feeling, a sensation; a place in time that may only have been for a short while but one that left a deep and impenetrable impression.

How did I come to this conclusion? Sitting snuggled under my wool blanket, with Simon curled up on my lap, I thought of the times in my life I was the happiest. And I didn't just mean laughing happy, I meant completely and utterly at peace with myself and the moment. That definition narrowed my list dramatically, and I found myself thinking about the common denominator between them all. Michelle. In her arms I was safe. There was no hiding. My heart was out there, to be loved and to be hurt. And yes, we certainly had our share of drama, but in those moments with her, talking, laughing, loving, I was complete, as whole of a man as I ever dared to be. I let myself be strong and I let myself be vulnerable. She infuriated me yet she calmed me. She made me believe in the essence of love, and that I deserved to experience it, no matter what had happened in my life. For me, in those moments we shared a rarity. We shared a home.

While I had my memories with Michelle, I had nothing with my son. No sense of belonging, no sense of sharing, no sense of love. I mean, I loved him because he was my son, and would always innately be a part of me, but loving him for the things he did, or the boy he'd become? I was never even given the opportunity. I'd fought my feelings about that for a long time, wrestling between understanding and anger. The process was exhausting and the only way I'd ever be able to find any sense of resolution was if I found him.

Having no clue where to start, I made a few phone calls back to my lawyers' office in England. They were one of the few people who actually knew the full details of my life, well most of the details.

"I apparently have a son."

"Apparently?"

"Well I've never met him personally," I said, "but I have no reason to believe he doesn't exist."

"Has anyone asked you for money?"

I couldn't help but laugh. "You lawyers, always thinking about the money."

"Well it's a valid point John. The last thing we want is someone extorting you for money."

"I know, and I appreciate the concern. I've never been asked for a cent, and that's what makes me believe that the child is real."

"Do you have any information at all?"

I told him the story of Rondell, and how I thought that Pierre had probably grown up in Germany. That's about all I had to go on.

"That's it?" said the voice on the other end of the phone.

"Yes, I'm sorry," I answered. "That's it. I have no idea where he might be now."

"Well I guess we'll start in Germany then. It'll be tough, and I can't give you any guarantees but we'll give it a shot.

"That's all I'm asking," I said.

"I'll let you know if we find anything, and John, do give us a ring if you remember anything more will you?"

"Of course."

I hung up the phone feeling strangely excited about the conversation. He didn't say the task was impossible, just tough, and that was enough encouragement for me; the tiniest of threads dangled, and right now, that was all I needed. At least I'd taken the first step and put the process in motion. There was a time when I thought I'd never even have the courage to do that.

The days drifted into weeks, and winter settled over the little farmhouse, mounds of snow sealing off even the tiniest of cracks. For once the place felt warm and cozy. There'd been no word at all from the lawyers' office, but I supposed these things took time, and I vowed to remain patient, a trait that wasn't always part of my repertoire. The writing continued, although not as fast or as furious as I would have liked. For some reason I'd thought the process was going to be easy once I got past my initial writer's block. Turns out I had writer's block more often than not. I just didn't know what to say? What was important and what wasn't. Then I remembered my conversation with Vincent.

"Write it all down John. Everything. It doesn't matter whether or not you think it's important, you can decide that later. Just write it all down and be safe. Sometimes the best thoughts are the ones we think no one gives a shit about!"

I missed Vincent. And looking outside at the stark white world, I missed his rooftop patio.

"What do you say Simon?" I said scratching him behind the ears. "I bet you're glad you're snuggled up in here with me instead of out there?"

The weather was awful. It hadn't stopped snowing and the wind was whipping it all up in a frenzy. I even felt bad for the damn donkey. When I went out in the morning the poor thing was covered in snow. I brushed him off as best I could and tried to fix the latch on the paddock window but I'll be honest, I'm not all that great with the handyman shit. I fed him some carrots as a treat, and broke the ice in his trough with the back of a shovel. That was the extent of my animal husbandry skills.

"Sorry buddy but it's cold out here," I said slapping his grey side before throwing a plaid blanket over his back. "This is the best I can do for you. I know it's Christmas, and I'd invite you inside if I could but I'm not sure that'd be the best idea."

The donkey sort of whinnied and shot a wad of snot out its nose and onto the sleeve of my coat.

"Well Merry Christmas to you too!"

I wiped my coat sleeve on the plaid blanket, gave him a couple more carrots, and another pat on the back. "Stay warm my friend, stay warm."

My own Christmas was a quiet affair, just me and the cat, and I was glad when I could finally turn off the light that night and go to bed. Holidays were the pinnacle for loneliness. I did manage to crack a fresh bottle of whisky to ring in the New Year, and since I had Simon, technically, I wasn't drinking alone. But the whole week was tough. I missed my father terribly, and felt bad that I hadn't made it back to England to celebrate with my mother. Christmas celebrations at my parent's place were spectacular. My mother would dress the house up with excessive Yuletide cheer to welcome the constant stream of revellers that stopped by the door for a drink or two. As a child I loved to hang off in a back corner of the room, just watching the action and trying to stay unnoticed, so I wouldn't get sent to bed. Inevitably, someone would spot me and make me come out and join the party for a round of carols. 'Only one round' my mother would say. Well before I knew it I'd be smack dab in the middle of the party, having a grand old time. More than once I remembered falling asleep on the front hall stairs, never quite being able to stay awake to say my goodbyes.

It was a clear, crisp January morning when I got the call. I'd been out at the paddock and heard the phone ringing as I opened the door.

"John. It's Max."

"Oh hello Max," I said sounding quite surprised. Max and I hadn't been on the best of terms for quite some time now, so hearing by brother's voice on the other end of the phone was quite concerning.

"It's mother. She's not well."

He didn't have to say another word. I immediately made arrangements for the young neighbour boy to take care of the donkey, gathered my belongings, and hopped on the first flight I could back to England.

"He's a good cat," I said handing Simon to the boy. "I'm not sure where he came from but I'd be very happy if you took care of him for me."

The boy grinned. "You mean I can have him?"

"He's all yours."

I gave Simon one last nuzzle, then sent the boy on his way home. There was no way I could bring him back with me, not with my mother being ill, and certainly not with Bobby. Bobby would have been right pissed off if I'd brought home an intruder. I was sort of sad to be leaving the farmhouse. I'd grown quite accustomed to its nuances and peculiarities, and in a strange way the house reminded me of myself; a little weathered, a few chinks in the exterior, but full of spunk and charm.

The plane landed in London after a short and easy trip over the English Channel. Anxious to get through Customs and make my train for Liverpool, I didn't hesitate handing the woman my United Kingdom passport. The U.K. and France were both part of the European Union, and travel within the European Union countries went unstamped on your passport.

I could have been flying in from Germany for all she knew, yet once again the Custom's Official stopped, checked the identification and smiled.

"Did you enjoy your time in France Mr. Coventry?"

I just shook my head and played the game. "Yes I did thank you. And I suppose you know exactly where in France I was and how long I'd been there?" A tilt of her ponytailed head and lingering smile gave me my answer.

"Welcome home sir."

I should have known that the Intelligence Services would never give up watching me. Although, I honestly had no idea what they could be after, or what they thought they might gain by keeping me under tabs. That part of my life was truly in the past. I had no contact with anyone I'd met during that time, and quite frankly I had no intentions of contacting any of them ever again. Well, except of course for Rondell. She really was the one who could unlock the mystery of my son. She could pick up the phone any minute and decide to tell me everything I needed to know. I could only hope and pray that she would.

CHAPTER SIXTEEN

Rondell heard the car pull up the driveway. She didn't bother getting up. There was no point. Pierre lifted the latch on the front door and strode in, ready for a battle. Fully expecting a tidal wave of fury, he was almost alarmed at the silence in the house. They couldn't be sleeping, it was still early evening. He set his bag on the front bench, and walked through the hall to the kitchen. Empty. Not a dish in the sink, not a coffee mug on the counter. His heart revved with anxiety.

"What the hell is going on?" he mumbled. "Where is everyone?"

The drawn curtains in the living room only furthered his uneasiness. Light burst into the room as Rondell clicked on the table lamp.

"Did you have a good time?" she said, her voice void of any emotion. The ice cubes clinked against the side of her glass; her eyes watching the steady movement as she tilted the glass. Back and forth. Back and forth. Back and forth.

Pierre just stood there, not knowing what to do or how to react.

"Answer me. Did you have a good time?"

"Yes I did."

"Well that's nice. Good for you. Glad you had a nice time. Berlin is such a fun city isn't it? Many good times there myself."

"Is everything okay? Why aren't you yelling at me? What's wrong?"

"What's wrong?" Rondell's laugh was harsh and raw. "Where do I even begin? How about you start? You tell me what you think is wrong."

"Well I know you're angry about me going to Berlin but I don't care. I wanted to go and I went. There's nothing you can do about it now." Pierre raised his guard. He wasn't going down without a fight.

"You're right," she answered calmly. "There's nothing I can do now."

"So that's it? I'm not in trouble?"

"Oh you're in trouble. Don't think you're going to get away with this nonsense so easily. What you did this weekend was inexcusable. I was worried sick about you. But that's another matter, and frankly I don't have the heart or the stomach to deal with you right now."

Pierre pulled up the footstool and sat in front of his mother. "What is wrong? This isn't like you? Please scream at me! Yell at me! Do what you usually do! Send me to Aunt Erika's office and let her whip me with the lash! Anything that seems normal! Please...you're scaring me!"

Rondell finally looked up from her glass and met her son's confused eyes. "There will be no more whipping Pierre. I am sorry you had to endure that all these years. Believe me I am."

"What are you talking about? I don't understand?"

"She's gone Pierre. Aunt Erika is dead." The blow almost knocked him off the footstool. "She died on Friday night while you were off doing whatever it was you were doing in Berlin. I had no way of getting a hold of you."

"I don't believe it?"

"Well I'm afraid it's the truth. She wasn't young anymore Pierre. Her heart just gave out on her."

Pierre sat motionless, unable to comprehend the news. "I can't believe I wasn't here."

Rondell just nodded her head in agreement. "You made the choice not to be here. Now you have to live with it."

She knew she was being hard on the boy but after a weekend of hurt and sorrow, she really didn't care whose feelings she hurt. Rondell was torn about Erika's death. On the one hand, she was happy she'd no longer have to put up with her commanding Nazi bullshit, but on the other, she was the last of her family, and the woman had taken her in as a child and saved her ass on many occasions. That they grew apart as time went forward was just a natural progression of two distinct and different personalities. Still, Rondell felt a huge sense of relief, and a spark of hope that maybe, just maybe, she'd be able to reel Pierre back into the fold before it was too late. The boy slumped on the stool, fighting back the tears. She hated seeing him so upset.

"Come here Pierre," she said holding out her hand. "I know. We're going to miss her. It's okay."

Pierre sank into Rondell's arms, the tears exploding from his sad brown eyes. She stroked the back of his hair, and kissed his cheek.

"I think you forgot to shave this weekend. You're a little scruffy." Her voice was soft and sweet and Pierre managed a quiet laugh. "It will be okay son. She lived a good life…and she loved you with all her heart. I know she could be a bitch…God don't I know it…but she did love you, and only ever wanted the best for you. Unfortunately, sometimes we didn't always agree on what was best."

Pierre looked up and smiled. "Sometimes?"

"Okay…most of the time," Rondell laughed. "We just had different views and wanted different things for you…that's all."

"I am sorry about this weekend Mom. I shouldn't have just left you a note like that. I wasn't thinking."

"It's over and done with Pierre. Let's not talk about it right now okay? But in the future you will be telling me where you are going. Is that understood? And in the next couple of weeks you and I will be sitting down and having a nice long conversation about what's been going on lately."

"Yes ma'am."

"Are you hungry? Have you had dinner?"

"I could eat."

"Of course you could," she laughed. "I never knew a time you couldn't!"

The two of them ventured out of the living room and into the kitchen; Rondell taking a spot behind the counter and Pierre pulling up a chair.

"By the way, where is everyone?"

"Gone," Rondell answered. "I got rid of them all. Well except for Marta. But she's only going to come around part-time from now on, and oh yes, I've kept the gardener. This is a lot of grass to cut. Unless of course you're up to the challenge?"

"Keep the gardener," laughed Pierre. "Grass isn't really my thing."

Rondell set a beef sandwich in front of him. "Sorry, the fridge is a little empty. With all the commotion this weekend, I didn't get to the market."

"That's okay." Pierre took a bite and began to chew. "So tell me about it. How did it happen?"

Rondell ran the damp dishcloth across the cutting board. "I was sitting in my room when Marta knocked and said that

Aunt Erika wasn't answering the call for dinner. She was in her office with the door locked as usual. I went with Marta and we banged on the door and there was nothing. Not a sound. Of course your Aunt never gave me a key to her office, so we had to break down the door...and there she was...slumped over on her desk. Pen still in her hand. Marta called the doctor, but I knew right away she had passed. She had this look on her face...I hadn't seen that look for a very long time actually. She looked happy and content."

"I've seen her look happy before," said Pierre.

"No," answered Rondell. "You've seen her smile. She's never really been happy since Uncle passed away. The doctor came straightaway and declared her dead. They removed the body and I got to work on funeral arrangements. That was it. I don't think she suffered. I think she went in peace. I must say it felt odd to be in her office without her there. That place was her sanctuary. I sort of felt like I was intruding."

"When is the service?"

"Day after tomorrow," answered Rondell. "She'll be buried in the family plot beside her husband. Just a small ceremony. Private. There's no need for a spectacle."

The last thing Rondell wanted or needed was a full out Nazi ceremony. Erika's affiliations weren't a secret, and some of her cohorts had tried to hijack the preparations but Rondell put her foot down. It was over. Erika would receive a nice family burial, and then they would get on with their lives. It was that simple. The reclamation of Pierre started the minute the old woman was in the ground. She would let him say his goodbyes in whatever way he wanted, then that would be it. No more Nazi indoctrination, no more lectures about the greatness of the past. It was time for Rondell to take back the reins and steer the wagon forward. The past was the past; their future began now.

The dark clouds hung low in the sky as the coffin made its way from the hearse to the burial site.

"God forbid she send a little sunshine," laughed Rondell to herself. "I suppose it's only fitting."

The service was short and to the point. Pierre looked handsome in his dark suit, standing so brave and tall, as he helped carry the remains of his beloved Aunt. The clergyman said his piece, and they all offered their thanksgiving for a life well-lived. Rondell tried to work up a tear for the old woman, but her brain just didn't want to connect with her emotions, and her eyes remained dry. Much to her chagrin, a host of Erika's Nazi friends showed up uninvited all decked out in their full regalia. The display almost made Rondell laugh out loud. So out of touch they were with the reality of the world. But Erika was their mentor, and now that they were here, Rondell wasn't going to deny them the right to say goodbye.

One by one they moved slowly past the coffin, throwing a rose, and offering a Nazi salute. If it hadn't been for the glaring arm patch swastikas, the procession might even have been considered lovely. The rain drops started slowly at first, just enough to make Rondell wish she'd worn her closed toe shoes. She placed her hand on the coffin and whispered softly.

"Goodbye old friend. You taught me much and you gave me a home when I had no other. For that I will always be truly grateful. You are as brave as you are stubborn, and I admire you for your conviction and devotion. You had a strength that amazes me still. I will miss you." She kissed the tips of her fingers, then with a gentle blow, sent the kiss floating through the rain on its way to eternity.

As she turned to walk away, Pierre was waiting with outstretched arms. They held each other for a moment, not saying a word, just letting the moment speak for itself.

"Take your time son. We're in no hurry."

Pierre stood silently at the grave, hands in his pockets, head bent forward. The intensity of the rain increased, but the boy didn't seem bothered by the drops exploding on his shoulders and down his back. Taking a rose from the wicker basket, he meticulously positioned it across the very front of the coffin, his hand lingering on the majestic wooden box. Softly through the pouring rain he began to sing.

The rotten bones are trembling,
Of the World before the War.
We have smashed this terror,
For us a great victory.

We will continue to march,
Even if everything shatters;
Because today Germany hears us,
And tomorrow, the whole World.

And because of the Great War
The World lies in ruins,
But devil may care;
We build it up again.

We will continue to march,
Even if everything shatters;
Because today Germany hears us,
And tomorrow, the whole World.

And the elders may chide,
So just let them scream and cry,
And if the World decides to fight us,
We will still be the victors.

We will continue to march,
Even if everything shatters;
Because today Germany hears us,
And tomorrow, the whole World.

They don't want to understand this song,
They think of slavery and war.
Meanwhile our acres ripen,
Flag of freedom, fly!

We will continue to march,
Even if everything shatters;
Freedom rose in Germany,
And tomorrow the world belongs to it.

When the song was over, he stepped back, clicked his heels together, and brought his right arm to his chest. With a quick arm snap forward, he saluted his Aunt Erika goodbye in true Nazi fashion. His mother closed her eyes, unable to watch what her son had become.

After the funeral, life settled into a more relaxed routine. In the time usually reserved for his studies with Erika, Rondell took to taking Pierre into town to catch a movie, go to the market, or for dinner. She enjoyed reconnecting with her son, and he seemed to enjoy the time with his mother. Rondell was careful not to forbid him contact with his right-wing friends, knowing full well what the consequences of that would be. Instead, she kept him as active as possible, hoping his need to interact with them would lesson with time. They enjoyed debating, and Rondell was always cognizant of bringing up situations and scenarios that directly conflicted with his 'Aunt Erika instructed' ideals. She knew his commitment was strong, but then again, so was hers. And so their life went on. And for the first time in a very long time, Rondell felt like she had her son back.

It was the second winter after Erika's passing that she began to notice how tired and lethargic she'd become. At first she thought she just wasn't getting enough sleep, so she went to bed earlier in the evening, cut out her nightly coffee, and took to drinking herbal tea. But she just couldn't shake it. Then came the back soreness, and loss of appetite. When the abnormal bleeding and aching pains in her abdomen persisted, she had to face the reality that something wasn't right.

"Cancer?"

"I'm afraid so Rondell," said the doctor. "It's quite advanced. We believe it originated in the ovaries but has spread to your uterus and liver. I'm so sorry."

Rondell stared motionless at the floor.

"I know that's not what you wanted to hear," the doctor continued. "But there is a course of treatment. Surgery to start, then chemotherapy. We will have to be aggressive and we will have to start soon. Let me talk to the surgeon and get back to you with a surgery date. How would you like me to proceed?"

Rondell continued to stare. Not hearing a word coming from the other woman's mouth.

"Rondell? I know this is difficult but I need an answer. How would you like me to proceed? Time is not on our side here."

Rondell lifted her wet eyes towards the doctor. All she could think about was Pierre and how this news was going to destroy him.

"You have a chance my dear. This is not necessarily a death sentence."

The sarcasm of the statement made Rondell laugh. "Not necessarily? Well that's hopeful now isn't it?" She was angry.

No, more like furious, and she had no intentions of hiding her emotions. "So let's be realistic. How much time do I have?"

"It's hard to tell at this point Rondell. Let's do the surgery and see exactly where we're at. We'll know better then what we're up against."

Eight days later, Rondell was lying in a recovery room; her ovaries, uterus, fallopian tubes, and a chunk of her liver gone. Pierre had been a tower of strength, hardly flinching when she told him the news.

"Well we're just going to have to get rid of it now aren't we? You'll have the surgery, some chemotherapy and all will be well. I just know it will."

Except all wasn't well. Rondell didn't respond to the chemotherapy like the doctors had hoped and the cancer continued to spread. And quickly. They suggested some new form of radical drug but Rondell said no. She was tired. The battle was over. The cancer had won. So Rondell began to make arrangements, she didn't want her son to have to worry about a thing. She planned her funeral to the last detail, picking out the music and the hymns, and even the menu for the small luncheon. Nothing elaborate, just the same simplicity that represented her life. With the proceeds of Aunt Erika's vast estate, the boy would never have to worry about money, but that really wasn't her main concern.

"Do you need any more tea?" Pierre said setting the cup on the side of her bed.

"No son. I'm fine for now. Thank you. You have been my strength and joy through these long, long months Pierre and I can't tell you how much I love you."

He smiled. "I would do anything for you. You know that."

"Would you? Would you really do anything?"

"Of course I would," he laughed. "Now you're just being silly."

Rondell marvelled at what a handsome man he had become, so unassuming, yet strong and confident. The way he sat in the chair and tilted his head to the side reminded her of the way Michelle used to look when she was playful and teasing. Rondell couldn't help but let the tears stream from her eyes.

"Mother what it is?" Pierre held her hand in his own.

"Will you forgive me?"

"Forgive you?" he said. "For what? The cancer wasn't your fault."

"No my son," she sighed. "It's not about the cancer. It's about you."

Pierre's eyes grew with curiosity. "Does this have to do with my father? Because if it does, then there is no reason to have to forgive you, you did nothing wrong. Like you told me a long time ago, circumstances happened and you did what you had to. I don't see him knocking down my door to come and see me."

"Don't blame him for anything Pierre. Your Aunt made sure he didn't get within twenty miles of you and she made me tell you that he'd been killed in a car accident. But eventually I told you the truth. That he was still alive. Poor man, she had him followed wherever he went. It must have been a nightmare for him…always waiting and wondering about you, and always finding a dead end to every lead. But that's about to change. I have hired a lawyer and he is currently trying to track him down. I want so much for the two of you to meet. I take the blame for so much of this…" She paused, took a deep breath and gathered her strength. "It is about your mother Pierre."

"My mother? You are my mother." The crease in his brow deepened.

"No I am not. I am the woman who raised you, and loved you, and loves you still…but I am not your true mother." The words barely made it through her tears. "Your real mother died when you were just a baby. She was my best friend. Her name was Michelle. Please let me explain!"

Pierre released Rondell's hand and stood abruptly from the chair, turning his back, shunning the words and the woman. He left the room without uttering a word.

"Pierre! Please! Pierre!"

But he was out the door and gone. Pierre had no idea where he was going; he just knew he had to get the hell out of there. Rondell wasn't his mother? What the fuck was that all about? How could she keep that from him for so long? Was there any truth to his life or had everything been just one big fucking lie? Then it hit him. Aunt Erika wasn't even his Aunt? He had no blood connection to the woman at all. All those times she told him that the blood of greatness ran through his veins. The blood of their ancestors. Their heroes. She was fucking lying the whole time! He pounded the gas, and the Mercedes responded with deft agility.

"Fuck them all!" he screamed. "I don't need them and I don't fucking want them! God damn fucking liars!"

He didn't see the other car until it was just about to kiss his front bumper.

"God damn it!"

He railed hard on the wheel, sending the car into a quick swerve right, and out of the path of the little red Fiat. One more second and the powerful Mercedes would have smoked the Fiat into oblivion. This day was not going as planned. Scared and unnerved, he pulled the car to the side of the road and shut off the motor. He needed quiet. He needed some time to think. Sort this shit through.

He had no idea how long he sat there, just staring out the front window, trying to make some sense of what Rondell had just told him. He thought back to the very first memory he could recall, and it was of Rondell. He thought of the time he fell off his bike and tore up his knee, and it was Rondell that picked him up in her arms, bandaged him up, and threw the hurt the away. Every memory, every moment of his past, was filled with her. Her smile, her voice, her laughter. He wiped the tears from his cheeks.

"She must have had her reasons. And it must have been difficult to raise someone else's child as your own...and love them...and do everything for them. Why did she take me? Where was my real mother's family? Didn't they want me either?"

Slowly he turned the key and started up the ignition. He wasn't going to find the answers sitting at the side of road. Rondell's room was dark when he returned home, so he snuck in quietly and took his usual spot in the chair by her bed. For the first time he really saw how much this wretched disease had ravished her body. The hollows of her cheeks sunk deep into her face like craters, making her nose more pronounced and distinct; the rosiness replaced by a grey pallor. Her skin just hung loosely over everything, like a wrinkled blanket. There was no spark. There was almost no life.

"You're back," she whispered, her voice tired and hoarse.

"Yes," Pierre answered. "I'm back."

"The top drawer of my dresser stand. There's an envelope. Will you grab it?"

Pierre turned on the small bedside lamp, then went to retrieve the envelope.

"Open it up."

His hand trembled as he fumbled with the paper sleeve.

"Photographs," he said softly.

"Yes. That cute little chubby guy there is you. And of course that's me. This photo was taken just a few days before we escaped."

"Escaped?" said Pierre.

"I'll get to that. Flip to the next one. Go ahead. It's okay." A weak smile etched across Rondell's lips. She has happy to finally be able to share this moment.

"She's beautiful."

"She's you Pierre. And let me tell you, you certainly have her spunk! She was quite a woman…quite a woman. I can't tell you how much I still miss her, and how I wish things had turned out differently."

Still staring at the photo, Pierre eased back into the chair. "Tell me about her."

They talked deep into the night, and almost constantly for the next few days. Rondell told him everything. She told him about the day he was born, and the day she watched in horror as Michelle was murdered. Tired of the secrets and the lies, she told him the good and the bad. She knew she didn't have long to live and she didn't want to leave Pierre with any unanswered questions.

"Did they love each other?"

"Your mother and father?" Rondell smiled. "By God they did, I can assure you of that. I had seen your mother with other men before but when John came along, that was it, she was hooked. I don't know if it was that British accent and charm, or just the fact that he was so different from all the other men she knew. He didn't want anything from her, except her. And unfortunately, at the time, she couldn't give him what he wanted. She was just so wrapped up in the cause…and everything it stood for. I tried to get her to leave Pierre, honestly I did…but she wouldn't listen. Not to me and not to John. He so desperately wanted her to run away with him, somewhere safe, where they could be together. He tried Pierre. Your father tried everything he could, but your mother was stubborn. He didn't even know your mother was pregnant. She refused to tell him and made me swear on my life."

"Why? Why didn't she want him to know?"

"Because she knew he would come for her. And in a way I think she was trying to protect him. Your father didn't live in our world Pierre. And he wouldn't have survived. I think that's why she didn't tell him."

"Is that why you and Aunt Erika clashed so much?"

"What do you mean?"

"You know what I mean," he laughed.

"I didn't want that life for you, no. I saw what it did to Michelle, and how she chose her ideals over her family, and I see some of the same convictions and stubbornness in you. I want you to have more than that Pierre. I want you to get a nice job, maybe even wear a suit and tie, and eventually...not too soon...find a nice girl that you fall madly in love with."

He took her hand. "And I want some of those things too Mom...I really do."

"I just don't want you living your life in fear like we did. It isn't fun Pierre. Always having to look over your shoulder. Never knowing who you can trust and who you can't. The day I pulled you from that burning farmhouse I vowed to never look back, and I haven't. I don't want that life for you! I don't want that!" The excitement sent her curdling lungs gasping for air.

"Shhh...shhh," said Pierre gently tapping her back with the palm of his hand. "You need to calm down." He reached for the glass on the table. "Here, have a drink. Just a few sips." He held the glass up to her lips, his hand supporting her frail head. "There. Better?"

"Yes. Thank you." She settled back down into the pillows and sighed. "I mean it though Pierre. Promise me when I'm gone you'll leave that lifestyle behind. Don't let it get you son. And it will get you. Maybe not tomorrow, maybe not next week…but it will get you."

Pierre leaned down and kissed her forehead. "I promise."

Despite her pain and failing health, the next couple of months were glorious for Rondell. Releasing the burden of the past had given her a bit more energy and spirit, and she spent as much time as she could with Pierre, just laughing and talking. She'd received a telephone call from her lawyer saying that they'd tracked down a man named John Coventry, and they were fairly certain it was the right John Coventry, but he was currently living somewhere in Los Angeles.

"Do you know where?"

"No I'm afraid we don't have an address," replied her lawyer.

"Oh that's too bad," answered Rondell. "Any idea when you might?"

"I'm sorry, we don't."

She hung up the phone feeling lost and discouraged. She knew if they could find John, he would come to Germany to meet them. Rondell had faith in the man; he would come through for her and for his son. She just had to stay alive long enough to make it happen. They needed to find that address quick. But time is cruel and always speeds up just when you want it to stop, if only for a second, if only to catch your breath so you can soldier on. And then, when you don't want it to stop, it takes its last breath and leaves you empty.

CHAPTER SEVENTEEN

I crunched the plastic cigarette wrapper in my hand and threw it on the little patio table. It killed me to see my mother so frail and fragile; her once vibrant self, worn down to skin and bones, a life evaporating. Except for fluffing her pillows and providing companionship, there was really nothing I could do but watch and wait, and at least hope that I was making her retreat from this life as simple and as comfortable as possible. When she wasn't resting, she liked to drink tea and just chat. In our intimate conversations, I struggled with not telling her about her grandson Pierre. I was just so uncertain about how she would react. No. That's a lie. I knew exactly how she would react. She'd be accepting and non-judgmental, just like she always was. I think it was my own anxieties that held me back. Why, I don't know. I should have trusted her with the truth. After all she had done for me, she deserved that much.

"I'm just going to run out for a few groceries if that's all right with you Mom? Won't be long."

"That's fine John," she answered. "I'll be all right."

Despite her failing health, my mother still enjoyed a semblance of independence, even if that meant staying home alone for half an hour while I ran an errand, or went for a quick walk. Sickness tends to strip the humanity away from a person, so I was always aware about giving her as much leeway and freedom as she could handle. Some days were better than others, and today was a good day.

"Are you sure?" I said. "I can see if Lillian can stop over until I get back?"

"You leave Lillian alone!" she smiled. "She has enough to do with those three little ones of hers."

"Okay. Well she's just next door. So promise me you'll ring if you need her. Be back in a bit!"

I knew my mother would be fine on her own, and I marvelled at her strength and tenacity. She wasn't going down without a fight, God bless her. I could only hope I would have half her courage when faced with such a battle. I was only about fifteen minutes late but arrived home to my mother in a terrible and frenzied state.

"What's wrong?" I said trying to calm her down. "Here. Let me help you to your chair."

"Those men. They were here asking where you were and something else I can't remember at the moment...I had no idea what they were talking about. But...but...they just kept on!"

"Calm down," I said pouring her a glass of water. "Now start from the beginning. What men?"

"There were two of them in dark suits. I heard a knock on the door but I couldn't see who it was. I tried to get there as fast as I could but I guess it wasn't fast enough because they just kept pounding and pounding. I got up so quick from the chair...I felt a little dizzy and had to sit back down again."

"God damn it!" I said.

"It's okay, I'm not dizzy now. When I finally did get to the door to open it, the one man...he was rather tall with wavy brown hair...well he was ready to bowl me right over and storm into the house. The other man...he had greyish hair, rather thin on top and a bit of a belly. Well he put his hand out and stopped the younger man. It was all rather disconcerting."

"I'm sure it was! My God Mother!"

"The grey haired man asked if you were here and I said no you were not. I didn't know who they were and quite frankly I didn't trust them one bit, so I told them that you went away to visit some people in London for a while. The dark haired man came right out and told me he thought I was lying! He said he didn't think that you would leave your 'poor sick mother' alone for that long. How they knew I was sick, I have no idea! I thought they were quite rude!"

I could feel the blood in my body begin to race, the intensifying pressure popping the veins in my neck, and exploding my white skin into a mass of red.

"Those God damn fucking bastards!" I said under my breath, although not quite quiet enough to elude my mother's still active ears.

"John Coventry!"

"I'm sorry Mother. I didn't mean to say that out loud. It just slipped. They had no right to treat you like that!"

"Do you have any idea who they might be?" she asked. "They didn't leave a card."

"I don't know for certain but I have my suspicions."

"Still the government men?"

"Possibly. Or a few others. You know when I was in Los Angeles, there were many, many times I felt like I was being watched or followed. I don't know why and I never confronted them because I never knew for sure. It was always just a feeling."

"Well whoever it was, they were certainly anxious to see you today."

"I'm sorry for that Mom. I never meant to put you in harm's way." The puzzled look on her face gave me cause for concern. "What is it?"

"I'm trying to remember what else they said? Something about a boy."

"A boy?"

"Yes! Yes! That's it." Her blue eyes sparked with life. "They asked me if I knew where the boy was? I said I have no idea what you're talking about. There is no boy here. Then they insisted I would know where he was? I said what boy! And the grey haired man said Pierre?"

What the fuck was going on? How did they know about Pierre? They might have known that Michelle had a son but how in the hell did they know I was the father? I didn't know I was the father right away, and I sure as hell hadn't told a sole. Rondell? No. She wouldn't talk. Unless of course they'd gotten to her? But why after all these years would they bother? The Baader Meinhof group had long disbanded and I couldn't imagine she had gotten involved in some sort of a splinter group.

"Do you know who they're talking about John?"

"No Mom I don't. I don't know why they'd ask about a boy." I hated lying to her. It made me sick. It just wasn't the time or the place for confessions.

"Well whoever the boy is, I hope he's okay," she said. "Those men sure seemed anxious to find him! Do you think maybe he's in some sort of trouble?"

"God I hope not Mother. I hope not."

I made us some dinner and tried to steer the conversation away from the events of the afternoon. I needed some time to digest the visit, and to figure out why they would want Pierre. I had no idea. Unless Intelligence thought he knew something? About what though? I needed to find him as soon as possible.

Maybe my mother was right, and the boy was in some sort of trouble. I knew nothing of his upbringing or what kinds of things he was involved in. As soon as I got my mother settled in for the evening, I picked up the phone to call Aaron, one of the trustee lawyers that worked for my father, and was now trying to locate my son.

"John, so nice to hear from you. I heard you were back in London. So sorry to hear about your Mother's failing health."

"Thank you Aaron. Yes it's a trying time for sure. Listen, I was wondering if there was a time we could get together for a chat to see where things are at?"

"I'm glad you called. I may have some information for you but nothing confirmed. How about Wednesday at around two pm? My office?"

"Still in the same building downtown?"

"Same one," he answered.

"Okay. I'll see you then."

Since I didn't know how long my meeting with Aaron would be, I arranged for Lillian, the neighbor to come and sit with my mom. Mom loved watching her three little kids play, and very much enjoyed a good 'woman to woman' chat every once and a while.

"I don't know when I'll be home exactly," I said straightening my tie in the front hall mirror.

"Take your time John," Lillian replied. "The kids and I are looking forward to a nice visit. I just hope Bobby is ready for all the excitement!"

"Yes he does tend to run and hide at the first sign of commotion doesn't he? Silly cat."

Warmth and friendship emanated from Lillian's smile. "Please don't hurry back on our account. Go out for a drink or visit a friend. Do something. You've been a real gent to stay here and take care of your mother like this. I know a lot of men who would have run away at the mere thought."

"Well those men don't have my mother for a mother now, do they?" I laughed.

"No they don't. She's someone special that's for sure!"

Chester was a beautiful place, an old historic Roman settlement, and one of the last towns in England to fall in the Norman Conquest. The architecture here and in fact in all of England is so much different than what I saw in Los Angeles. Compared to Chester's' two thousand years of existence, LA was practically a newborn baby, still whining and crying, desperately trying to fit in and find its place in the world. Chester had no such issues or pretensions. It didn't have to pretend to be anything other than what it was. What a comforting thought.

I arrived at Aaron's St. John St. office about fifteen minutes early, just enough time to have a cigarette and calm my nerves. He said on the phone that he might have some information. I didn't want to get my hopes up, but still it was hard not to feel a twinge of excitement. What if he'd found him? Would the boy even want to meet me was the real question. I took a last long deep drag, then butted out on the side of the old brick building. It was time for the moment of truth.

"Hello John," said Aaron with an outstretched hand. "Nice to see you again."

"Aaron. Thank you for fitting me in on such short notice."

"Have a seat," he said pointing to the high back leather chair. "Can I get you a drink?"

"A nice tall glass of whiskey would be ideal…but I'll settle for some water."

Aaron filled a couple of glasses from the decanter. "Oh a little midday smidge isn't going to kill you. How is your mother?"

"She's hanging in there I guess. Good days and bad days. Although lately I think the bad days are starting to outnumber the good."

"I'm sorry to hear that," he said taking a drink. "Wonderful woman your mother. And I can't tell you how much I do miss your father. He had such a way about him."

"That he did," I said. "I miss him too. I think about him often, especially now that I've begun the search for my own son. Makes me wonder what kind of a father I would have been to the boy."

"There's still time to forge that relationship John. Never give up hope."

I really didn't have a decent reply, so I busied myself with my drink.

"And on that note," he continued. "I think we may have a lead. My sources are in the process of trying to track down a woman by the name of Rondell Seidel. Apparently she has some ties to organized crime in Germany and spent some time in her youth in a French jail. It looks promising."

"Seidel? That's not a name I remember hearing."

"Well it's easy to change a last name these days…and for someone like her, with her connections, I imagine it would have been a piece of cake."

Still, I wasn't convinced. No particular reason, just a gut feeling. Aaron could sense my apprehension.

"We'll check it out. You never know John. Maybe we'll get lucky and nail it on the first shot, and maybe we'll have to keep digging."

"Well for money's sake, I hope this woman is the right Rondell. This digging around certainly isn't cheap."

"I know John and I've instructed my sources to be as prudent with their expenses as possible. Here is the amount so far."

"Good God Aaron! Is your detective eating prime rib for every fucking meal? I don't know how much longer I can afford this. I honestly don't. I'm not exactly working these days you know."

"We'll work something out John. Don't stress about it."

"I'm sorry…this whole ordeal has been stressful and now with my mother…I think I'm just tired."

"I totally understand," answered Aaron. "Go home and get some rest my friend. I'll call you when I know something more."

I left his office feeling somewhat discouraged and a little pissed off. These lawyers think that money is just so easy to come by. At the rate they were blowing through my budgeted funds, the search would be over by Christmas, and I'd have nothing to show for it but a stack of receipts. Unfortunately, as much as I wanted to throw every penny I had into the search, I just couldn't. And there was no way in hell I was asking my mother for any kind of financial help. I was on my own and would just have to make it happen with what I had.

As the dog days of August drifted away, my mother's health seemed to drift away right along with it. By the middle of September she was completely bedridden. Her independence gone; her strength waning. My heart ached for her, but she seemed to be at peace with what was happening. We spent much of our time chatting about the old days, growing up at 'Townfield' and going away on our many family adventures. Those were good times, and memories that I'll hold close to my heart forever. She didn't seem afraid of death, and at this point almost seemed to welcome the next stage in her journey.

"I won't be alone son," she said softly holding my hand. "Your father will be with me. Oh how I've missed him."

"I know you have," I said. "I've missed him too."

"And one day, a very long time from now, you and Max and the rest of the family will join us. And we'll all be together again."

The words barely squeaked past my lips. "I would like that very much."

"But not too soon," she laughed. "Your father and I are going to need some time alone first!"

I bent in and gave her a kiss on the cheek. "Trust me...I'll try to hold on as long as I can!"

A few short weeks later, she was gone; her brief moment in time ending peacefully in her sleep, a mischievous grin etched on her face. My father must have kissed her hello. Her death was a devastating blow. Of course, I knew it was inevitable but that didn't stop the pain or the sorrow, or the incredible sense of loss and loneliness. If my father had been the rock in the family, my mother was the foundation. She was the one that brought stability to my life, a sense of place to come home to, and a sense of belonging. Her wit, her charm, and her joviality; parts of her that remain parts of me. Mom was the map on my road of life, always guiding and pushing me to go in new directions and discover the undiscovered, both on the surface, and in my heart. Without my map, the road ahead was going to be a whole lot messier, and a whole lot more lonely.

After my mother's death, I moved into a small apartment in Chester with Bobby, my faithful feline friend. The original lead on Rondell turned out to be a dead end, which for me, wasn't much of a surprise. There was some information about a boy named Pierre but the child didn't quite fit the age profile, so I told Aaron to concentrate my funds on something more promising. When he called me for a meeting at his office, I was certain it was to tell me that I was out of money and would have to give up the search.

"How are you doing John?"

"I'm doing all right I guess," I said. "Just trying to figure out what I'm going to do."

"Well I have some news that I think you're going to like. As you know, when your father passed away, the majority of his estate and holdings passed to your mother."

"Yes of course."

"Well as we've been going over your mother's will, it seems as though your father had set up some sort of a trust fund for your son."

"What are you talking about? My father never knew about Pierre?"

"Apparently he had his suspicions," said Aaron. "I don't know for sure since the will was drafted by one of my dear old colleagues, who has since passed away himself.   But there is a clause in your mother's will, that links to a safety deposit box. The safety deposit box contained a letter addressed to you and account information for the trust fund. I have the letter right here."

My trembling hands could hardly keep the page straight.

Dear John,

If you are reading this, then it is safe to say that both your mother and I have left this earth. Do not be sad for us. We have both lived incredibly fulfilling lives and are grateful for everything, especially our wonderful children. You and your brother have truly been a gift in our lives, which is why some day I hope you have the courage and strength to find and connect with your own child. I never told you that I knew of their existence. I didn't want to interfere or pressure you in any way. You'd been through such an ordeal, and I felt you needed time and space to recover. We had a couple of visitors at the house one day. You were out in the back gardens for a walk with your mother. As soon as I saw the dark suits I knew they were after something and it probably had to do with you.

One of the men asked me if the child was here. I told them that I knew nothing about a child. Then he said the strangest thing. He said they knew there had been a child there but it was missing. Of course, I had no idea what he was talking about and promptly kicked them off the property. But then I got to thinking. Why would they come here looking for a child? Unless they suspected that you were the father? Like I said, I didn't want to burden you with the knowledge of my visitors, so I kept the information to myself, and when I didn't ever hear you mention a woman or a child, I thought maybe our visitors were mistaken. John, I don't know the full story or the reasons behind it all…that is your business and yours to sort through, but I wanted to do something to help.

This trust fund is my way of saying we welcome our grandson or granddaughter into the family. Use the money as you see fit, in the child's name, for their education, care or whatever you need – the fund will cover the amount. And remember what I always told you John, "Family comes first". There have never been truer words.

I hope this letter finds you well my son. Take care of yourself and find the happiness you deserve.

Your loving Father

I didn't know what to say, my brain having a total disconnect from my mouth. Why didn't my father tell me about the visitors and his suspicions?

"I don't understand," was all I could manage.

"It's really quite simple," said Aaron. "Our firm has been put in charge of the execution of the trust fund, subject to your stipulations for the needs of the child."

"This is all such a shock," I said. "The money, the letter, the whole god damn thing!"

"I can imagine." Aaron smiled and poured me a drink. "You look as though you could use this."

I read the letter again, letting my mind digest each and every word of the handwritten script. It had been a long time since I'd seen that familiar scribble, and as much as I tried to hold back, the tears would not be defeated.

"I'm sorry," I said. "Reading this just brings back so many memories. Here he is, my father, still taking care of things from beyond the grave. Always trying to protect us, never wanting to see us hurt."

"He was a good man, your father."

"Yes he was. And you know...that was his favourite saying, 'family comes first'. It was the code he lived by and now apparently I see the code he died by. Amazing."

"So what do you want to do with the money John?"

"Go find my son so I can bring him home."

CHAPTER EIGHTEEN

Pierre brushed the loose curl back from the side of his face and tried to focus his bloodshot and weary eyes. Uwe was somewhere in the bar, but he'd lost sight of his friend in the haze and dim lights. It had been a rough couple of months for the boy, and he was having trouble adjusting to life on his own. Lonely and looking for direction, Pierre took off for Berlin to find his much older friend Uwe Boehnhardt, an ardent Neo-Nazi supporter he'd met at a rally some years before. All the bedside promises he'd made to his mother were thrown out the window, and Uwe became his guiding force and unwavering mentor. Uwe was hard-core, and represented everything Rondell did not want for her son. German Intelligence had been monitoring his activities since the mid 1990's, along with the other members of the 'National Socialist Underground (NSU)', and there were rumours abound that Uwe and his crew had been responsible for the horrific 'Doner murders'. Targeting mainly Turkish immigrants, the gunmen would storm their various shops and stores in broad daylight, and shoot the victims in the head at close range with a CZ 83. There was no rhyme or reason for the murders, the victims were just ordinary citizens working and trying to make a living but to Uwe and his crew they were abhorrent people who deserved to die, strictly because they weren't pure-blooded

Germans. And Pierre, wide-eyed and looking for acceptance, hung on Uwe's every word.

With his money from Aunt Erika's estate, Pierre rented a small apartment in the heart of Berlin. He loved the city. The constant buzz and sizzle invigorating his lonely and sad heart, his pain lost in the dirge of the dirty streets and seedy bars. Not quite ready for the Neo-Nazi superstardom of the NSU, Pierre had joined a lesser group called the 'Immortals' who were loosely affiliated with the NSU, factions of the National Democratic Party of Germany, and other rising radical 'Free Forces' groups.   It didn't take long for Pierre's Nazi indoctrination to cut through the sensibilities of his mother, and he found himself roaming the streets of Berlin in an organized chaos, dressed in a black coat and white mask, warning anyone who would listen about the impending extinction of the German people and death to the 'anti-German Government and the migrants'. These weren't the Neo-Nazi's of old with their shaved heads and combat boots, but a new breed who wore suits and ties during the day, and used social media to organize rallies and demonstrations. The Immortals were a savvy bunch, and someone like Pierre, young, impressionable, and looking for a reason to be, fit their recruiting profile to a tee.

Owned by an ex-pat British man, 'The Executioner' was well known in Berlin as the meeting place for all sorts of right-wing extremists, and as a place where guests could freely exhibit their Nazi paraphilia and pride. Pierre had taken a real liking to the windowless pub, finding it the perfect place to hide from the world and his true self.

"I see you've been helping yourself to the 'Himla's' my young friend," laughed Uwe pointing at the empty glasses on the table. Named as a tribute to one of Hitler's Nazi police chief Heinrich Himmler, the 'Himla' was one of the bars most popular drinks.

"What can I say," slurred Pierre. "I'm a fan of raspberry rum."

Uwe slapped him on the back and turned his eyes to the stunning blond girl beside him. "This is Anna. She and I go way back. Anna, this is Pierre."

"It's so nice to meet you Pierre," said Anna sliding in across the table.

"Good to meet you too," he answered, his eyes fixated by her sea-blue gaze.

The two of them chatted while Uwe took off again to join another table for a while.

"So Uwe tells me you are a rising star in the Immortals?" said Anna.

Pierre blushed. "Uwe said that? Well I don't know if I'd call myself a rising star but…"

"Yes. He says you're really going places."

Inflated by pride, he kicked back the rest of his drink like a pro and leaned across the table, his drunken stutter invading the poor girl's personal space.

"Well the Immortals…that's my group…but I just told you that right? Are you an Immortal? I've never seen you at a rally before?"

"No," said Anna. "I belong to the Thüringer Heimatschutz. We are dedicated to building a Fourth Reich and ridding Germany of all the fucking immigrant bastards!"

"I totally fucking agree Anna! They drive me fucking crazy. The whole thing drives me fucking crazy. The government. The fucking globalization of everything. Democracy."

"Spoken like a true Immortal!" said Anna.

"Like what is democracy? Where everything is supposed to be fair and right? Well guess what? The world ain't fucking fair, and people just need to deal with that. You're in our country, so act like it. Don't parade your fucking dirty culture and people around here like you own the fucking place."

"I couldn't agree more Pierre. So young, yet so informed and passionate! I'm impressed."

Pierre smiled. "I have strong opinions."

"That's always a good thing my friend. Tell me about yourself. About your family."

"There's not really much to tell."

Anna noticed the solemn drop in his voice. "You sound sad about your family? It's okay if you don't want to talk about it."

"It's just that I don't have any family left," said Pierre with a shrug of his shoulders. "Well I have a father but I don't know where the fuck he is. My mother was trying to track him down before she died but I guess they couldn't find him."

"Oh Pierre! I'm so sorry to hear that!" said Anna taking his hand.

"I'm fine you know…I get by. It's not like I ever knew the guy, so what does it really matter. Some Englishman."

"But it does matter Pierre! Family is important. You should keep trying to find him."

"Apparently, my mother hired a lawyer to look. I don't know if he's still looking or not."

"I hope you find him Pierre. It would be nice for you."

"Ya…I suppose." Pierre tried not to let on how much he really did want to meet his father. He thought somehow it would make him seem weak and needy, like he couldn't survive on his own. And he could survive on his own. He'd been doing okay so far and there was no reason for him to believe that it wouldn't continue.

"So you've lived in Germany your whole life?" said Anna.

"That's right," he lied. "My mother was a proud and staunch German Nationalist! And my Aunt Erika? Well she was the one who really taught me about things you know? How they were and how they should be. She even met Hitler once. My Uncle was a decorated Nazi officer. She had so many stories to tell. You would have liked her."

"Would have?" said Anna.

"Ya," she died about a couple of years before my mother.

"Oh my God Pierre? So you have no one?"

"Nope. Just me."

"You poor thing," she said kissing the top of his hand. "Well you stick with me! I'll take care of you!"

A devilish grin slid out of the corner of his mouth. "Would you? I promise to be good?"

"You cheeky thing," she said laughing. "I have to ask though...how did a German boy like you end up with the name Pierre?"

His mind raced for an acceptable answer. He didn't especially want to bring up the idea that his real mother was French and he in fact, didn't have an ounce of true German blood flowing through his veins. It was a minor glitch in his true Germanic identity. He grew up German. He lived like a German, and to him, he was a German. Still, not everyone, especially in this crowd, would share his same thought process.

"Oh you know parents," he said laughing. "There was some actor or singer or something like that that my mother liked at the time, and she liked how the name sounded, so she thought it would be a good idea. I guess she just wanted something different."

Anna laughed. "That's funny. My parents named my sister after the neighbour's cat, so I totally understand where you're coming from."

Before their conversation could continue, the pub fell silent as a tallish man with light brown hair strode in, surrounded by bodyguards. All eyes were on his every move. He stopped, turned towards the swastika hanging on the wall, and gave a one-armed salute.

"Heil Hitler!" The room responded with a deafening chorus of "Heil Hitler's" then raucous cheers and applause.

"It's Karl," said Anna ripped with enthusiasm. "I'll be right back." She jumped from the table and was at the man's side in the snap of a finger.

"She's awfully excited," said Uwe sitting down and taking a gulp of beer.

"I guess she must know him? Who he is?"

"Only one of the nastiest son of a bitches in the whole movement. He does good work Pierre. He heads up one the most active groups in Germany. It's not often you see him in person. He usually stays pretty much in the shadows."

"So you know him then?" said Pierre, his eyes struck wide with awe.

"Not personally. But we certainly all know of him. He's the big time Pierre. One of the highest in the entire Neo-Nazi movement."

"Holy shit man. I would love to meet him!"

"Looks like you're going to get your chance. Anna is bringing him over."

The crowd parted like the Red Sea as Karl followed Anna over to the table. Pierre stood dumbfounded and lost for words.

"Uwe, Pierre," said Anna. "This is Karl."

"I'm Uwe. Pleasure to meet you," said Uwe holding out his hand. "Can I get you a beer?" Karl nodded. "Paul! Need a round for the table please!"

Karl's hazel eyes bore down on Pierre's. "And you young lad, must be Pierre?"

"Yes sir!" said Pierre snapping up into a soldier's stance.

Karl laughed. "I see he's a product of the old Nazi summer camps. They've taught you well."

"Yes sir! Every summer since I was fourteen sir! Well except for the last two. But I loved the experience sir!"

"You can relax Pierre," said Karl with a smile. "And please, call me Karl. The sir is so formal…and we are all friends here are we not? Here for the same purpose? Here for the same reasons."

"You can count on me to do whatever you need to be done Karl!" said Pierre.

Karl glanced at Anna. "He's an enthusiastic one isn't he?"

"Yes he is," said Anna. "I think he's going to be a great asset. Isn't that right Uwe?"

"Definitely," Uwe answered. "Great potential and very good discipline. Whoever taught him, taught him well."

"That would be my Aunt Erika."

"Erika?" said Karl. "That name sounds so familiar. Older lady?"

"Well she's dead now, but yes she was older. Erika Zschape."

"You are the nephew of Erika Zschape?" said Karl. "She is a legend!"

"You knew my Aunt?"

"I met her a few times, years ago, when she would come to Berlin. Amazing woman. So dedicated and such a visionary!" Karl took a big swig of beer and paused before swallowing, letting the full flavour of the liquid swish around in his mouth. "But your Aunt was of the old school. Things have changed. Yes we are still trying to attract the youth to the movement but not just the disenchanted and rebellious. We are looking for the doctors and lawyers of the future, people that are sympathetic to the cause who can instigate change from within, and draw others in. That is key. Violence has its place of course, but sometimes it can give people the wrong idea about what we are trying to achieve. We are not just a bunch of thugs with skinned heads and combat boots. We are a movement that the people of Germany can take seriously. The far right is no longer a fringe group my friends. We are moving mainstream. We have a political party and sympathizers all throughout the government and police forces. When necessary violence does occur, they will turn a blind eye, and now, that it is all part of the master plan. You can't tell me that any true-blooded German is happy with all the fucking Muslims and Turks and Africans and God knows who else is living in our sewers. We need to take back what is ours. Reclaim the Fatherland and return the country to righteousness."

"What more can be done," said Uwe.

"Tell me about your operation Uwe," said Karl.

"I am second in command of the Zwickau cell," said Uwe, "After Mundlos."

"Ah yes, I have heard of your cell. You are doing great work."

"Thank you," said Uwe with a wide grin.

"We need to keep recruiting efforts up. Increase our membership. There is definite strength in numbers." Karl lit a cigarette and took a deep drag. "We must be where the people are suffering the most. Where unemployment is high and there is little hope. We must swoop in and give those people hope. Assure them that we are the way out. We will give them hope! When you give people hope, they will do anything to make that hope come true."

"Those are brilliant words Karl," said Anna. "Truly inspiring."

"Yes, yes," he replied. "Hope from disparity is the key. As Pierre can attest and as I'm sure you two already know, the National Socialist Union has stepped up its 'summer camp' programs, offering refuge for children from poor families. A place where they can send their kids for free! Now what parent doesn't like that? They are gaining in popularity. We start them out young…learning the importance of discipline and self-control. Young minds are eager and willing. They listen if you tell them the right thing and engage them in a way they want to be engaged. Once the kids get a little older, weapons and military training is introduced."

"Yes," said Pierre. "We learnt all of that and so much more."

"So you found the camp beneficial then?" said Karl.

"Fuck ya! It was the best thing ever!"

Karl slapped his hand on the table. "I just love his youthful enthusiasm! He's exactly the type we need to take this movement to the next level."

"You just tell me what you want me to do sir and I'll do it!" said Pierre. "No questions asked!"

"Well tell me what you're doing now," said Karl.

"I'm clearing the fucking Turks off the streets is what I'm doing. A few in my crew, we go out at night on patrol and let them know that they're not wanted in this country and that they should just leave."

"Fucking right Pierre, fucking right!" said Uwe. "Beat the fucking shit out of them. Or better yet…put a fucking bullet through their brain. That'll shut them up for good!" He reached across the table and gave Pierre a high-five. "Let me know when you want that gun Pierre. I can hook you up no problem."

"Might be a good idea Uwe," said Karl. "I think Pierre is ready to take that next step. Do you think you're ready Pierre?"

"Yes I do. I can't wait for the opportunity to make you proud sir."

Karl patted the boy on the shoulder, "You've already made me proud son. Just remember, biology is our priority! Our Germany is not a Germany filled with fucking Africans, Arabs, and Asians. Weed them out, and shut them down. That is our mission. For our future. For our Germany! Make it happen. Make it happen!"

Pierre left the bar later that night inspired by Karl, and full of confidence for the cause. Karl's words gave him direction, and assurance that he was part of something that was going to change Germany forever. Without even trying or knowing, for that matter, he was stepping right into the shoes of his mother; not Rondell, but Michelle. The cause eventually killed her, and Pierre would have to be careful to avoid the same fate. History has an odd way of repeating itself.

"Are you interested in a road trip?" Anna and Pierre were sitting in a café having lunch.

"Sure," said Pierre. "Where to?"

"Jamel. I want to show you what all of Germany can be."

Jamel was a small rural town north of Berlin, once part of communist East Germany. Years before, Sven Krüger, a notorious neo-Nazi had begun the process of weeding out all of the non-Nazi sympathizers from the town through oppressive and violent means. Once the intruders were gone, Krüger and his associates would buy up the empty properties and offer them to other Neo-Nazi's from all over Germany. With the goal of a pure and homogeneous society, Krüger had no qualms about using violence or oppressive measures to scare off any outsiders. Jamel was the Mecca for Neo-Nazi's, a destination place where they could come and worship Hitler and the Nazi ideals. Left alone by police and state officials, Krüger was free to run the village as he saw fit, and to build on the concept for neighbouring towns and villages.

"Jamel is the only nationally liberated zone in Germany," said Anna as they made the turn onto Am Berg road. "But that's just for the time being. Soon there will be many Jamel's scattered all over Germany. Krüger is doing incredible work. He really is a shining star in the movement."

As they pulled off Am Berg road and onto the main road leading into the village, Pierre was amazed at how rundown and shoddy everything looked. Empty beer cans and garbage were strewn along side of the houses and one of the houses looked charred and ready to fall in.

"Not what you expected?" said Anna, her voice tinged with sarcasm.

Pierre shrugged his shoulders. "No, it's not that, I guess I just thought it would look different. The summer camps were always so neat and clean…"

"Don't be so judgmental Pierre. It is the ideals behind the movement that matter. Jamel is just the beginning.   Is it perfect? No, of course not. But we will get there. Once we get into government, we can take care of infrastructure. For now we make do with what we have. The point is, in Jamel, we are free to do as we please. If you want to leave your beer can on the side of the road, then so be it. No one is going to say anything one way or another."

Anna slowed to halt in front of a large boulder just off to the side of the road.

"Read that plaque."

"Jamel village community - free, social, national"

"That's right Pierre. Think about that. Everyone here shares the same goals. For a free Germany. You will not see a black or brown face here. No fucking turbans or hijabs. This will be the birthplace of the new Germany."

Pierre craned his neck to read the myriad of sign markers nailed to the wooden post. "Paris – 1547km, Breslau, Königsberg, Braunau am Inn – 855 km. Braunau am Inn, that's where Hitler was born! Very cool."

"I think you're going to like Jamel Pierre. Wait until the bonfire rally tonight! You will be blown away!"

"Look at that mural," said Pierre pointing to a painting on the outside of one of the buildings. "I think I saw that exact painting in one of the old Nazi textbooks my Aunt had. And it has the same slogan as the rock."

"The painting symbolizes the need for Germans to get back to our roots. See the woman cradling that newborn child, while her husband and other children look on? That's what Germany needs…to have more pure children and espouse true family values. If Germany needs more people, then that need should by filled through pro-creation, not immigration!"

"German children need our country," said Pierre reading from a campaign sign stuck in the ground near the centre square.

"It is the truth Pierre. Look at what our parents have left us? A fucking soft left-wing country full of pussies and punks too scared to stand up for us and our needs. They live with constant war guilt, not wanting to offend anyone. Who fucking cares? As far as I'm concerned, Germany should have never conceded to the fucking Russians and Americans. Communism on one side. Democracy on the other. And neither had anything to do with what Germany wanted or needed. They say as Germans we should be tolerant because of the past. Fuck that! Tolerance doesn't make the changes we need. Tolerance has filled our country with a bunch of immigrant assholes who think they run the God damn place. I am fucking sick and tired of it!"

"So there are no immigrants here at all?" said Pierre with a wide grin.

"Not a fucking one," Anna smiled. "There are a few non-sympathizers who live in an old farmhouse on the outskirts of the town…"

"Why don't we drive the bastards out?"

"Because it's sort of fun to watch them live in fear," she laughed. "And they are German, and pretty much mind their own business. I suspect one day they will up and leave or Sven will take of it. Right now it's not a top priority. I think with Sven around, they never get too comfortable. It's the fucking Turk mafia that's causing us all problems."

"The Turkish mafia is here in Jamel?" said Pierre.

'No. In the cities. Berlin especially. We need to do something about it."

"I say we chop their fucking heads off?" said Pierre. "I know Uwe would be game!"

"I agree with you Pierre but I don't want you getting in over your head. The Turkish mafia…as much as I hate the fuckers…are mean and organized. They don't mess around."

"Well neither do I!"

"I know," she laughed. "I can see that."

"Let me step up the patrols…cause some more shit. That'll get them real pissed off. And then we can hit them hard! With full force."

"They have strong leadership Pierre. I don't know…"

"So we take out the leader. Seems like a pretty simple solution to me."

CHAPTER NINETEEN

Pierre had found his purpose. Taking out the head of the Turkish mafia in Germany was a sure fire way to move up the organizational ladder, and show the leaders that he was someone to be counted on to get the job done. The thought consumed him. Over the next few months, he planned and plotted, practicing his shooting at a secret neo-Nazi warehouse range, intent on taking the shot that would take down the Turks. It was a risky proposition but Pierre's arrogance these days knew no boundaries. He would not fail. He could not fail. He was the 'chosen one' as his Aunt always said, and now Pierre believed it was time to fulfil his destiny.

He fuelled his courage with drugs, booze, and sex with any women who would open her legs on his behalf, and there were many. He shot off his mouth at every opportunity, bragging about his exploits and his future plans.

"You know Pierre," said Anna. "It might be best if you leave Berlin for a while." Her voice was crisp and clear. "Maybe go back to your Aunt's estate and lay low for a while."

"What are you talking about? I ain't going nowhere."

"You know that kid you beat the living shit out of the other night?"

"Of course," he smiled. "It was so bad the blood was coming out of his fucking eye. Brilliant."

"Well that kid just happened to be the son of Irem Kaya, a very important and very nasty man in the Turkish underworld. You don't even want to know some of the shit that he's done."

"So what?" said Pierre, his stoned eyes barely beyond slits. "Am I supposed to be scared?"

"I'm just saying be careful. My sources are telling me they don't know it was you but they're going to find out, and I just think it would be best if you weren't in Berlin when they did. What about Munich or going to Jamel? You'd be safe there. Sven would protect you."

"I don't need any fucking protection Anna. I can handle this. There's no way they know it was me. I had on my black coat and white mask. I looked like every other person in the Immortals."

"You really think that your friends aren't going to give you up when Kaya has a chain around their balls and is pulling as hard as he can? Don't be stupid Pierre."

"Honestly, I don't even care. I'll fucking kill him too!"

"I think you've been taking too many of those pills and smoking too much of your funny cigarettes. Your mouth has no idea what it is saying."

"I know exactly what I'm saying. You just don't think I can do it." Pierre finished his bottle of beer, then smashed it against the side of the building, sending shards of glass to the street.

"God damn it Pierre! Control your temper. One of those pieces could have hit me! Holy fuck!"

"I'm sorry, I'm sorry," he answered sprawling his drunken arms around her in an attempted hug.

Anna pushed him hard against the wall. "Get off of me!"

His balance compromised, he fell to the ground, his hand catching a piece of glass. "God damn it! Look what you did?"

"I didn't do a thing," she said. "It was your drunken foolishness that got you there." She bent down and examined the hand. "It's just a scratch. You'll live. But I warn you my friend, you need to get your shit together. Look at you? Drunk and stoned sitting in a pile of glass on the dirty street? And you expect to be someone in this organization? I look at you and I see weakness. You can't handle your booze. You can't handle your drugs, and you flap your mouth too much about everything! It's got to stop Pierre or you're going to get yourself killed. Or worse. You're going to get one of us killed! You are out of control. I don't think I can trust you anymore. And you had such promise."

"I am NOT weak!" His boot slammed hard on the ground.

"Go home and get some sleep Pierre," she said turning away. "We will talk more later…when I get back to the city. I have business in the south I have to attend to."

Pierre refused to look at her; his eyes welling in anger. "I am not weak."

"No? Then maybe just stupid and immature. We need leaders Pierre. Not useless punks."

Anna walked away knowing she'd been hard on her friend, but it was time for him to hear the truth. These last couple of months he'd been so unpredictable and downright big-headed. She wondered if it had anything to do with the telephone call he'd received from his lawyer, saying they had what they thought was a good lead on his father but it had fallen through. Pierre acted like he didn't give a shit but Anna knew he was hurting inside. The drugs and the drink were just masks, hiding his pain, allowing him to shut off his head and his heart. Despite his ardent denials, Anna knew how disappointed he was at the news, and her heart broke when she saw the wet glaze form on his sad eyes. She worried about him constantly, and had begun to care for him deeply. While violence was always a part of their life, Pierre had foolishly and unnecessarily put a huge target on his back. She wasn't against his crusade against the Turks by any means, she just wished he'd thought things through a little more, and used a little bit more discretion. His angst and fury were going to get him in a tonne of trouble.

Pierre picked himself off the ground and wiped the blood from his hand.

"Weak? She seriously thinks I'm weak? She doesn't know what the fuck she's talking about." He was pissed; pissed at Anna and pissed at himself for losing control. He adored his friend but sometimes she treated him like a child and it drove him crazy. He wasn't a child anymore, and he didn't need her to tell him what to do.

Fighting the effects of that last pill he'd just popped, he braced himself against the wall, words flying from his mouth like sparks on a fire.

"You're not my fucking mother…I have no mother anymore…and to think I once had two mothers…and now I have none. And my father?   Who the fuck is he? Some Englishman who doesn't give a fuck about me obviously. If he did, why isn't he here? Why doesn't he come find me?" His voice got louder and louder. "It's not like I'm hard to find! I'm right fucking here Dad. RIGHT FUCKING HERE! Do you hear me?"

"You all right man?" The man's voice was gentle and kind. "Do you need any help?"

Pierre's eyes burned with rage. "Are you saying something to me nigger?"

Shocked and scared, the man took a few steps back, then turned to walk away. It was too late.

"Was there something you wanted to say to me nigger?"

"No, no," the man answered. "I see you're fine. I'll be on my way."

"Like hell you will!"

Before the man could move an inch Pierre was on him, fists flying, legs kicking. The poor man tried to defend himself but fuelled by chemical courage, Pierre was just too strong. Every cell in his body raged with fury, and it no longer became a fight against a black man and the purity of the Fatherland, but a release of all the emotion and anger he'd bottled up since he'd found out about his true identity. With a final blow, the blood spurted from the man's mouth as he whiplashed against the brick wall, a stream of red trailing the descent of his head down the wall. Pierre wiped his foaming mouth with the back of his hand and laughed.

"Too weak? I don't fucking think so!"

Once he'd unleashed the demon, his wrath was unstoppable. Armed with his anger and a lead pipe, Pierre took off into the Berlin night, hell bent on proving his strength and his worth. Anything or anyone that even slightly resembled a Turk or Turkish property got a hack with the lead pipe or a punch to the face. Storefront windows, slashed tires, nothing escaped his rampage. He was proud of his accomplishments, yelling and screaming like a crazed banshee, in his black coat, his mop of curls drenched with exhilaration. If he had just gone home, or taken Anna's advice and gotten out of the city for a while, everything would have been okay, and the incident probably would have been chalked up to some random acts of violence by some random neo-Nazi's.

But once again, he couldn't keep his mouth shut, and bits and pieces of his escapade escaped in casual conversation. He wanted people to know it was him, and the need to prove himself, and seek acceptance had almost become a sick obsession. Of course, the others in the Immortals heralded him as hero, and Pierre's head swelled with the praise, creating a sense of invincibility.

"We need to kill him. Just think what will happen if we do?" Pierre was holding court with a bunch of his friends in a back alley. "Everyone will know us. That we were the ones to kill the leader of the Turkish Mafia in Berlin."

"I don't know Pierre," said Marco tugging the pockets of his leather jacket. "It all sounds good but how in the hell are we going to pull it off. He always has a fuck load of bodyguards around him."

"I say we just storm him and start firing," added Stefan. "They won't know we're coming and they won't know what hit them."

"I like that idea Stefan," said Pierre. "But we can't dress as Immortals. They'll see us coming for sure."

"But don't we want everyone to know it was us?" said Marco.

"Of course," said Pierre. He paused and took a drag of his cigarette. "We leave a mask. Like just sort of throw it on the ground as our calling card."

"Brilliant man!" said Stefan.

"Ya I like that," said Marco. "So when do we do it?"

"We need to have a plan," said Pierre. "And we need to do it somewhere where we'll have easy access to an escape. Like this alley would be no good because it's fenced in at the end. Nowhere to go. We need to think about things like that."

"So what do we do?" said Stefan.

"We spend some time following them. Find out where he goes and what he does. Get to know any of his patterns. But we need to switch it up, so it's not always the same person. They'd get suspicious then. I can go first. Then you Marco and then Stefan. We can ask Niklas too. I'm sure he'd be game. He's been dying to fire off his new semi-automatic at something other than a red target."

"No doubt!" laughed Marco. "That thing is a beast."

"I know," said Pierre. "I'm going to see if Uwe can't hook me up with one just like it."

For the next couple of months the crew planned and strategized. Pierre became an expert at gathering information and working this information into a well thought-out plot. He wasn't going to fuck this opportunity up. It was his chance to rise to the top, and he was determined to make that happen, no matter the cost. He knew that one or two of his friends would probably get shot and even killed in the process, but was willing to sacrifice them for his own ascension. His dependency on the drugs and the booze intensified, his morning coffee replaced by a shot of rye and a few of his favourite 'blue butterfly' ecstasy pills. When he'd come down from the high, he was a bastard, mean, cold, and nasty. The warm, kind-hearted kid of old was gone; dead and buried along with his mother.

Pierre flipped his grey hoody up over his head, shielding away the cold November mist. He was on his way to meet Anna at The Executioner. While he had forgiven his friend for treating him so poorly and questioning his strength, he still got the feeling that she was holding things back from him. He was no longer her confidante, and it annoyed him that he always seemed to be the last to know about issues and plans within the movement.

"What's up?" said Pierre sliding into a chair across from the blond. Her eyes were blank and red.

"They're dead."

"Who's dead? Anna what is wrong?" Pierre gently reached across the table and lifted the woman's chin upward.

"They were attempting to rob a bank in Eisenach and something went wrong. I don't know for sure."

"Who Anna who?"

"Böhnhardt and Mundlos."

"Uwe?"

"Yes."

"He is dead?"

"Mundlos too."

"I don't understand," said Pierre gasping for breath. "Did the police get them?"

"No," said Anna wiping her tears. "It appears they shot each other in the head. They were found in a mobile home…"

"What the fuck are you talking about? They shot each other? Why? I don't understand!" The tears streamed down his dirty cheeks.

"I don't know all the details Pierre but Uwe was involved in much, much more than you think. Perhaps he thought things were closing in on him. I don't know. I wasn't there."

"I can't believe it."

"You know Pierre that it was Uwe and Mundlos, and their friend Beate that were responsible for all of the Doner murders don't you?"

"No I didn't," said Pierre quietly. "Why didn't you tell me? Why didn't he tell me?"

"Some things are better left not talked about my friend. One of those people they killed was a cop, so you know the police would have jumped on anyone who had the slightest bit of knowledge."

"I can't believe they're dead." Pierre pulled his hoody further over his head. "It just doesn't make sense to me. If you're going to die, why not go down, taking as many people with you. Committing suicide? They were fucking cowards to do that!"

"Pierre! Watch your words!" she scolded. "Did you ever think they were trying to protect the rest of us and all the work we've done for the movement? Their secrets die with them. Are you going to call Hitler a coward too? After all, he committed suicide in his bunker. Is the Führer a coward?"

"Of course not," he said dropping his head. "I didn't even think."

"It's okay," said Anna reaching for his hand. "I know you're upset. I am too."

"I looked up to him. I wanted to be him. And fuck man, everyone in my life ends up dying! I'm sick of it!" Pierre stormed from the table.

"Pierre! Where are you going?" Anna screamed after him. "Pierre!"

By the time Anna burst out through the doors, Pierre was gone; lost in the streets, embroiled in his own self-pity, looking for a way to mitigate the pain.

****

I set down my coffee and picked up the phone. Probably one of those God damn telemarketers again trying to sell me something. They'd been awful since before the Christmas holidays, like it was a New Years' Resolution to piss off as many people as possible.

"Hello."

"Hi John, it's Aaron. I think we've got something concrete this time."

"You're kidding me?"

"We think he's in Berlin."

"I'll pack my bags and get on the first plane out of here!"

"Not so fast," said Aaron. "We don't know where in Berlin and it's a pretty big city, so you roaming the streets probably wouldn't be a good idea."

"I see your point."

"And John…there's something else." His voice went quiet. "And I'm not sure you're going to like it."

"What? Just tell me Aaron. What? He has a record for shoplifting or something?"

"It appears as though he's a member of the right-wing group the Immortals. They are a band of neo-Nazi's…anti-capitalist, anti-democracy, anti-immigration. Basically they hate everything and everyone that isn't German."

"Oh my son. Just like your mother…just like your mother." I couldn't believe the words coming from the other end of the telephone. "Enough Aaron. I don't want to know anymore. Just find out where he is specifically so I can go get him the hell out of that rats nest."

"It might not be that easy," said Aaron. "He might not want to go."

"Leave that to me. I'll think of something."

"You could lure him with the trust fund?" said Aaron. "At least to get him interested…"

"Possibly…but I don't want him to come just because of money."

"I understand," said Aaron, "but some of these kids are so committed to their cause, it's hard to pry them away."

"You don't have to tell me that Aaron," I sighed. "I've already lived it first-hand. So how are you going to go about finding him?"

"Well to start we're going to place some advertisements in the local papers…see if that drums up any hits…and I'll also speak to the constable in charge of the Immortals and neo-Nazi task force…just to see if they have any indication of where he might be. The problem is we don't have a picture at the moment, so that might slow the process down, and we can't assume he is using his real name."

"So you're saying I shouldn't wait by the phone".

"No probably not," he laughed. "But these developments are good John! We're finally getting somewhere."

"Any word on Rondell? I'd like to have a word with her, especially about this Nazi business."

"I'm afraid she passed away a little while ago."

"Oh dear God! So the boy is out there alone, with no one to take care of him? You must work as quickly as you can Aaron. I don't care what it costs. I just have a bad feeling about this."

"Try to stay calm John. I'll work as quickly as I can. I give you my word."

"Stay calm? You just told me my son is a Nazi? How in the hell do you expect me to stay calm?"

****

Pierre tapped the toe of his shoe against the right leg of the leatherback chair. He hated the whole look and feel of the lawyer's office, but as a condition of his mother's estate, he had to come and check in periodically to receive some money and give the lawyer an update. He was always certain to tuck his iron cross necklace under the collar of his white dress shirt and pin-striped tie, knowing the Nazi paraphernalia probably wouldn't go over well in the conservative office.

"So how are things Pierre?" said the lawyer, a middle aged man with a slight balding spot near the back of his head.

"Things are good."

"Keeping yourself out of trouble?"

"You know me," said Pierre with a smile. "Always an angel."

"Yes I'm sure you are," said the lawyer, with a half serious laugh.

"So let's get this money business out of the way. Here is your cheque for living expenses and I've paid your rent up until the end of the year. I just thought it might be easier that way since you seem to have trouble remembering to pay it on your own."

"It was only once or twice," said Pierre. "And I just got busy."

"I understand, but I don't think your mother would be too happy with the prospect of you getting kicked out and living on the streets."

"I'm not worried," Pierre laughed. "I have tonnes of friends that would let me crash."

"No matter. It's taken care of and you don't have to worry about it."

"Thanks."

"On another matter," said the man shuffling some papers. "My investigator has come across the most interesting advertisement in the paper. I think it might be from your father."

"What?" said Pierre almost falling off his chair. "My father?"

"Yes. I won't go into details but the ad states a man by the name of John Coventry is looking for a boy with the birth name of Pierre. It goes on to say the name of your mother and your approximate age. There is a number here for a law firm in Chester England, which I believe is located somewhere near Liverpool. Do you want me to call?"

****

"It's him John," said Aaron. "We've found Pierre."

"You're sure it's him?"

"Yes. I just spoke to a trustee lawyer in Berlin. He saw our ad in the paper and after confirming all the details, we're both one hundred per cent certain that it's a match."

"Oh my God," I said reaching for the arm of chair. "I can't believe it. You've found my son...after almost twenty years. My God Aaron, my God."

"I know John. I told you to have hope."

"I know but I honestly didn't think it would happen. I mean things like this never turn out right for me."

"Well this time they did my friend, this time they did."

"So now what?" I said.

"You book a flight to Berlin. I'll give you the number of the lawyer and you can call him as soon as you get there. He'll set up the appointment with Pierre, and you can go from there."

"Splendid Aaron. Splendid."

I hung up the phone needing a minute to process the conversation. After all this time, I was going to be reunited with my son. It was almost more than I could ever believe. What would he think of me? Would there be anger? I was sure there was going to be at least some anger and resentment for not having been there his entire life. Hell, I was angry and resentful myself. But we could move past all that couldn't we? And form a relationship? I wasn't saying he'd have to call me Dad, and I didn't expect him to live in my spare bedroom, but maybe this could be the beginning of a new life for both of us? I knew there was a reason I desperately held on to my memories of Michelle all these years; it was so I could share them with our son. Those memories kept me going and those memories were going to be key going forward. My hand shook as I tried to light a cigarette. I hadn't felt these sorts of nerves since I got out of prison. I wondered how much Pierre really knew about his past. Did Rondell ever tell him the truth? Dear Lord! I hadn't even thought of that. What if he knows nothing of Michelle? And I have to be the one to break the news that Rondell really wasn't his real mother? How was I going to manage all those emotions?

The questions and uncertainties just kept flying through my head like firecrackers, shooting one way then the next, my mind a jumbled mess of missed connections. For a brief second I wondered whether I should have just let the child be. Maybe this meeting would be more than he could handle? Maybe it would be more than I could handle. Then as I walked to the cupboard to get down a glass for a shot of whiskey, I saw the metal framed picture of my parents, standing in front of the old estate, huge smiles on their faces.

"Yes, you're right," I said with a quiet laugh. "Family comes first."

It didn't matter what had happened in the past, what Pierre knew and what he didn't. All that mattered was the future. The other stuff would sort its self out, it always did.

CHAPTER TWENTY

My flight arrived to Tegel Airport in Berlin about thirty minutes late but I wasn't worried, I wasn't supposed to meet Pierre's lawyer until two, so I had plenty of time to spare. I'd booked a room at the prestigious Hotel Adlon, a short walk away from the famous and historic Brandenburg Gate, built in the late 1700's by King Fredrick William II of Prussia as a sign of peace. When Hitler and the Nazi's came to power, they used the Gate as a party symbol, and when the Communists ruled East Germany, the Gate was incorporated into the Berlin Wall as a means of shutting the gate figuratively and physically against the West. Today, the gate stands as a symbol of the reunification of Berlin and Germany, although the neo-Nazis use the Gate as a rally point for demonstrations and events. Pierre's lawyer's office was just a few blocks west of the hotel, so instead of sitting around in a nervous twitter, I decided to get out and walk for a bit, taking in the sights and the place my son called home.

I explored a few of the quaint little shops and found a wonderful deli that served me delicious salami on 'Sonnenblumenkernbrot' or dark rye bread with sunflower seeds. As I was eating my sandwich, I noticed a tall, darker skinned man enter the deli, look around, and then take a seat a few tables away from mine. His dark eyes looked at me in a curious way but did not smile. I tried not to pay any attention, but the man wouldn't stop staring, and I was becoming unnerved. Suddenly the man got up and walked towards me. I could feel the sweat breaking out under my arms and in the little crevice in my back.

"I'm sorry to bother you," said the man sporting a closely cropped black beard. "But do I know you?"

I couldn't quite place the accent but it wasn't German. "I don't think so," I answered. "This is my first time in Berlin." I steadied my voice. Why was this stranger talking to me?

"I'm not from here either. You're from England obviously? I can tell by your accent."

"Yes I am." I wanted to keep my answers short and sweet, since I didn't have a clue what this man wanted. Had he followed me here? For what reason? My mind went back to the strange visitors at my mother's house before she died.

"Did you happen to ever work at the BBC in London?"

"No I haven't had the pleasure."

"Well you look exactly like a man I once worked with there. Very odd."

My shoulders dropped as the tension eased. "Yes that is funny. They say everyone has a double in the world somewhere."

"Well you have one that works for the BBC," the man laughed. "I'm so sorry to have interrupted your sandwich. Please forgive me."

"No problem." I looked at his watch. "Oops...I've got to get going. Have an appointment across town and I don't want to be late."

I rose from the table, brushed past the stranger, and headed out the door without looking back. I didn't have the best feeling about my encounter. It was probably nothing, but then again it could have been something. Just to be safe, I went into a few more shops, dilly dallying around, pretending to be interested, but keeping a watchful eye over my shoulder.

"Maybe I am being paranoid," I mumbled paying for the pack of gum I tossed on the shop counter. "Just calm yourself down Coventry. It's going to be okay."

"Danke," I said reaching out to collect my change.

"Bitte," replied the clerk.

Positive that my current paranoia was a figment of my imagination, I left the store for the short walk to the lawyer's office. With each step I could feel my heart pound and my chest tighten. I was nervous. Damn nervous. The lawyer thought it would be best if we met at a neutral location like his office; Pierre had been there many times before and wouldn't feel intimated. I was fine with that since I didn't really know my way around Berlin and was a little leery of any place that Pierre might choose on his own. For the first meeting, this was a perfect compromise.

The receptionist smiled as I approached the desk. "John Coventry, I presume?"

"Yes," I said. "I hope I'm not too early?"

"Not at all. Mr. Bercker is just on the phone with another client. Follow me and I'll take you back to the waiting area."

"Is Pierre here yet?" I could feel the moisture draining from my lips.

"No, not yet," she smiled. "I certainly see a resemblance between the two of you."

"Really?" I grinned. "In what way? I've never even seen a picture of him before, so I have no idea?"

"Well to start, you both have the same smile...and I think you even walk alike!"

This weird sense of warmth crept into my cheeks, causing an unwanted blushing sensation. "Well, I'll certainly be interested in seeing for myself."

"Here you go," she said opening a solid oak door. "Can I get you anything? Glass of water? Coffee?"

"Some water would be great thanks."

"He shouldn't be too long."

"No problem," I said. "I've been waiting for this moment for a long time. A few minutes more isn't going to kill me!"

She smiled then closed the door a little, leaving me alone with my apprehensions, the four walls seemingly getting closer and closer. I didn't have to wait long.

"John Coventry. Nice to meet you. Hans Bercker."

"Mr. Bercker. My pleasure."

"Please call me Hans." He shook my hand firmly and motioned to one of the leather back chairs. "Have a seat. I spoke with Pierre yesterday and he said he would meet us here at two. He's not usually late for our appointments but we'll give him a bit of time. He might have missed the bus or something."

"I'm in no hurry." My palms glistened as my nervousness exploded."

We engaged in some small talk and Bercker filled me in on as much background information as he could legally indulge.

"I do believe in my heart that he is a good kid," he said. "I think he has lost his way somewhat since Rondell passed but that's understandable, and he has of course gotten in with the wrong crowd."

"Yes, I have heard of his affiliations. It certainly disappoints me but I'm not sure what I can really say because I haven't been there for him. You have no idea how much I wish I had been."

"I can tell by the pained expression on your face." Bercker checked his watch. "Let me call his cell phone." He flipped through some papers looking for the number. "Ah here it is." He pushed the metal rims of his glasses back against his nose and began to dial. We waited in silence. Silence greeted us from the other end of the phone. "He's not picking up. That's not like him." He hung up the phone.

"Perhaps I should just go and try and find him? Where does he usually hang out?" My naivety was obvious.

"I don't think that's the best idea John," said the lawyer shaking his head. "In his world and with his people, you are an outsider. And to be frank with you, I wouldn't advise it. Pierre believes that I don't know about his association with The Immortals, and tries desperately to hide it while he is in my presence. He also doesn't know that his mother and I had a long chat before she died, and I know everything about his childhood."

"What about it? Was it horrible?" Panic and guilt hit me like a wave.

"Unfortunately I can't divulge any more information. That's up to Pierre. Let's just say that he was exposed to alternative political views from a very young age."

"Damn Rondell! I trusted her! I knew I should have never let her take him…"

"Not Rondell, John," Bercker interrupted. "Her Aunt. Because of certain circumstances, Rondell had to make some very difficult concessions to insure the boy's safety. It was done out of love, I can assure you of that. She was a good mother. She did the best she could."

"And that's probably better than I could have done."

Bercker checked his watch again. "Look I have another appointment scheduled but you are free to wait in the lounge for as long as you like. I'm so sorry he's so late."

"Yes maybe I will wait for a bit longer. No harm."

Bercker led me back out to the main waiting room. "Sondra please make sure Mr. Coventry is comfortable.

Maybe some coffee? I think we still have some pastries from lunch?"

"Just some coffee would be great," I said.

Sitting in that chair waiting was one of the most painful experiences I'd ever had in my life. I knew he wasn't coming, yet I waited, holding out the tiniest hope that maybe, just maybe he would prove me wrong. I suppose I deserved the heartbreak. I can't imagine living life knowing that your father was out there somewhere but didn't have the balls to come and find you before now. What kind of a person does that? I'd convinced myself that I had my reasons and they were damn good ones, but were they really reasons or just excuses. I could have come sooner. I could have done so many things differently. He was punishing me, and I get it. I deserve it. I probably would have done the same thing. There was no point in waiting any longer.

"Thanks so much for the coffee," I said quietly setting the cup on the corner of the front desk.

"You're leaving?" Sondra tried to force a smile. "I'm sure something came up. He was excited about meeting you. He honestly was."

"I guess he changed his mind," I shrugged.

"Where are you staying in case he calls in or shows up?"

"I'm at the Hotel Adlon. I plan on staying for at least a couple of days, if not longer. I really don't want to go back to England without at least having had the chance to say hello…and I'm sorry."

"He'll show up eventually. I know he will!"

I laughed at her enthusiasm. "I sure hope you're right. And if he does, how will I know it's him?"

"Just look for the kid with the mop of dark curly hair, and a smile that's just like yours."

By the time I'd gotten back to the hotel I was distraught and feeling incredibly sorry for myself. My mind had jumped to every conceivable conclusion and assumption as to why he didn't show up, and everything pointed back to me being a horrible person and a worthless father. I couldn't help it. I just couldn't shake the self-doubt and self-loathing. I didn't feel like going back up to my room, so I found a stool at the bar and drowned my sorrows in vodka. It wasn't the first time and it certainly wasn't the last.

****

"Jesus!" said Pierre taking another drag of his cigarette. He was on his way to meet Marcus and Stefan. "Who the hell keeps calling me?" He pulled his phone out of his pocket and checked the number. His glossy eyes didn't recognize the numbers, especially in the darkness of the street, so he shoved the phone back into his pants. He had more important things on his mind anyway, like figuring out just how he was going to get away with murder, literally. The time was close, he had to either make his move or back away. Word had gotten out that someone from The Immortals was responsible for the all that vandalism, and there was a price put on the perpetrator's head. So far, no one had given him up but he did walk a bit more cautiously when he was out at night.

"God damn it! Hello?" he screamed into the phone.

"Pierre? It's Hans Bercker. Are you all right?"

"Mr. Bercker…umm…yes I'm fine. Sorry I didn't realize it was you that was calling. What's up?"

"What's up?" Bercker's voice was stern and harsh. "So did you purposely blow off the meeting with your father today?"

"Oh my fucking God," thought Pierre. He'd totally forget. And it didn't help that he was high as a kite when Bercker called a few days ago to make the appointment. His memory tended to be a tad foggy during those moments.

"I'm so sorry," said Pierre. "Is he still there? What's he like? I am sorry…" His voice started to crack. "I didn't mean to blow him off…I've just had so many things on my mind…Oh my God…he's going to think I'm such an ass! Fuck!"

"He's staying at the Hotel Adlon. He said he'll be there for a few days."

"Thank God! I'll go right now!"

"No," said Bercker. "You will not go near that hotel and that man until you are stone sober. Do you hear me? Don't think I don't know Pierre. He's a good man and he was heartbroken when you didn't show today. Spare him the sorrow of having his son show up too stoned to even carry on a conversation."

Pierre was silent.

"Do you hear me Pierre?"

"Yes I hear you," he answered. "Can I at least have his number?"

Pierre never saw the two men sneak up behind him. Nor did he see the eight inch blade glisten in the dying sunlight. He only felt the excruciating pain as the blade plunged into his side and ripped through his liver.

"This will teach you to fuck with us and our people, you stupid little fucking Nazi boy!" The violent breath was close and hot against Pierre's neck, staccatos of tobacco laced spit settling deep into his curls. "You don't look so tough now do you punk ass?"

"Hold him still," said another much deeper voice. "He's squirming around too much. Pull his arms back. Ya like that." He pulled out another knife and pointed the laser sharp tip against Pierre's throat. "We have a saying in Turkey, 'Ýðneyi kendine batýr çuvaldýzý baþkasýna' which means 'stick the needle into yourself to see how much it hurts before you thrust the needle into others'. You should have thought twice before messing up the son of my boss Irem Kaya…"

"I swear," Pierre gasped. "I didn't know."

"Tell me you're sorry," he growled sending the tips of his long moustache half way up his cheek. The boy stayed silent. He wasn't about to give in to some fucking dirty Turk.

"Tell me you are sorry!"

Pierre gritted his teeth; every pain, every sorrow, every hurt and every anguish, concentrated in his locked jaw.

"Fuck you Turk bastard!"

The movement was short and swift. Pierre crumpled to the ground.

"Get the fuck away from him!" screamed Stefan, his semi-automatic pistol peppering the area with bullets.

With a bullet lodged in his shoulder and another grazing his forearm, the man accidentally dropped his knife, yelping in pain.

"Haydi! Hadi buradan çıkalım! Acele edin! Acele edin!"

The two scrambled from the ground and took off down the alley, Stefan hot on their trail. Marcus followed in behind.

"My God Pierre! Are you all right?"

Pierre tried to open his eyes and speak, but the words wouldn't come. Marcus ripped off his shirt and held it against Pierre's neck in a vain attempt to stop the bleeding.

"Hold on man! Hold on!"

"The ambulance is on its way," said a panting Stefan, his cell phone to his ear. "Holy fuck Pierre! Don't you die man!"

Pierre inched his right arm out from under his body, his hand still clutching his own cell phone.

"My father." The words were mumbled, disoriented by the coagulating blood.

"What?" Marcus leaned his head close to Pierre's mouth. "Say it again buddy."

"My father…" Marcus watched Pierre's eyes drift towards the cell phone in his hand.

"The cell phone!" yelled Marcus. "He's looking at the cell phone!"

Stefan took the phone from Pierre's bloody hand and put it to his ear. Nothing.

"Call the last number!" said Marcus. "Maybe that's who he was talking to? Hurry!"

With sirens wailing in the background, Stefan pressed redial. "It's ringing! It's ringing!"

****

"Mr. Coventry," said the clerk. "There's a call for you at the front desk."

I polished off the rest of my drink and followed him out to the lobby.

"Hello?"

"John, it's Hans Bercker. It's about Pierre."

****

"Can't you go any faster? My God! I need to get to the hospital!

"I'm going as fast as I can sir!"

"I know! I know! My God! I'm sorry! It's my son! I have to get there!"

The taxi driver swerved left, then right, manoeuvring in and out of traffic like a mad dog. Panic seized every part of my body and I wanted to throw up. This couldn't be happening. This could not be fucking happening! Not now, not when I was so close. Tears streamed from my eyes, sweat flooded my pores.

"Almost there," said the driver. "It's just down the street a bit more." He saw me fumbling in my wallet for some money. "No way. This trips on me my friend!"

The car skidded to a searing halt in front the gigantic double emergency room doors. I was out of the car before I could even say thank you.

"Good luck!" yelled the driver. "I hope he makes it."

I flew through the doors, screaming at anyone who would listen. "My son! I need to find my son! They brought him in by ambulance. Dear God where is he?"

"Sir! Sir! Please! Calm down!" A short haired lady whipped around from her reception desk.

"I need to find him! Please help me!"

"Follow me."

The first thing I noticed was the trail of blood on the pristine white floor, leading straight to the trauma room.

"Jesus Christ no..."

People flashed across the room in waves of constant motion, the air ripe with blood and antiseptic. The woman disappeared amongst the flurry, leaving me to watch through the rectangular door window in horror. Two seconds later the door burst open and I felt someone tug my arm. I was lost. I couldn't focus, I couldn't breathe. The voices were jumbled and far away, like I was in a dream, watching it all in a haze. The first thing I saw was his hair. The mop of curly dark hair. I smiled.

"He's been drifting in and out of consciousness," said a male voice. "Talk to him. We're taking him up to surgery as soon as they clear the room. You only have a few moments."

I took the boys' blood soaked hand in my own. It still felt warm. I tried to ignore the mass of blood stained cloth wrapped around his neck, and the grimacing nurse, trying to stop the bleeding. I only saw the sweet face of my son. My God he looked like his mother. My breathing slowed, trying to find peace.

"Pierre. It's me. It's your Dad. I'm here. Everything is going to be okay. I promise. You just stay strong and fight hard. I know you have your mother's spunk…I can just tell. Please Pierre please…we have so much to talk about…so much catching up to do." I had no idea where the words were coming from but they came in a constant stream. The boy was so still. Unnerving.

"Pierre…listen to me. Open your eyes for just one second if you can. I want to see you and I want you to see me…so you know I was here…so that when you get out of surgery, you will know it's me…and that I was here." My tears fell shamelessly on his shoulder.

"We have to take him now sir," said the nurse.

"Just one more minute," I pleaded.

"We may not have one more minute."

I bent over and placed a kiss on his forehead. "I'll be here when you wake up son. I'll be here." I felt a sudden pressure on my hand. Pierre was squeezing back. "Yes that's right son. I'm here."

The nurse flipped up the metal safety bars on the side of the bed and the crew began to roll him forward. All the while his hand gripped tightly around mine, my heart a wretched mess.

"Stop!" I yelled. "He just said something! Please! Just for a second! Quiet please."

"Hi Dad…"

EPILOGUE

The deep December chill seeped through every nook and cranny of the rental car as I drove down the dirt road toward the old churchyard. It had been a long time since I'd been in this area, but nothing had really changed much. The trees were a little bigger, the paint on the signposts a little duller. I parked the car down the beach a ways, preferring to finish the journey with a walk along the sea swept sand.

"Here we are son."

Never in a million years did I think I'd be making the trip back to Jersey to visit with my Michelle, under these circumstances. For the first time, we would all be together; maybe not physically but certainly in spirit.

"Your mother and I had the most wonderful time in Jersey, Pierre. So carefree and so much fun. God I miss her. This is where we truly found our love, and I knew without a doubt that she was the woman for me."

I could still picture her running on the sand, her dark hair flying wildly behind her. Her smile and her laugh. Enchanting me deeper and deeper under her spell.

"She used to think I was so naïve about so many things…and looking back, maybe I was. But is it wrong to believe in love? Is it wrong to believe in happiness Pierre? Did you ever believe that things would turn out this way? Don't answer that," I sighed. "I know…I'm just a hopeless romantic who believes in happy endings. But things don't always turn out the way we want them to do they son?"

I reached over and gently rubbed the top of the small pine box. That was all I had left; a small non-descript box filled with his ashes and what if's. What if I had never given him up? What if his mother had come with me when I begged? What if? What if? What if? Those two little words caged me like a prison, tormenting me, taunting me, making me wonder if I had ever done anything right in my life at all. Michelle was dead. Pierre was dead. And I was left with a whole bunch of what ifs?

I tucked the little box under my arm, and made my way out into the night; the cold angry sea spraying icy tears matching my own. I had come to Jersey to reunite Michelle with her son, in the spot where our love shone like a thousand stars. I had been dreading this moment, putting it off and putting it off, thinking that the longer I waited, the less it would hurt. I was a fool.

"See the lights Pierre? Down the beach in the distance. The church…it's all decorated for Christmas."

I'd never been to Jersey in the winter time and despite the solemn occasion, I marvelled at the beauty of the snow tipped sand dunes dotting the beach, and the constant crash of waves against the shore, a subtle reminder that time does not stop – not for a minute, not for a second, and certainly not for me. Why I picked the Christmas holiday season, I'll never really know. Maybe it was the promise of peace and happiness. Maybe it was just old sentiments. At any rate, here I was, trudging along the beach, my wool coat pulled tight around my neck, the tip of my scarf flapping in the wind with a mind of its own. The closer I got to the old church, the more my heart started to pound.

The large evergreen guarding the corner of the churchyard was bright with a multitude of twinkling coloured Christmas lights, illuminating the sky with the sentiment of hope. As I walked closer, I could hear the melodic sound of voices, rising up against the cruel bitter wind, each element crashing against the other in a crescendo of glory to the Almighty.

"Must be some sort of church service going on tonight Pierre. Hear the beautiful carols? Did you ever listen to carols growing up? I hope so."

Of course I had no idea, but my imaginary picture of Pierre sitting around a massive Christmas tree, drinking hot chocolate and listening to carols, afforded me some sort of solace as to what his life may have been like. I couldn't stomach even the briefest thoughts of him being unhappy. His life had already been cut too short, and I prayed to God that the special moments he had were good ones. I shook the snow from my hair and soldiered on. The church was not my final destination.

Even with the snow now falling like a white wall, it wasn't hard to spot the old tree. Our tree. Seeing it again made my heart ache. Its tall reaching branches stood firm against the sweeping surf, a symbol of strength, a symbol of our eternity. I searched desperately for our initials, carved deep into the wood by Michelle on that magical summer day, but like a protective mother, nature had shielded our love, entombing it forever under a fresh growth of bark. It was only fitting. With Pierre's death, that part of my life was over. Gone in body, but forever entombed in my heart. At least we had been given the chance to look upon each other's eyes, and know that our connection was not just blood alone, but spirit and strength. The moment was brief but poignant. And in his eyes I saw forgiveness, and really that's all I could have ever asked for. He never made it out of surgery; the wounds too deep, the blood loss too severe, but he died knowing that I was there…that I had searched, and searched, and searched until I found him, never giving up the hope or the dream.

I don't know how long I sat under that tree, putting off the final moment as long as I could. I wasn't good at goodbyes. Not with my father or mother, nor Michelle or my son. I never knew what to say. I never knew what to do. So I sat up against that tree, alone with my thoughts, and lost in the moment, just waiting for a sign. I knew it would come. I knew she would come. As the snow began piling up around my legs, I listened to the choir sing something about peace on earth, and I wondered after all that had happened, if I would ever find peace in my own life.

"You will find peace my love." The voice was soft, yet so distinct and so familiar.

"Michelle?"

"I am here John…right beside you, where I have always been."

Startled, I twisted my head to the side but saw nothing. Yet, I knew that she was there.

"It's time John."

With a heavy heart, I brushed the snow off the lid, and stared aimlessly at the inscription on the gold metal plate. 'Pierre'.

"Open the box."

Bracing my body against the old tree, I stood up and opened the pine box, tilting it ever so slightly. Michelle caught the ashes on her breath, and danced with them high into the tree tops, a lullaby of love, a mother's warm hello. I closed the lid and gently nestled the empty box into the snow at the foot of the tree. With tears streaming down my frozen face, I turned to make the lonely walk back down the beach to my car. This would be the last time I would come to this place. I just couldn't endure the pain it brought any longer.

I stood at the edge of the churchyard and looked out onto the roaring sea. The falling snow was no match for its fury, gobbling up each flake before it even hit the water. Wrapping my scarf tight around my neck, I took a few steps forward then stopped. I just couldn't leave. My feet cemented in the sand. The waves grew louder and louder as the snow danced wildly on the shore; the carollers reaching a feverish pitch in their exaltation. I heard none of it. I was in a vacuum, concentrating solely on the image of two figures hovering peacefully above the wild surf. A mother and her son. Both with outstretched arms. Both beckoning me to come.

ABOUT THE AUTHORS

John Coventry

John Coventry was born near Liverpool, England. He's led an incredible life, traveled extensively, met many interesting people and as Jackie Stallone says, 'John really has shaken hands with highest and the lowest from Kings, Queens, Presidents and Prime Ministers to drug runners, IRA terrorists and worse.'

John Coventry's life began to unravel as he began to mix with some unsavory people in an attempt to fraudulently remove a considerable amount of money from the British Government and having to work for them in an attempt to stay out of prison. The Customs offer was simple, "work for us, become involved with some of your friends who are druggies, find out who the dealers are"......It did not take long for his involvement to become much deeper as John enters the world of drug runners and terrorists and worse, and this starts the first part of his thrilling book.

In 1999, John left the clutches of the Security Services and arrived in Beverly Hills, California where he lived for the next 10 years, meeting and making lasting friendships with many celebrities both within and outside the movie industry. After the advice of several of these people, John left the United States in 2008 and moved to live in France, there in a a secluded farmhouse in Normandy and using the original notes, documents, photographs and secret recordings that his late father had made and placed in a vault, he started to write the first book,"I Was, I Am, I Will be".

John, the eldest of two sons, was brought up within an established English family dating back to 1460. He was sent away to boarding school when he was six. His school life was unhappy; while the school that he attended was owned by an Admiral of the Fleet and run by a Lord, he was sexually assaulted by the Masters (this is recorded in his book).

John met and had tea with British Prime Minister Harold Wilson while still at school and since then has met every Prime Minister from Wilson to Margaret Thatcher to Tony Blair. When John was 20 he led the first group of Young Conservatives ever to visit the then Communist Russian Soviet Union on an official engagement. During their stay John became friends with a young man from Leningrad (now St Petersburgh) University. The Young boy was called 'Putin' and he was, of course, to rise to become the Russian President.

The United States was his next port of call and again leading a British fact finding mission, was received at the White House by President Nixon. This was the first of a long list of United States Presidents, Governors and Senators that he was to meet.

Trish Faber

Trish Faber was born in Markham Ontario, Canada, the youngest of five children. She began to write at the age of five, using her family as characters in her first epic novel, "The Rabbit Family". Although never formally published, the single, handwritten, and self-illustrated copy of "The Rabbit Family" did make appearances at the local school, grocery store, bowling alley and bridge club meetings, courtesy of an enthusiastic mother and her large purse.

Trish is grateful to her family for allowing her to develop her imagination and creative flair without ever passing judgment. She realizes that at times this must have been difficult. Trish holds an Honours Degree in English and History from the University of Western Ontario, and a life degree in the trials and tribulations of being a restaurant owner, an academic tutor and life skills coach, as well as a business owner. She likes music, sports, tomato soup, and has secret aspirations of one day becoming a rock star. Most of all, she loves spending quality time with her friends and family.

TITLES
"Songs About Life" (1st Edition 2006, 2nd Edition 2016)
"I Was, I Am, I Will Be" (2010) (Print 2016)
"Pierre's Story" (2013) (Print 2016)
"Ghost – The Rick Watkinson Story" (2016)

Connect with Trish Online:
Website: www.trishfaber.com
Facebook: www.facebook.com/pages/Trish-Faber-Writer
Twitter: @trishfaber
Wonder Voice Press: www.wondervoicepress.com

For updates and more information on both authors, go to www.coventryandfaber.com.